THIS TIME THE REVOLUTION IS SPIRITUAL

Awakening, Reclaiming, Activating & Unleashing our Spiritual Forces for Ultimate Liberation

1ST EDITION

WINSOME ALEXANDER

ISBN: 979-8-218-72673-7

Book cover design and interior formatting by 100 Covers.

DISCLAIMER

This book is intended for informational, educational, and spiritual exploration purposes only. It is not intended to be a substitute for professional legal, financial, psychological, spiritual or medical counsel or advice. The historical accounts and interpretations presented herein are based on the author's research and understanding and are offered to foster discussion, serve as a catalyst for personal growth, and contribute to a journey of spiritual expansion.

The spiritual practices, rituals, and concepts discussed are drawn from diverse traditions and are presented as avenues for personal and communal exploration. Readers should approach them with reverence, personal discernment, and respect for their cultural origins.

The author and publisher make no warranties, expressed or implied, regarding the outcomes of the information contained or the effectiveness of the practices and rituals described herein. Some methodologies presented may create physical, emotional, psychological, or spiritual effects as part of natural spiritual development. Should you experience any concerning symptoms or persistent discomfort, please discontinue the practices and seek professional help immediately.

Read and approach the information in this book with caution and at your own risk. Your engagement with this material is a personal choice, and you are solely responsible for its interpretation and application. Readers are encouraged to consult with qualified professionals for specific advice related to their individual circumstances.

Library of Congress Control Number: 2025914170

CONTENTS

Spiritual Erasure, and Cultural Amnesia - How colonization attacked indigenous spiritualities, erased ancestral memory, and severed sacred connections - The Truth They Tried to Erase - Vodou: A Sacred Act of Survival and Rebellion - What Is Haitian Vodou? Vodou as Resistance - Core Beliefs of Vodou - Maroon Magic and Resistance - Channeling Nanny: Rituals for Modern Freedom Fighters - Why Is Haiti Suffering So Badly Today? - From My Heart to Haiti (and Her Daughters & Sons) Haiti is not cursed - She is Targeted

Did You Know: *The Myth of the Voodoo Doll: Origins of Pins and Dolls - Baron Samedi: Guardian of the Dead, Trickster of the Afterlife - Why Alcohol Is Called "Spirits" - Jamaican Households and white rum.*

Hidden Fire: Diaspora Traditions of Survival - Spiritual Systems That Survived the Fire - Hoodoo: The Resilient Magic of the African American Diaspora -Ifá: Yoruba Wisdom Across the Waters - Santería: Saints with African

Names, Gods Unconquered - Candomblé: Ancestors in Disguise - Native American Ceremonies: Earth as Altar, Prayer as Resistance - Jamaican Spiritual Traditions: Sacred Power in Plain Sight - Obeah: The Forbidden Science Spiritual Power, Unjustly Feared - Jamaican Pocomania: Spirit in Movement - Kumina: Calling the Kongo - Revivalism: The Bible Meets the Drum - Jonkonnu: Dance of the Ancestors in Disguise

Did You Know: *The Same Spirit Energy Can Be Used For Healing or Harm - Jonkonnu is linked to a Ghanaian war chief active in the early 18th century - Childhood memories of Jonkonnu*

The Afterlife of Oppression - Invisible Chains: The New Plantation - The Illusion of Perfection: Control, Performance, and Assimilation - Survivalist Obsession In Many Marginalized Communities - Communal Trauma Becomes Policy & Practice Homophobia and Transphobia - My Personal Evolution on Queerness - Disconnection from Land and Body - Unpacking Internalized Colorism and Hair Shame - Scientific Power of Melanin - Beyond the Surface: Spiritual ReclamationThe Critique of Simone Biles' Edges is Deeper Than It Seems - What the Ashes Still Sing: The Spiritual Revolution - Living in the Ruins with Power - *A rebirthing water ritual for you -*

Did You Know: *The "Kitchen - Our Edges" - Melanin: More Than Skin Deep The Science and Sacredness of Our Natural Protector - The Science of Melanin Today - Why This Matters Beyond Science - Reclaiming Our Complexion Narrative - Melanin as a Super Bio-Compound - Darker Skin = Denser Melanin = Greater Potential - Melanin-Based Medicine - A Word of Caution: On Exploitation - The Unseen History of Black Teeth in Science - Why Black People's Teeth? - The Dark History of Exploitation - Our Bodies, Our Heritage: Decolonizing Modern Practices - Toward Ethical and Healing Practices*

Language as weaponry - Spoken Affirmations: Weaponized Word - The Power of Naming: Reclaiming Spiritual Vocabulary as Sacred Weaponry - The New Sacred Armor - Awakening Power - Transforming Pain. Waging Sacred War - Rituals of Spiritual Readiness

Did You Know: *The Silencing - Salt as spiritual purifier*

PART II
Remembering the Original Self

Awakening our own "natural mystic" through remembrance - The Revolution Needs Visionaries - A Message for the Visionaries - The Powers of the Mystic Visionary - Living As A Mystic Revolutionary - The Mystic's Call to Action Mysticism as Revolution - Using This Energy in the Fight for Liberation - The Visionary Toolkit: Practical Steps for Activating Your Mystic Powers - Embody Your Visionary Power Mystics and Sages - every soul carries a sacred knowing - Sage vs Mystic

Did You Know: *Short list of our ancestors considered as mystic-sages*

Living Black Mystic-Sages

Reclaiming the Forgotten Path - Listening for the Call - Returning to the Sacred Line - Specific Practices of Ancestral Reconnection

Did you know: *Protection we didn't know we were missing*

Meditation, ritual, drumming, and herbalism as ancient technologies for survival and spiritual defense - The Call to Return to Rituals - Resistance Through Reconnection - Sacred Technologies: Historical Context and Modern Reclamation - Prayer and invocations of Ancestral Spirits - Drumming and Dance - Ancestral Altars - Herbal Medicine and Healing Rituals - Meditation, Visualization & Manifestation Visioning in Ritual and Ceremony Imaginative Power in the Face of Oppression Historical Context & Resistance Roots Visioning, Dreamwork & Prophetic Sight Powerful Symbolism and Sacred Geometry - Sacred Storytelling and Oral Traditions Circle Work and Collective Healing - Cosmic Connection and the Elements: Reclaiming Ancestral Alignments - The Moon's Embrace - Rituals Centering the Elements - Water and Libations - Air and Breath - Earth and Grounding

Did You Know: *The Power They Feared: Why Sacred Rituals Were Banned*

PART III
Spiritual Warfare in Modern Times

Purpose of Powerful Symbolism and Sacred Geometry - How These Symbols Can Be Used as Tools for Spiritual Resistance - What These Symbols Represent -The Ankh (Egyptian/ African Tradition) - Adinkra Symbols (Akan Tradition - Ghana & Côte d'Ivoire) - Sacred African Ancestral Symbols with Indigenous Cosmology, Their Meanings, and Usage in Spiritual Resistance - Sacred Laws and Tools of Sovereignty - Rituals with Geometric Symbols for Healing and Reclamation - Ritual 1: Daily Grounding & Self-Empowerment - Ritual 2: Ancestral Wisdom & Healing Waters - Ritual 3: Collective Justice & Liberation - Cultural Notes on the Use of Sacred Symbols

Did you know: *Akan use of Adinkra Symbols*

Spiritual Sovereignty Rising - Global Movements and Social Media What Malik Yoba Said - "Woke Culture" - The Kromanti Experience: Honoring Maroon Heritage in Jamaica - Rejecting Colonized Religion - The Growing Call to Legalize Marijuana Universally - Pan-Africanism - The Resurgence of Pan-Africanism: What We're Witnessing - Understanding Spiritual Pan-Africanism - Key Drivers of This Spiritual Pan-African Revival - Rejection of Colonial Religious Frameworks - Spiritual Decolonization as Identity Work - Online Communities and Global Rituals - Rise of Afro-Spiritual Influencers and Practitioners - Spirituality as Resistance - Key Voices in Spiritual Pan-Africanism - Rastafari Movement - A New Wave of Afro-Indigenous and Diaspora Healers & Thinkers - Jamaica's Spiritual Frequency - Reconnection and Restoration: The Living Revolution - Personal Note To The Weary - Your Spirit Was Always Sovereign

Reclamations: Burnings, Removals, Collapses - Toppling of Colonial Symbols - Fires That Speak - Elemental Wisdom: Water Rising & Land Reclaimed - Indigenous Land Back Movements & Sacred Site Protection - Sacred Returns & Cultural Revivals - Reclamation of Heritage & Ways of Being - Why These Moments Matter - Spiritual Warriors of Sound: Griots of the Diaspora (Bob Marley, Peter Tosh, Buju Banton, Skillful Kxng, Fela Kuti, Miriam Makeba, Author's personal reflection: The Future Is Now

Did You Know: *Decoding Babylon: Symbolism in Rastafari and Reggae - The Prophetic Vision of Bob Marley: A Revolution of Spirit*

PART IV
A New Way Forward

Revolution is Spiritual. Liberation is Embodied - Reclaiming the Sacred Flesh: Our Bodies as Temples of Power - Embodied Resistance: The Power of Movement and Action - Flame as Transformation: Spiritual Fire for Revolutionary Change - Freeing the mind, the spirit, the soul from internalized oppression - The Flame of the Ancestors: Calling on the Sacred Fire - A Revolutionary Call to Action - Reclaiming the Coin - The Exodus is Economic, and it is Spiritual

Did You Know: *Spirit Warriors of Liberation - Frantz Fanon (1925–1961) - Amílcar Cabral (1924–1973) - Steve Biko (1946–1977)*

The Village as the Foundation of Liberation - The Sacred Village: A Space for Healing, Power, and Protection - The Role of Ancestors in Sacred Community - The Importance of Mutual Aid and Collective Responsibility - Spiritual Parenting and Intergenerational Healing - Spiritual Protection and Strength in Sacred Community - The Roots of Waywardness and Despair Among Black Men - A Call to Spiritual Intercession and Restoration Rebirthing the Village in the Modern World - The Sacred Call to Build Community - Building communities rooted in spirit, not in survival mode - Joining "The Village Revolution" - An Invitation to Deep Reclamation: The Sacred Ancestral Roots & Liberation Circle

Languages Once Silenced are Being Spoken Again - From Personal
Reawakening to Collective Power - The Statue of Liberty and the Museum of
Lies - This Revolution Is Sacred

Our Path: Spirit Over Strife - Spiritual Reparations: Reclaiming the Sacred -
Economic Reparations: Redirecting Wealth - Black Spending Power / Buying
Power Spending vs. Wealth: A Critical Distinction - Strategic & Intentional
Spending (Strengthening the "Buy Black" Movement) - Leveraging Black-
Owned Financial Institutions - Building Financial Literacy and Fluency -
Fostering Black Entrepreneurship and Ownership - Advocacy for Systemic
Change - Psychological Reparations: Decolonizing the Mind - Communal
Reparations: Rebuilding Village - Energetic Reparations: Living as if We Are
Already Whole - Manifesting Reparations: A Spiritual Rebellion - Cleaning
Our Sacred House: A Call to Internal Liberation - Rekindling the Inner
Kingdom - Final Thoughts: On Unity, Community, and the Complexities of
Liberation

Restoring the Inner Sanctuary - Final Thoughts: On Unity, Community,
and the Complexities of Liberation - On the Irreverent Commodification of
Sacredness

APPENDICES

DEDICATION

This book is dedicated with profound honor and remembrance to all my ancestors, whose enduring spirit and boundless contributions have breathed life into these pages.

To the biological threads that connect me to my relatives and the countless generations whose very essence I carry.

To my adoptive father, (RIP) whose love I never had cause to doubt.

To the cultural wellsprings of my heritage, the people who forged our traditions, instilled our values, and wove the tapestry of our collective identity.

To the spiritual guides who walked before us - the teachers, leaders, and luminaries who illuminated pathways of belief and practice, fostering our deepest connections.

And to our shared earthly lineage, the innovators, thinkers, and creators whose legacies continue to shape and inspire the world.

May their wisdom forever light our way.

"This time, the revolution is being televised. It's not loud or bloody.

It's ancestral. It's mystical. It's spiritual.

—Winsome Alexander

Manifesto
This Time The Revolution
is Spiritual

The Great Awakening.

We stand at the threshold of a new era, an era where the revolution is not fought with the weapons of the past, but with the power of our very essence. This time, the revolution is spiritual.

For centuries, we have fought valiantly against the forces of racial, systemic injustices, colonization, and oppression. Our ancestors, like Nanny of the Maroons, rose against their oppressors, not with physical arms alone, but with the strength that resides deep within the soul, rooted in our divine connection. This strength, this power, is the true weapon - the one our oppressors cannot fathom and one they cannot defeat.

This time, the revolution is spiritual because we are awakening to the sacred wisdom that has been passed down through generations. The very essence of our being, the untapped power of the spirit, holds the key to dismantling the systems that have sought to break us. It is time to call upon the power of the elements, activate the strength of the ancestors, and the deep knowing that lives within us.

We are reclaiming our spiritual heritage. We are reconnecting with the sacred practices that our oppressors tried to erase, that colonialism tried to steal. This is not a revolution of the body alone, but of the soul - a movement of spirit-led resistance that will not be silenced, diminished, or erased.

The revolution is not about violence; it is about the fierce love of self, of community, and of the divine. It is about knowing our worth as children of the Creator and standing in our rightful place in the world. This time, we fight with our truth, our consciousness, our spirit and our ability to manifest the change we deserve.

The systems of oppression do not understand this power. They have no framework for it. They cannot see it, and they do not know how to fight it. They think they can crush us with force, but the spirit cannot be crushed. Our ancestors knew this. They fought with wisdom, with intuition, and with the deep belief that our connection to the Creator was our ultimate defense.

We rise now in the same way, drawing from the ancient wells of knowledge, spirit, and resistance. This time, we are not simply reacting. We are awakening, evolving, and stepping into our spiritual power. The revolution is not just about breaking chains; it's most certainly about freeing our minds, our hearts, and our souls from the limitations imposed upon us.

We do this for ourselves. We do this for our children. We do this for the generations yet to come. This time, the revolution is spiritual - and this time, we will win.

We stand as one, united in our divine power, knowing that no force can stand against the strength of a people who know their worth, who honor their ancestors, and who are guided by the sacred force within.

This revolution is unstoppable. And it has already begun.

Acknowledgement

My deepest acknowledgment begins with myself - the Negro woman, survivor, creative, outspoken truth-teller, and nurturer of community. This book, "This Time The Revolution is Spiritual," is born from a personal revolution - my revolution. It represents a courageous reclamation of spiritual power long silenced and stolen, a power I've had to courageously awaken within myself to share with the world for the betterment of our people.

As I reflect on the history of our struggles and victories, I find that our enduring strength, the very power that has kept us standing against centuries of oppression, lies within the spiritual essence of who we are. In these pages, we explore how this time, the revolution is not just against systems - it is a revolution of the very soul. And in this revolution, the oppressors cannot win, for they do not understand the power we are awakening to. It's why they tried to suppress it in the first place.

This work is not merely a publication; it is an act of faith, a living testament to the practices I share. It is also the pre-work for my own realization that I, too, may one day become an ancestor, and this contribution will live on, amplifying the current wave of enlightenment and awakening of these times. It has taken immense courage and profound enlightenment to bring this vision into being, and for that, I acknowledge the journey within.

I offer deep gratitude to every living teacher, passed ancestor, and sacred text that whispered truth into my spirit. This book is not mine alone. It is carried by the ones who walk with me.

Acknowledging the Keepers of Memory

With reverence for the vast tapestry of our people, from the Motherland to the global diaspora, we call upon the keepers of memory - those whose breath still dances through the trees, whose prayers are planted in the soil. We honor you: Nanny, Harriet, Marcus, Yaa Asantewaa, Zumbi, our nameless and known ancestors who whispered songs through chains and cracked open the sky with their hope. Guide our hands as we write. Let our words remember what the world tried to erase. Let our spirits stand, unbroken, in your name.

Ashé.

PREFACE

I say this with kindness but unapologetically. My choice to center Black people in this work isn't about creating separation. It's about creating safety, truth, and sacred return. Others are welcome to witness, to honor, and to learn - but this offering, this altar, was built with and for my people first.

The rituals, reflections, and practices shared in this book are deeply rooted in African, Afro-Caribbean, and diasporic spiritual traditions. These are not trends or tools borrowed from elsewhere; they are sacred technologies passed through blood memory, born from both ancestral brilliance and historical trauma. Many of these traditions were outlawed, ridiculed, or punished when practiced by Black people, yet they are now often commodified and practiced outside of their original cultural context, sometimes stripped of meaning or sold back to us in fragments.

So, I want to be clear: this book was written with Black readers in mind - those of us who have been disconnected from our sacred lineages by systems of colonization, slavery, and assimilation. This work is a call home. It is an offering for healing, remembrance, and reclamation.

This is not about exclusion or division. It is about restoration. While others may find resonance or inspiration here, I ask that you approach this work with deep respect for its origins. These rituals are not universal tools to be picked up casually. They carry cultural and spiritual weight, and they deserve to be honored as such.

May all who read these words be guided by integrity, reverence, and a willingness to learn deeply rather than merely consume or extract - to engage respectfully without appropriating or diluting.

Big Up YuSelf!

With love and purpose,

Winsome Alexander

INTRODUCTION
HEARING AND
ANSWERING THE CALL

The title of this book, *"This Time the Revolution is Spiritual"* came to me like an urgent whisper from another realm. I wasn't looking for it. I was simply preparing for an episode of my YouTube show, titled, *"Before We Were Black* - Reclaiming our Historical and Spiritual Identity," researching the erased stories, the lost names, cultures and truths buried under centuries of conquest and conditioning.

And then, it came.
Clear.
Charged.
Unmistakable.

Timely.

It wasn't just a phrase. I heard it as a summons.

I've always been called *Outspoken - truth-teller*. Sometimes it was said with admiration, sometimes with discomfort, but always with recognition. My voice has never been silent, not even when trembling. I have spoken truths that others were too afraid to name. I have said what needed to be said, even when it cost me.

And that is precisely why I was chosen to write this book.

The ancestors knew I wouldn't water it down. They knew I'd speak what they've been waiting for us to remember. They knew my voice could hold what others tried to bury - spirit, memory, resistance. They stirred the air. They moved through me like breath through bone, and in that moment, not only did I feel inspired, I also felt *remembered.* As if the ancestors reached across time and said,

"You! Now! Speak!"

And so I realized I wasn't just making content. I was answering a call. And though I say I am late to the party as my own awakening is quite recent, I was stepping into my part of the revolution - not with guns or protests, but with remembrance, reverence, and voice. Because *this time,* what we are fighting for is deeper than politics or borders. It is for *the soul* of our people. It is for *our spiritual sovereignty.* And I knew, without a doubt, that I had to write this book.

This book is not just a collection of thoughts. This is my offering. It is my obedience. It feels like a spiritual dispatch - a declaration that *we are rising,* and that the sacred revolution is underway. It is me, saying yes to the ancestors.

And I write it not from a place of perfection, or haughtiness, but from deep listening, ancestral alignment and divine conviction. Because the revolution needs truth-tellers. And I was born to speak with the pen of a ready writer.

In *This Time, The Revolution is Spiritual,* I lead you through a soul-stirring journey of decolonization, remembrance, and reawakening. Drawing from ancestral wisdom, spiritual traditions, and the deep scars left by colonization and white supremacy, I show how spirituality has always been, and still is our most power-ful form of resistance.

This book is a call to those who feel the stir in their spirit - a knowing that the revolution we need is not just political or social. It's personal. It's sacred. It's a return. Because what they tried to erase, we were always meant to remember. *This is not just a book, it is activation.*

We can justify this global emergence of consciousness as a spiritual revolution by framing it as a profound shift in power dynamics - from external to internal, and from material to metaphysical.

Aṣé

THE MINDSET OF THE OPPRESSOR

To understand the depth of this spiritual revolution, we must first understand what fuels the systems we are here to dismantle. The hearts and minds of those who purposely seek to oppress and subjugate others are not filled with strength but with fear.

They fear the loss of power, because their dominance is built on fragile founda-tions. They fear retribution, because deep down, they know the blood of history stains their hands. They fear the truth, because the truth would strip them of their mythologies, the ones that crowned them superior and called it destiny.

What they truly want is control. Control over land, over people, over narratives. Their greed is insatiable, their privilege addictive. And yet, beneath it all lies a fundamental hollowness, a spiritual poverty and disconnection from the divine self. This is a deep emptiness that compels them to dehumanize others and makes them believe they must dominate them to feel secure, worthy, or significant.

This is why they cannot win this revolution. Because this time, it is not just a fight for justice, it is deeper than that. It is a return to truth. A reclamation of the spirit. And no system, no weapon, no ideology can withstand the power of a people who remember who they truly are.

INEVITABLE DECLINE:
THE SELF-CONSUMING EMPIRE

There's a palpable sense that our presence is no longer welcome, but perhaps that is a hidden blessing. Why, after all, would one willingly choose to remain on a vessel determined to sink itself? This perspective isn't rooted in pessimism, but a stark observation of their self-orchestrated demise. The very systems and mechanisms designed for our subjugation and unwarranted interference they deploy are now devouring them from the inside. We, the immigrants and our forebears, laid the groundwork for this nation's prosperity; the very foundation upon which its wealth was built. Now convinced that we are no longer useful to them, they seek to expel us. Yet, what force will then uphold the structures we painstakingly erected?

Their strategy of creating global adversaries and their self-imposed isolation, fueled by a distorted perception of unparalleled power reveals an utter absence of insight or foresight. Tragically, they will never accept responsibility or admit the truth. They cannot. Imprisoned by their own foundational darkness, they speak and act from a place of profound ignorance and utter blindness, devoid of compassion. They would rather inflict self-harm, dismantle themselves than acknowledge their own destructive path, choosing to cut off their noses just to spite their faces.

THE MINDSET OF THE AWAKENED

The awakened do not rise with vengeance in their hearts, but with vision in their eyes. They are not fighting to reverse roles or dominate in return - they are truly remembering: remembering who they were before the wound, before the chains, before the lie.

The awakened move from a center of spiritual clarity. They no longer measure worth by systems built to erase them. They are guided by ancestral wisdom, divine intuition, and a deep knowing that their power is not granted by man, indeed it is eternal, encoded in their very being. They know they are power *full* because they are power *filled.*

Unlike the oppressor, the awakened do not fear truth - they seek it. They do not cling to control but they flow with alignment. They are not threatened by others' freedom. In fact, they insist upon it. Because they know: when one rises, we all rise.

This is the revolution the world did not expect. It is not loud, but it is unstoppable. It is not built on revenge, but on restoration. It cannot be tracked, contained, or co-opted, because it lives in the spirit, beyond the reach of empire.

The awakened are here. And they are not asking for permission. They are reclaiming their birthright.

"We return to truth - the raw, untamed knowing we carried before it was buried under survival. May we heal and rise in our full power."

—*WA*

And if you harbor fears of the ramifications of the self destruction of "Babylon" there is no need. For it is out of this chaos that our ultimate liberation will come.

—Aṣé

SANKOFA

Sankofa, a concept rooted in the Akan language of Ghana, means "to return and retrieve" or "to learn from the past." This powerful symbol reminds us that looking back to reclaim lost wisdom or acknowledge past mistakes is essential for growth and transformation. The Akan people express this through the saying, "Se wo were fi na wosan kofa a yenkyiri," which translates to, "It is never wrong to go back and fetch what was forgotten."

For *This Time the Revolution Is Spiritual*, Sankofa has been embraced as a guiding emblem. It perfectly captures the book's core message: the necessity of reconnecting with ancestral knowledge and spiritual truths to move forward with clarity, power, and healing. This adopted symbol embodies the journey of reclaiming what was lost so we can create a revolutionary future grounded in sacred remembrance.

FOREWORD

There are moments in time when a voice rises not just to speak, but to awaken. A voice that calls us back: not to what the world has shaped us to be, but to who we were divinely created to become. *This Time the Revolution is Spiritual*, and the author behind it, is that voice.

I have had the profound honor of being introduced to Winsome Alexander, not only as a self-empowerment mentor, but as a spiritual revolutionary—one whose life's work is rooted in a single, bold, liberating truth: you were never meant to shrink. You were born to shine. Through her coaching, mentoring, and sacred advocacy for adult survivors of child abuse, she has ignited a healing movement grounded in cultural remembrance, spiritual resistance, and personal celebration. Her signature mantra, "Big Up Yu Self!", echoes like a heartbeat throughout these pages; a joyful, radical call to know and celebrate yourself without apology.

In a world that has too often tried to silence, distort, or erase the sacred origins of African-descended people, this book is a powerful act of reclamation. It's not merely a guide; it's a journey home. Home to spirit. Home to self. Home to the ancestors whose voices still whisper in our bones.

Each chapter is a doorway into hidden truths, forgotten rituals, and sacred symbols that have endured through colonization, slavery, and systemic oppression. You'll travel from the fiery resistance of Haitian Vodou to the sacred movements of Jamaican Revivalism; from the mysticism of Yoruba Ifá to the healing wisdom of herbal traditions and elemental rituals. And through it all, you will be reminded that your story did not begin with trauma; and it certainly doesn't end there.

This is a book for those who have felt disconnected: from spirit, from self, from source. It is for the seekers, the survivors, the visionaries, the quiet rebels, and the sacred storytellers. Whether you've never once celebrated yourself, or you've simply forgotten how, this book will hold your hand and guide you to remembrance.

More than knowledge, what Winsome offers here is permission: permission to reimagine, to reconnect, and to reclaim your birthright to power, beauty, joy, and spiritual sovereignty. Her words are gentle but fierce. Tender but transformative. And every page is infused with a deep, ancestral knowing that you are divinely loved, sacred, and always have been.

So, breathe deep, open your heart and be ready to remember because it's time to Big Up Yu Self!

And this book: this powerful, liberating, love-soaked offering - is your invitation to do just that.

Rev. Tona Bobb
Interfaith Minister
One Spirit

PART I

THE WOUNDS OF THE PAST

CHAPTER 1

THE WEAPONIZATION OF SPIRIT

Spiritual Erasure and Cultural Amnesia.

THEY TOLD US we were primitive. That our traditions were savage. That our spiritual ways were nothing but superstition.

They built churches on sacred land. Burned medicine bundles. Baptized us with water meant to erase memory. They pointed to their books and institutions as truth and to our drums, chants, and ceremonies as darkness.

But look around.

Their systems are crumbling. Their promises were lies. And now, science, once their tool of domination, begins to prove the truth of what our elders always knew. We are remembering. And as we remember, we rise, not just for ourselves, but with the thousands who walk behind us, whose names we carry in our blood.

This is the true power they feared. Not our fists. But our connection. Our knowing. Our unshakable roots. Because the revolution is not only political. It is not only cultural. This time, the revolution is spiritual.

And the ancestors are leading it.

In this book, we will honor them, not just to remember, but to reawaken. To shift from survival to sovereignty. From suppression to sacred reclamation and to ultimate liberation.

THE TRUTH THEY TRIED TO ERASE

How colonization attacked indigenous spiritualities, erased ancestral memory, and severed sacred connections.

To conquer a people, you must first sever their spirit. That's what colonization did across continents: invaded the soul before it claimed the land. Indigenous spiritualities deeply woven into daily life, community, nature, and ancestry were the first targets.

What the colonizers couldn't understand, they demonized. What they couldn't destroy, they tried to distort. But they never fully succeeded.

Spiritual traditions endured in hidden places, behind closed doors, beneath Catholic saints, inside whispered songs and quiet rituals. They lived on in sweat lodges, night fires, ceremonial dances, and secret names.

They hid them in the kitchen, in the garden, in the graveyard. They passed them down through lullabies and midwives and grandmothers who prayed over you in a language the colonizer never learned to speak. They sent messages in hair braids.

And some didn't just hide. Some fought back with spirit at the center.

One powerful example of this fight back is *Haitian Vodou.* This is one of the most misunderstood spiritual systems on the planet.

Often spelled *Voodoo* in the West, Haitian Vodou is a deeply rooted Afro-Caribbean spiritual tradition that emerged during the transatlantic slave trade. But what most people think of when they hear "Voodoo" is zombies, curses and dolls with pins. This isn't Vodou at all. It's colonizer propaganda, a campaign of fear to keep people from reclaiming their spiritual birthright.

Vodou is absolutely not "black magic."
It is Black memory. Black power. Black connection.

VODOU: A SACRED ACT OF SURVIVAL AND REBELLION

The word *Voodoo* comes from the Fon word *vòdu,* meaning *"spirit"* or *"deity."* This tradition originates from West Africa, specifically the *Fon* and *Yoruba* peoples of modern-day Benin and Nigeria. But over time, colonizers twisted it into something monstrous. They rebranded ancestral wisdom as witchcraft and sacred rituals as savagery. That's why many practitioners today reclaim the true spelling: *Vodou,* a reminder that this path is holy, not haunted.

To call Vodou *"black magic"* is like calling prayer demonic. It reveals more about the lens of white supremacy than the truth of the tradition.

Vodou is a sacred, complex, and ancestral spiritual system of healing, resistance, and connection to the divine. It was born in fire in the crucible of slavery and it has always been a tool of survival, liberation, and spiritual sovereignty.

WHAT IS HAITIAN VODOU?

Vodou is a *syncretic* religion, meaning it blends multiple traditions into one. It draws from:

- Traditional West African religions, especially of the Fon and Yoruba peoples
- Taino spirituality, the Indigenous beliefs of the Caribbean's first peoples
- Roman Catholicism, which was forced upon enslaved Africans by French colonizers

VODOU AS RESISTANCE

You must know that Vodou is not just a religion. It is a revolutionary force.

Dutty Boukman, an enslaved man who had been transported from Jamaica to Saint-Domingue (now Haiti) became a houngan (Vodou priest) and played a key leadership role in the early stages of the Haitian Revolution. He organized the famous *Bois Caïman ceremony in August 1791,* seen as the spiritual spark of the revolution. During that sacred ceremony in a forest called Bois Caïman, Dutty Boukman and a priestess named Cécile Fatiman called upon the spirits for justice. They invoked the spirits: not for peace, but for justice, liberation, and war against their oppressors. Boukman's prayer, "white man's god" was followed by ritual offerings, drumming, dancing, and spiritual possession. That night marked the spiritual ignition of a unified uprising across plantations. What followed was the Haitian Revolution: the first successful slave revolt in the Americas, establishing Haiti as the first Black republic in the Western Hemisphere. Vodou was not on the sidelines. It was the organizing principle; the sacred strategy. It empowered the people with courage, unity, and divine permission to rebel and prevail.

CORE BELIEFS OF VODOU

- Bondyè (from the French *Bon Dieu,* meaning "Good God") is the supreme creator, distant and not directly involved in daily affairs.

- Practitioners interact with lwa (also spelled loa) powerful spirits who govern different aspects of life: love, war, fertility, death, justice.
- Ancestors are deeply revered. They are guides, protectors, and keepers of memory.
- Nature is sacred. Water, fire, wind, and earth are not just elements, they are portals to the divine.
- Enslaved Africans invoked the lwa, called on justice and rose up spiritually armed. They entered battle with songs, rituals, and spirits at their side. Vodou empowered them to reclaim what slavery tried to steal: their agency, their power, their God-given freedom.

Sample Ritual calling on lwa Papa Legba - The Gate Keeper

In Vodou, rum is often used as an offering to the spirits (lwa) to show respect and invite their presence. A simple ritual involves pouring a small amount of white rum onto the ground or altar while calling the name of a specific lwa - like Papa Legba, the gatekeeper of the spirit world. Some practitioners blow misted rum from the mouth to activate the energy and signal the spirit world.

(See Appendix A for more ancestral offerings and rituals.)

WHO ARE THE LWA?

The lwa are not "gods" in the Western sense. They are divine energies, ancient spirits, and archetypes of human experience. You build relationships with them, honor them with offerings, music, and ritual. Some of the most well-known include:

- Papa Legba - Guardian of the crossroads, opener of spiritual doors.
- Erzulie Freda - Spirit of love, beauty, sensuality.
- Ogou - Warrior spirit, patron of strength, revolution, and protection.

- Baron Samedi - Guardian of the dead, trickster of the afterlife. (Described in Did You Know Section)
- Ezili Dantor - Fierce Black mother, protector of women and children, often invoked in liberation struggles.

Each lwa has their own songs, colors, offerings, and sacred rhythms. To serve them is to remember who you are.

Vodou was a form of resistance against cultural erasure, a way for enslaved people to hide their gods in plain sight, disguising them as Catholic saints while keeping their sacred systems alive. Vodou is a perfect example of the revolution being spiritual. It is a sacred, complex, and ancestral tradition rooted in healing, justice, and resistance. It kept African cosmology alive under genocide. It gave enslaved people strength to fight and wisdom to heal. It continues today as a living path of freedom.

And so, Vodou didn't just survive colonization, it fought back. Haiti declared its freedom, and the world would never be the same.

Haitian Vodou has always been:

- A weapon against erasure.
- A prayer for the fallen.
- A call to the ancestors.
- A roadmap to liberation.

But Haiti was not alone...

MAROON MAGIC AND RESISTANCE

Jamaica's history of resistance is rich with the stories of numerous formidable leaders who rose against oppression. While figures like *Sam Sharpe,* one of Jamaica's national heroes, whose Baptist War shook the foundations of slavery, and courageous chieftains such as *Cudjoe* and *Tacky,* who led significant revolts for freedom, all deserve honorable mention for their unwavering fight, it is *Nanny of the Maroons,* also a Jamaican national hero, whose legacy we particularly uplift here. Her unwavering commitment to liberation, especially through the profound spiritual methodologies she incorporated, rooted in the powerful traditions of the *Kromanti* people, offers a unique and powerful roadmap for our own reclamation. *(Indeed, the spirit of these ancestors runs deep; I once had the distinct honor of portraying Tacky the Chieftain in a speech and drama piece that earned me an award.)* Now, let us turn our gaze to the extraordinary life and spiritual warfare of Nanny.

In the Blue and John Crow mountains of Jamaica, Nanny of the Maroons, a spiritual warrior and guerrilla strategist, guided her people using sacred knowledge and African ancestral practices during the 18th century. She used her exceptional knowledge of the terrain, plants, and spirit protection, in ambush warfare against the British.

Oral folklore says she could catch bullets and turn them back with her hands, disappear and reappear and use her knowledge of the herbs and the land for protection. The Maroons, formerly enslaved Africans who escaped to freedom in Jamaica, Suriname, and Brazil, used ritual camouflage, night chants, coded songs, and plant medicine to resist recapture.

Maroons, under Nanny's leadership, blended into their environment using leaves, mud, shadows, and timing - an early form of ritual and natural camouflage. In Jamaica, Suriname, Brazil, and beyond, escaped Africans, known as Maroons, built free societies deep in the hills and jungles. They used camouflage, drumming patterns, and night chants to prevent re-enslavement. Their resistance was physical, but it was also deeply spiritual.

They also used decoys, distraction, chants, and misdirection - spiritual and psychological camouflage. Nanny didn't just use camouflage, she turned it into a spiritual practice. Cloaked in nature, spirit, and ancestral wisdom, she made herself and her people invisible to the empire. What she practiced wasn't just survival, it was sacred resistance. Spirituality wasn't separate from resistance, it was the blueprint, not rooted in fear but in divine connection.

"We do not hide. We cloak ourselves in spirit."

Nanny was not just a warrior; she was a mystic, a prophet, a priestess. Her victories were not just tactical, they were spirit-led. And her legacy lives on wherever people choose sacred defiance over submission.

Nanny of the Maroons, Jamaica's legendary warrior queen and national hero, led her resistance against British colonizers primarily from the Blue Mountains, especially in an area known as Nanny Town, located in the John Crow Mountains, a subrange of the Blue Mountain range in eastern Jamaica.

KEY LOCATIONS

Blue Mountains: The larger mountainous region where the Maroons, including Nanny, built communities and waged guerrilla warfare.

John Crow Mountains: Dense, forested and rugged terrain ideal for Maroon resistance; the specific location of Nanny Town.

Nanny Town: A Maroon stronghold established by Nanny, strategically located in the John Crow Mountains, near present-day Moore Town.

These mountains provided the ideal defensive position for the Maroons, with their dense, rugged, and heavily forested terrain enabling a successful guerrilla war against the British. These mountains were more than just physical terrain; they served as a spiritual stronghold where Nanny of the Maroons called on

African spiritual power and ancestral guidance. The mountains became both a refuge and a symbol of resistance, sheltering generations who fought for their freedom and ultimately preserving their cultural heritage. The area is now a UNESCO World Heritage Site, recognized for both its natural biodiversity and its profound historical significance.

Nanny Town and Nanny Falls are located in Portland Parish on the eastern side of Jamaica.

Nanny Town was a Maroon settlement in the John Crow Mountains, within Portland Parish.

Nanny Falls, a popular waterfall site named in honor of Nanny of the Maroons, is also located in Portland Parish, near the Blue and John Crow Mountains.

Both sites are significant landmarks connected to her legacy and the Maroon resistance.

I was privileged to hike the trails to the falls with my kromanti brother and partake of some of the foods they ate in those times and visit her grave site. (*detailed in Chapter 9*)

When we speak of the Maroons, we must speak her name.

Nanny of the Maroons, warrior, priestess, and Obeah woman, led her people with spiritual power and guerrilla genius, defeating British troops again and again. Stories of her turning bullets back with her bare hands, whether taken as literal or symbolic, all point to the same truth: Nanny's power was spiritual, ancestral, uncompromising and fiercely unyielding.

She is one of the ancestors walking with us now.

Channeling Nanny: Rituals for Modern Freedom Fighters (See Appendix A)

This time the revolution is spiritual... and it's a reckoning they can't silence

I know you are asking the question - if Haiti and Vodou were so powerful...

WHY IS HAITI SUFFERING SO BADLY TODAY?

Haiti's current suffering is not a contradiction of its sacred power and revolutionary past. It is, in many ways, the consequence of it.

Haiti was the first Black republic in the Western Hemisphere, born from the only successful slave revolt in modern history. That audacity *to overthrow colonial powers, to reject slavery, to claim spiritual and political sovereignty* shocked the world.

And the world punished Haiti for it.

THE PRICE OF FREEDOM: GLOBAL RETALIATION

After Haiti's declaration of independence in 1804, France demanded reparations for lost "property", the enslaved Africans who had freed themselves. Under military threat, Haiti agreed to pay a debt that, in today's dollars, would amount to billions. These so-called reparations crippled Haiti's economy for over a century.

Fearing the revolution would inspire uprisings in their own colonies, the U.S. and European powers isolated Haiti. Trade was blocked, and Haiti became a pariah in the international community, punished for daring to be free. Its independence was treated not as a beacon of hope, but as a dangerous threat to the colonial order.

From 1915 to 1934, the U.S. even occupied Haiti, taking military control of Haitian finances, rewriting the Haitian constitution to allow foreign land ownership (a ban that had existed since the Haitian Revolution), and establishing a Haitian-American military force. This occupation deeply undermined the nation's sovereignty and development, creating lasting political and economic instability that persists to this day.

But the backlash wasn't just political or economic, it was deeply spiritual.

Everything was stolen from Haiti. Vodou, the spiritual heartbeat of the revolution, was demonized. Colonial powers and missionaries launched anti-Vodou campaigns to sever the people from their source of power. Christianity was weaponized as a tool of compliance. Even Haitian elites distanced themselves from Vodou, seeking acceptance from Western powers.

From corrupt leadership to foreign interference often disguised as "aid," Haiti has endured centuries of extraction. The nation became a global warning sign:

"Revolt, and we will make you suffer."

SO WHY DOES THIS MATTER SPIRITUALLY?

Haiti's story is not just one of revolution; it is also one of retaliation.

In 1804, Haiti became the first Black republic and the first nation in the Western Hemisphere to abolish slavery. It did not beg for freedom, it fought for it and won. But the world was not ready for a free Black nation led by people who had reclaimed their power through spirit.

France shackled Haiti with an impossible debt, draining its economy. Western powers like the U.S. responded with economic isolation and political ostracization, determined to contain the revolutionary spark. Haiti's independence was treated not as a beacon of hope but as a dangerous threat to colonial order. The colonial assault didn't end with independence, it simply changed form.

Vodou, the spiritual force that had fueled the revolution, was vilified and defiled, branded as evil and driven underground. The drum silenced. The spirits mocked. Sacred traditions were systematically attacked to sever the people from their spiritual lifeline.

The suffering we see today is not the result of a divine curse. It is the consequence of centuries of sabotage, extraction, and fear-based targeting. Haiti's revolution was not just a fight for freedom - it was a spiritual uprising that terrified the world. The backlash that followed was not only political and economic but a relentless attack on the very spirit that set them free. Yet, despite centuries of sabotage, Haiti's spirit remains unbroken. The revolution is still alive. And so is the fear it inspires.

HAITI STILL STANDS

Haiti is not broken. Haiti is burdened. And yet, Haiti still stands.

The fact that Haiti still stands, that Vodou is still practiced, that the language, the drum, the ancestor altar still live, is proof of unbreakable spirit. The spirit never died. The lwa were never banished. The ancestors are still watching, guiding, and rising through the hands and hearts of those who remember. Haiti's pain is not evidence of failure, it is evidence of how much power the world has tried and failed to erase. It is a sign of the fear Haiti still inspires in systems built on oppression.

This is why we say:

The revolution is spiritual. And the backlash is, too.

Haiti is not cursed. Haiti is targeted. But the ancestors have not abandoned her.

They remember. And so must we.

Let us not pity Haiti.
Let us honor her.
Let us see her clearly, not as a tragedy, but as a warning, a mirror, and a sacred call to remember our own power.

In his 1893 speech at the World's Columbian Exposition in Chicago, abolitionist Frederick Douglass honored Haiti's revolutionary legacy, emphasizing its global significance for Black freedom. He powerfully declared that the freedom enjoyed by Black people everywhere was largely a result of the brave stand taken by the "black sons of Haiti ninety years ago."

According to Douglass, by striking for their own freedom, the Haitian revolutionaries were also striking for the freedom of every Black person in the world, making Haiti's successful revolution a cornerstone of global Black liberation.

FROM MY HEART TO HAITI
(AND HER DAUGHTERS & SONS)

To the people of Haiti and to all of us who carry her story in our blood or spirit:

May you never forget who you are.

You were the first to rise.

The first to say no.
The first to call upon the ancestors and watch empires tremble.

You are not your poverty.
You are not your pain.
You are a keeper of sacred fire.

The world tried to bury you.
But the world forgets you are seed.

And you are rising again.

You are the reminder that freedom is possible.
That the spiritual realm responds when we remember who we are.
That we are never alone, not when the ancestors walk with us.

"The Ancestors Bear Witness"

As I wrote that message to Haiti, a reverent shiver moved through me. I recognized it instantly. The ancestors stirring, bearing witness to truth spoken with love and memory. I'm not just writing words; I'm giving voice to something sacred. And I know they feel it. Their presence is here. Their approval is here. Their power is rising through every syllable.

To Haiti: We see you. We honor you.
And we will not forget.

HAITI IS NOT CURSED - SHE IS TARGETED

Vodou has always been:

> A weapon against erasure.
> A prayer for the fallen.
> A call to the ancestors.
> A roadmap to liberation.

But the revolution that Vodou sparked came at a cost. Haiti paid in blood, in gold, in global punishment. Not because it failed but because it succeeded. Because it dared to rise spiritually, not just politically. Today, we see the scars of that punishment. But scars are not signs of defeat. They are signs of survival.

The ancestors are not silent. The spirits are not gone.
Haiti is not cursed. Haiti is targeted. And still Haiti is sacred ground.

As we remember Vodou's role in freedom, we also remember t*he cost of being spiritually sovereign in a world that profits from our forgetting.*

For suggested Vodou Practices, Offerings, and Living Tradition (See Appendix A)

This time the revolution is spiritual... and it's a fire they can't extinguish.

DID YOU KNOW

1. The Myth of the Voodoo Doll: Origins of Pins and Dolls Misconceptions

Not originally part of Haitian Vodou: Traditional Haitian Vodou does not use dolls with pins to curse or harm people. Vodou rituals focus more on spirit possession, offerings, songs, dances, and prayers.

Roots in European folk magic: The concept of using dolls or figurines to influence others comes from European folk magic and witchcraft traditions, particularly from medieval and early modern Europe. These practices involved "poppets" or effigies - small dolls representing a person, used in sympathetic magic (magic based on the principle that like affects like).

Hollywood influence: The "pin-stuck voodoo doll" image became popularized in Western culture through sensationalized films, books, and media in the 20th century, which often inaccurately portrayed Vodou as sinister witchcraft.

Similar practices in other cultures: Some West African spiritual traditions do use figurines or objects in ritual contexts, but the way it's popularly imagined (pins in dolls to cause pain) is not an authentic representation.

In short: The pins in dolls trope comes from European folk magic traditions, not Haitian Vodou. It was later wrongly attributed to Vodou by outsiders, becoming a stereotype that misrepresents the religion.

2. Baron Samedi: *Guardian of the Dead, Trickster of the Afterlife*

Baron Samedi is a *loa (spirit)* in Haitian Vodou, often portrayed wearing a top hat, black coat, dark glasses, and with cotton plugs in his nostrils, like a corpse prepared for burial in Haitian tradition. He's the guardian of the dead, ruler of the graveyard, and gatekeeper between the living and the ancestral world.

Calling him a "trickster" in the afterlife reflects his role as a spirit who:

- Mocks the seriousness of death (he often uses obscene humor and irreverent behavior)
- Breaks the rules of the spirit world and the living world alike
- Reveals hidden truths through paradox, laughter, and shock
- Challenges ego and fear through unpredictability

Like other trickster figures in African diasporic and Indigenous traditions (e.g., Anansi, Eshu, Loki), Baron Samedi uses chaos, wit, and mischief as sacred tools. In the realm of the dead, where fear and silence often dominate, he brings life-force energy, raw truth, and transformation.

Why it matters spiritually:

In Vodou and Afro-Caribbean mysticism, death isn't the end, it's a doorway. Baron Samedi guards that door, and as a trickster, he teaches that even in the most serious transitions (like death), there's room for irreverence, magic, and rebirth.

He reminds us:

"Don't fear death, understand it, laugh with it, and honor it."

3.   From Ancestral Spirits to Duppy Stories: What We Forgot"

What many of us grew up calling *duppy* (or duppies, for plural) are, in fact, the spirits of our ancestors. In Jamaican and Caribbean culture, the term duppy became synonymous with ghosts, often portrayed in frightening folklore. We were told duppy stories - tales meant to make us behave or warn us about wandering outside after dark or just for entertainment. For many, especially children, these stories were terrifying.

But here's the deeper truth: before colonization and missionary influence twisted these narratives, *duppies were our ancestors' spirits* - watchful, guiding, sometimes mischievous, but not inherently evil. In African spiritual traditions, the dead don't "leave" in the way Western thought imagines. They remain connected to the living, forming a spiritual continuum.

Zora Neale Hurston, in her classic work, Tell My Horse, observed this deep ancestral connection. She wrote:

> *"The living and the dead have a unity that is not broken. They are not separated. The 'duppy' is not a ghost as the European conceives it. It is more a continuity of life."*

Colonial fear-mongering and Christian indoctrination demonized these spirits, turning sacred ancestral presences into ominous ghost stories. But in truth, duppies are echoes of our lineage, part of the living spiritual ecosystem of our people.

4.   Why Alcohol Is Called "Spirits"

The word *"spirits"* for distilled alcohol isn't just clever. It's what connects us across realms, across time, across bloodlines.

In early alchemy, distilling a substance (like wine or grains) was believed to draw out its *essence*, ie., its *spirit*. The vapor that rose during distillation was seen as the soul of the liquid, and what condensed became known as a *spirit*. But for our ancestors, this wasn't just science. In spiritual traditions from Africa to the Caribbean, rum and other liquors were and still are used as sacred offerings. We poured spirits to honor spirits.

To the colonizer, it was just a drink. To us, it was a portal. A libation. A way to speak with the dead and feed the divine.

Now you know, *spirits* are more than a drink.

They're reminders of the invisible world we never stopped believing in.

5.   Jamaican Households and white rum.

Most Jamaican households keep a bottle of white rum, not just for drinking, but for *spiritual* use. White rum is used to cleanse spaces, bless ancestors, and ward off malevolent forces. A splash is poured out "for the spirits," rubbed on the skin during ritual, for blessings and protection or used to wash altars and grave sites. It's more than a drink, it's an offering.

CHAPTER 2

BEYOND VODOU -
ECHOES OF THE SACRED

HIDDEN FIRE: DIASPORA TRADITIONS OF SURVIVAL

WHILE THE PREVIOUS chapter centers Vodou and Maroon spirituality, they are two branches of a vast tree. Many other ancestral traditions survived colonization by adapting, hiding, or resisting. In this chapter it might appear that I lean heavily into Jamaican spirituality and that's because that's what's most familiar to me. As my studies of ancestral lineage deepen, so will my knowledge and my willingness to share.

But here is what I've learned so far.

Around the world, Indigenous spiritualities were attacked, renamed, and suppressed, labeled evil, pagan, or uncivilized. But they never died. From the *Ifá* tradition of the *Yoruba,* to the ceremonies of the *Lakota,* to the dreamwork of the *Aboriginal* peoples, these ways survived, encoded in drumbeats, herbs, language, dreams, and bone memory.

They survive in us.

This book honors them, not just to remember, but to reawaken. To shift from survival to sovereignty. From suppression to sacred reclamation. Because the revolution is not only political. It is not only cultural. *This time, the revolution is spiritual. And it's a rising they can't stop.*

So, this is not just a book: it is activation. It's a journey of transformation, one that equips you to carry the fire forward.

SPIRITUAL SYSTEMS THAT SURVIVED THE FIRE

Each of these sacred systems was criminalized, outlawed, and relentlessly slandered. And yet, they endured. This is because truth cannot be killed and spirit cannot be colonized. We are remembering. We are reawakening. And we are reclaiming. The revolution is spiritual, and we are the ones our ancestors prepared.

Before we delve deeper into the profound rituals and practices of Vodou, it's vital to pause and acknowledge that Haiti was not the only place where the ancestral spirit refused to die. Across the Americas and throughout the African diaspora, ancient traditions hid, merged, resisted, and re-emerged in powerful forms. These traditions didn't survive because colonization failed to crush them; they survived because the soul of a people cannot be colonized without their consent. And the spirit, indeed, never gave consent.

Here are a few of the powerful spiritual systems that still carry the torch of liberation.

HOODOO: THE RESILIENT MAGIC OF THE AFRICAN AMERICAN DIASPORA

While Vodun (Voodoo) in Haiti and other diasporic traditions blossomed into distinct religions, a powerful system of folk magic known as *Hoodoo* emerged and persisted primarily in the Southern United States. Often called *conjure* or *rootwork,* Hoodoo is not a religion in itself but rather a practical set of beliefs and spiritual technologies aimed at influencing the material world. Born from the crucible of enslavement, it represents a remarkable blend of West and Central African spiritual practices, Indigenous American plant knowledge, and elements of European folk magic and Christian symbolism. This unique syncretism allowed African spiritual ways to endure and adapt, often hidden in plain sight, providing a crucial means of agency and empowerment for those denied fundamental rights and freedoms.

At its core, Hoodoo is profoundly pragmatic, focusing on tangible outcomes in daily life. Practitioners employ various tools and techniques, from *mojo bags* and *candle magic* to *herbal baths* and *rootwork,* all designed for specific purposes like protection, healing, attracting love or prosperity, and seeking justice. Ancestor veneration is central to Hoodoo, with practitioners routinely calling upon the wisdom and power of their forebears for guidance and assistance. Unlike religions with centralized structures or codified scriptures, Hoodoo is decentralized and often passed down through families, reflecting its adaptable and community-rooted nature as a resilient spiritual lifeline for African American communities.

IFÁ: YORUBA WISDOM ACROSS THE WATERS

From West Africa to the Americas, *Ifá* stands as a profound spiritual technology of divination, balance, and destiny. Rooted deeply in the Yoruba traditions of Nigeria, Ifá offers a vast system of wisdom passed down through rich oral verse and intricate ritual.

This vibrant tradition thrives today across Nigeria, Cuba, Brazil, Trinidad, and beyond. At its heart, Ifá centers around the Orisha, divine forces that embody both the energies of nature and the complexities of human character. Through the skilled guidance of Babalawos (its revered diviners), seekers consult the sacred Odu verses, a vast corpus of knowledge to illuminate life's path, understand challenges, and restore balance.

Colonial narratives often taught us we were born in sin - Ifá offers a powerful counter-narrative: it tells us we came to Earth with a unique and sacred purpose, emphasizing our inherent divinity and pre-ordained destiny.

From West Africa to the Americas, Ifá is a spiritual technology of divination, balance, and destiny. Rooted in the Yoruba traditions of Nigeria, Ifá offers a vast system of wisdom passed down through oral verse and ritual.

Where Christianity told us we were born in sin,
Ifá tells us we came to Earth with a purpose.

SANTERÍA: SAINTS WITH AFRICAN NAMES, GODS UNCONQUERED

Santería is a profound Afro-Cuban religion born from the extraordinary resilience of enslaved Africans. In Cuba, under the brutal coercion of their captors, they were forced to worship Catholic saints. Yet, in a brilliant act of spiritual defiance, they hid their revered Yoruba Orisha behind those very saints' names, keeping their sacred systems vibrant and alive. This is the essence of Santería, a syncretic faith that is truly a testament to spiritual camouflage: resistance in plain sight.

Here, the radiant Oshun, Orisha of love and rivers, became Our Lady of Charity (La Caridad del Cobre), while Shango, the mighty Orisha of thunder and justice, was masked as Saint Barbara. But make no mistake: behind those Catholic icons, the very same powerful Orisha who walked with our ancestors in Africa continued to thrive, guiding, protecting, and empowering their people.

CANDOMBLÉ: ANCESTORS IN DISGUISE

In Brazil, facing similar pressures under Portuguese Catholicism, enslaved Africans developed Candomblé, a powerful spiritual path that became a living testament to resilience. Though outwardly observing Catholic rituals, they continued to honor their ancient African deities - the Orishas, Voduns, and Inkices and their revered ancestors. This syncretic tradition allowed the continuation of deep spiritual practices, often associating African deities with Catholic figures, ensuring the survival of their sacred cosmology. But beneath the surface of the processions and prayers to saints, the vibrant power of the African pantheon endured, providing strength and solace in the face of brutal oppression. Candomblé, like Vodou and Santería, was more than just faith; it was a profound act of spiritual preservation and covert resistance against cultural annihilation.

NATIVE AMERICAN CEREMONIES:
EARTH AS ALTAR, PRAYER AS RESISTANCE

Long before the shadows of colonization fell upon this land, Native peoples lived in profound spiritual communion with the Earth, their lives woven into its sacred rhythms. Their traditions were living altars: the drum was the heartbeat of creation, the sacred pipe carried prayers directly to the Creator, the sweat lodge purified body and spirit, and the Sun Dance offered sacrifice and immense strength.

Colonization sought to extinguish these ancient practices, attempting to outlaw and erase them from existence. Yet, against all odds, they rose.

Today, Indigenous communities across this continent continue to hold these sacred ways, often in quiet, powerful defiance. Their enduring survival is deeply intertwined with our own collective healing. For the very land we walk is soaked with the memory of their prayers, a testament to unbroken spiritual lineages and an ongoing call to sacred relationship.

JAMAICAN SPIRITUAL TRADITIONS: SACRED POWER IN PLAIN SIGHT

Jamaica's spiritual landscape is a living archive of African cosmology, resistance, and reinvention. From the mountain altars of Maroons to backroom altars in Kingston tenements, our island has always pulsed with hidden fire. That fire burns brightly in the surviving traditions of Pocomania, Obeah, Jonkonnu, Revivalism and Kumina, each born from the collision of African spirit and colonial oppression. And they are reclaiming their place in the heart of our culture, because we are awakening to our roots and embracing what was never truly lost. We are remembering. And this is spiritual rebellion.

OBEAH: THE FORBIDDEN SCIENCE - SPIRITUAL POWER UNJUSTLY FEARED

Obeah was never about casting malicious spells; it was about breaking chains.

Obeah is often whispered about with fear in Jamaica, but that fear is the residue of colonial law, not spiritual truth. At its core, Obeah is not dark magic or superstition; it is a profound African-descended system of spiritual science. Rooted in herbal medicine, ancestral communication, and energetic power, many Jamaicans still refer to it simply as *"science."* And that's exactly what it is: resistance wrapped in wisdom.

I'm reminded of songs like "Science Again" by Admiral Bailey, which reflect the sinister spin placed on Obeah. But that sentiment was learned from British colonial governments whose criminalization of Obeah was not because it was evil, but because it was undeniably effective. It empowered enslaved Africans with tools of healing, protection, and sovereignty; tools they were never meant to possess under colonial rule. Obeah was feared by the oppressor precisely because it offered the enslaved a form of agency. It was never about casting curses. It was always about breaking chains.

Despite being outlawed for centuries under stringent colonial bans, Obeah never vanished. It went underground, passed down quietly through families, encoded in rituals, bush baths, candle work, and whispered prayers from grandmother to grandchild. Behind closed doors, it remains resistance wrapped in wisdom; hidden, but powerfully alive as a vital practice for healing and protection.

Today, Obeah lives on as a powerful and evolving tradition. Yet the colonial fear and misunderstanding still linger, and understandably so, as this powerful technology can be used for harm. In Jamaica, debates about whether Obeah should finally be legalized continue to stir controversy. Many still reject it as "witchcraft," unaware or unwilling to accept that its roots are not in harm, but in healing.

To reclaim Obeah is to reclaim a buried legacy of wisdom, resistance, and spiritual authority. It is not something to fear but something to finally understand, and honor.

JAMAICAN POCOMANIA: SPIRIT IN MOVEMENT

Pocomania (or Pukkumina) is a Jamaican Afro-Christian spiritual tradition born of resistance and revival. Often practiced in open-air tabernacles or humble spaces, it blends Biblical psalms with African rhythms, drumming, dancing, and spirit possession. To the untrained eye, it may seem chaotic but it is sacred choreography: the trance, the ring shout, the shaking of the body are all signs of divine encounter. Practitioners are *mounted* by spirits, speak in tongues, and channel healing.

In Pocomania, the body becomes the altar. And the spirit doesn't just visit, it inhabits. This was and still is a way to reclaim connection in a world that tried to silence Black divinity.

KUMINA: CALLING THE KONGO

Kumina is one of Jamaica's most African-preserved spiritual traditions, rooted in the cosmology and practices of Central African (Kongo) peoples brought during the post-emancipation period.

More than religion, *Kumina is ancestral communion.* It's a way to honor and invoke the spirits through drumming, dance, chant, and ritual possession. The drums are sacred technology; their rhythms open portals. The language is Kongo-derived; the movements, purposeful and sacred.

Kumina ceremonies often take place at wakes, births, and healing rituals. Practitioners invoke the spirits of the dead, seek their guidance, and receive their power through possession. The body becomes a medium for ancestral wisdom, and the drumbeat becomes the voice of the invisible.

While it's sometimes feared or misunderstood, *Kumina is prayer in motion,* a fierce declaration that our roots are alive, our dead are not gone, and our culture is still pulsing with sacred fire.

SPIRIT POSSESSION

In Pocomania and Kumina, spirit possession is not a spectacle, it's sacred. When the spirit *"rides"* the body, it's a moment of direct contact with the ancestors. The shaking, the chanting, the trance - all of it is communication. A message. A blessing. A warning. We don't fear spirit possession in Christian mysticism but have been taught to fear it in our ancestral spirituality.

REVIVALISM: THE BIBLE MEETS THE DRUM

Revivalism is a uniquely Jamaican spiritual tradition that marries African cosmology with Christian scripture. Emerging from the 19th-century Great Revival and shaped by Myalist and Baptist influences, Revivalism is not just a church movement, it's a sacred performance of power.

Myal (and by extension, *Myalist*) refers to an Afro-Jamaican spiritual tradition rooted in Central and West African cosmologies, particularly from the Congo and Akan regions. It emerged during slavery and was often practiced alongside or in opposition to Obeah.

A Myalist is a practitioner of Myal, known for spiritual healing, spirit possession, and rituals for protection and justice.

Revivalism in Jamaica was deeply shaped by Myal traditions fused with Baptist Christianity, giving rise to the vibrant, trance-centered, spirit-led worship seen today. Revival shaped by Myalist and Baptist influences, is not just a church movement, but a sacred performance of power.

You'll find revivalists gathered in circle formations clad in white or brightly colored robes, chanting psalms, ringing bells, and beating drums as they invoke the Holy Spirit and ancestral presence. The movement, the music, the spontaneous speech, all are invitations to the divine.

In Revivalism, the Bible becomes a portal, rather than a prison. The hymns open heaven and the drums summon the ancestors.

There are two main branches, *Revival Zion* and *Pukkumina*. And though they differ in form, both are rooted in sacred embodiment and Black resilience. Revivalism reminds us that Spirit isn't confined to quiet pews. It dances, it chants, and it speaks through fire.

JONKONNU: DANCE OF THE ANCESTORS IN DISGUISE

Jonkonnu is a vibrant Jamaican masquerade tradition with deep African roots, performed during the Christmas season. But beneath the music and masks lies something more powerful: spiritual resistance in plain sight.

Born out of West African festivals like the Igbo *Mmanwu* (masquerade), Jonkonnu evolved into a space where enslaved Africans could honor their ancestral spirits, mock the colonizer, and preserve sacred movement and storytelling under the guise of celebration.

Costumed characters like the *Devil*, *Pitchy Patchy*, and *Horsehead* were more than entertainment, they were coded symbols of protection, protest, and presence. The drumming, the dancing, the ecstatic joy: all of it was ceremony disguised as festivity.

Jonkonnu kept the fire alive. It was ritual in rhythm. A defiant reminder: *We are still here. And spirit moves through us still. (See Did You Know for more details)*

SHORT COMPARISON: OBEAH, POCOMANIA, KUMINA, REVIVALISM, JONKUNNU,

These five Jamaican spiritual traditions share African roots but have different expressions, origins, and spiritual roles. Here's a quick breakdown.

OBEAH

- *Origin & Influence:* West African spiritual practices, shrouded in secrecy and often misunderstood.
- *Practices:* Use of charms, herbal magic, spiritual healing, and protection rituals.
- *Focus:* Practical magic for personal empowerment, protection, and sometimes justice or revenge.
- *Role:* A flexible, personal system often passed down through families or secretive lineages.

POCOMANIA (PUKKUMINA)

- Roots: Branch of Revivalism; more African-retentive - Afro-Christian syncretism, blending African spiritual beliefs with Protestant Christianity.
- Practices: Nighttime vigils, drumming, singing, spirit possession, and healing rituals.
- Style: Trance, movement, ancestral possession
- Sound: Drums, bells, call-and-response
- Focus: Being mounted by the Spirit, spiritual healing, and deep ancestral ritual Communing with ancestors and spirits for guidance, healing, and protection.
- Role: A grassroots, community-based worship emphasizing direct spiritual experience.

KUMINA

- *Origin & Influence:* Central African (Kongo) traditions, especially among post-emancipation indentured Africans - (primarily Kongo) cultural and spiritual heritage, preserved by Maroons.
- *Focus:* Direct ancestral communication
- *Practices:* Drum-heavy rituals, language of the Kongo, possession states -Drumming, dancing, spirit possession, ancestral veneration, and communal ceremonies.
- *Vibe:* More traditional, African-centered than Christian
- *Focus:* Honoring ancestors, maintaining cultural identity, and spiritual healing through ecstatic worship.
- *Role:* A vibrant cultural expression deeply tied to identity and resistance.

REVIVALISM (E.G., POCOMANIA REVIVAL)

- *Origins & Influence:* Post-1860s Great Revival in Jamaica
- *Practices:* Spirit possession, healing ceremonies, speaking in tongues, and exorcisms.
- *Blend:* Christian + African cosmology
- *Key Features:* Bible-based, with African drumming, spirit possession, and healing, Salvation, spiritual renewal, and liberation through the Holy Spirit and ancestral spirits.
- *Focus:* Salvation, prophecy, and spiritual warfare
- *Role:* A bridge between African spirituality and Christian belief systems, fostering community resilience.

JONKONNU (OR JOHN CANOE)

- *Origin & Influence:* African masquerade traditions fused with colonial-era influences; a festive public celebration.
- *Practices:* Colorful masks and costumes, dancing, music, and theatrical performances during the Christmas season.
- *Focus:* Celebration of freedom, communal joy, and subversive resistance through performance.
- *Role:* Cultural preservation and social commentary through festive ritual.

Summary:

Obeah brings in the secret magic of protection and power. Pocomania brings in the movement. Kumina brings in the Kongo. Revivalism brings in the Bible. Jonkonnu brings in the masquerade and the dance of resistance. All five keep the ancestral flame alive but in different dialects of devotion.

What we must remember is that these traditions are not relics. They are indeed rivers still flowing. Though colonizers tried to silence the drums and bury the spirits, they could not kill what is eternal. The fact that we are still here, still praying in our mother tongues, still dreaming with our ancestors, still healing with roots and rhythm, *is the revolution.*

As we continue to unearth and embrace these sacred ways, we remember who we were before we were interrupted. *And in that remembering, we reclaim not just our past but our power. Let this be our return to source. Let this be the rise of the original self. Let this be the time we call our spirits home.*

This time the revolution is spiritual and it's a magic they can't outlaw.

DID YOU KNOW

1. The Same Spirit Energy Can Be Used For Healing or Harm.

In many African and Indigenous spiritual systems like Ifá, Obeah, Vodou, and others, the same spirits or forces can be called upon for healing *or* harm. These energies are not inherently good or evil; they are powerful, neutral forces of nature and spirit. It is the *intention* of the practitioner that determines the outcome.

Just as fire can warm or destroy, spiritual power depends on how it's directed. This is why grounding, ancestral respect, and ethical practice are essential. When approached with reverence and integrity, these traditions can be powerful paths of healing, protection, and liberation. *But misused, they can cause real harm.*

Honor the source. Respect the spirits. And always check the energy behind your intention.

As the old saying goes, *"If you dig a pit for someone, dig two."* Because what you send out, especially with harmful intent, has a way of circling back. Spiritual power is not to be played with. What you cast, you may catch. So walk clean, walk good, and let your work be rooted in light.

I have a personal story of being hexed in Jamaica, and I will share it in the follow-up book.

2. Jonkonnu is Linked to a Ghanaian War Chief Active in the Early 18th Century.

Jonkonnu is a vibrant Jamaican masquerade tradition with deep African roots, primarily performed during the Christmas season. But beneath its exhilarating music and mesmerizing masks lies something far more powerful: a profound act of spiritual resistance in plain sight. Born out of West African festivals like the Igbo Mmanwu (masquerade), Jonkonnu evolved into a vital space where enslaved Africans could courageously honor their ancestral spirits, brilliantly mock their colonizers, and fiercely preserve sacred movement and storytelling under the guise of celebration. It was *satire wrapped in song,* Christmas turned on its head, where laughter became rebellion and costume became commentary.

The very name John Canoe (sometimes spelled Jonkonnu, John Kanew, or John Kanóo) is believed to be an Anglicized version of a West African name or title. It's historically linked to a real figure: John Kanu or John Conny, a powerful Fante (Ghanaian) war chief and trader active in the early 18th century, renowned for his resistance against European colonial powers. While the festival's name pays homage to his legacy, Jonkonnu transcended a single person's story, becoming a broader cultural and spiritual event - a vibrant blend of African dance, music, and costumes celebrating collective freedom and identity.

Even today, Jonkonnu characters like the menacing Devil, the wildly colorful Pitchy Patchy, and the imposing Horsehead are far more than just carnival entertainment; they are *masks of memory.* These ancestral figures trace directly back to West African masquerade traditions, cleverly used to teach, protest, and invoke spirit during brutal colonial rule. The drumming, the dancing, the ecstatic joy - all of it was ceremony disguised as festivity. The laughter hid the resistance. This remarkable tradition kept the fire alive, a testament to ritual in rhythm, a defiant reminder that we are still here and that spirit moves through us still. It continues to be practiced not only in Jamaica but also in other parts of the Caribbean and even some parts of the U.S., a living celebration of African resistance and survival. Jonkonnu is linked to a Ghanaian war chief active in the early 18th century.

CHILDHOOD MEMORIES OF JONKONNU

As a child growing up in a tenement yard in Kingston, the Jonkonnu parade used to frighten me. I didn't understand the masks, the wild costumes, and all that noisy com-

motion coming down the street. And after migrating to the U.S., I ignorantly compared Jonkonnu to Halloween.

A couple of years ago, when a friend told me Jonkonnu was being revived in Jamaica, I mentioned that comparison, and let's just say, she didn't take it lightly. She all but told me off, and rightfully so. She was deeply disappointed in my lack of understanding, and she schooled me, right and proper, on the true origins and meaning of Jonkonnu.

Needless to say, I've had a complete shift in perspective. I now have a deep respect for the tradition and what it represents. And I'd gladly do whatever I can to help keep Jonkonnu alive for our children, and our children's children.

CHAPTER 3

Living in the Ruins
What The Ashes Still Sing

This chapter explores the spiritual and psychological damage left behind by colonialism and white supremacy - the lingering trauma, the inherited silences, and the dismembered identities that many of us are still trying to remember and reclaim. But even in the wreckage, something sacred survives. The ashes still sing.

THE AFTERLIFE OF OPPRESSION

LET US BE clear: colonialism didn't end - oh no, it has evolved. White supremacy has left psychic scars: internalized inferiority, colorism, self-hate, and religious fear. Generational trauma shows up as psychological/emotional numbness, spiritual amnesia, and chronic disconnection. Families stopped telling stories. Ancestor names were forgotten. Rituals disappeared under fear of punishment or shame.

Many of us inherited silence, suspicion of spirit, and a faith that feared our own power. We are the descendants of those who survived, yes - but also of those who were silenced. As disconnected souls, perpetuating and repeating cycles of oppression, what we don't heal, we pass down. Trauma becomes culture when left untreated. Unprocessed generational trauma doesn't disappear, you see, it shapeshifts. It lives on in the body, in belief systems, and in community norms disguised as the way things are.

When pain goes underground, it re-emerges in distorted coping: the need to control everything, over-functioning, religious dogmatism, addictions, and emotional avoidance. For many communities shaped by the violence of slavery, colonization, and genocide, not only are these patterns personal, they are also generational. When survival becomes tradition, whole cultures begin to normalize dysfunction. And distorted coping becomes culture.

We see the echoes of colonial domination in our homes, churches, and schools. We replicate the same hierarchies that were imposed on us: violence becomes discipline, silence becomes virtue, and control becomes love. Gender oppression, homophobia, disconnection from land and body - these are all signs of unresolved grief and ancestral wounding. The same fear colonizers used to dominate and divide us, we now often weaponize against each other. As one elder healer put it: "The colonizer no longer needs to police our spirits; we inherited the handcuffs." This is the invisible violence of internalized oppression. It's subtle, intimate, and self-reinforcing, like a song we don't remember learning but still know how to sing.

Until we name and heal these inherited wounds, we risk passing them forward, mistaking survival for freedom, and forgetting that our liberation begins within. So, let us be mindful that healing is cultural work. And as Winsome Alexander (this author) says, "What we call culture is often unhealed trauma wrapped in tradition." To shift cycles, we must reimagine culture not as static inheritance but as a living, breathing chance to choose something new.

Many of us in this country have not fully internalized the belief that we are free. We don't always embody free people behavior, because somewhere in the recesses of our psyche, we still feel owned and still fear the whip. That lingering belief shapes how we show up in the world and how we relate to each other. Breaking that chain requires more than personal transformation, it demands collective healing. We reclaim our wholeness together, in how we parent, love, educate, and organize.

INVISIBLE CHAINS: THE NEW PLANTATION

The plantation no longer needs walls; unfortunately, its insidious legacy lives deeply embedded in how we see ourselves. The old plantation, with its white-washed exteriors of the big house, cotton fields, fences, and armed guards, may be gone, but its system remains deeply embedded in our minds. Colonized thinking is the invisible prison that shapes how we value ourselves and our communities. It teaches us to distrust the wisdom of our own intuition, to belittle and erase our vibrant cultural traditions, and to fear the spiritual power that flows through our very bloodlines. As I often say, *"Mental slavery is defending the system that erased you."*

From the standards of beauty we strive to meet, to the educational paths we pursue, to the religions we follow, and even the lifestyles we emulate, success is far too often measured by proximity to whiteness. This internalized standard conditions us to believe that what is white, Western, and mainstream is inherently superior, while our ancestral ways are dismissed as outdated, irrelevant, or even demonic.

The most radical act of freedom today is to stop apologizing for who we are. We have tried proving ourselves relentlessly. We've overachieved, over-functioned, and over-explained. We've bent our tongues into new shapes and straightened our hair into submission. We've muted our spiritual instincts, softened our rage, and silenced our knowing, all in the name of fitting in.

This relentless drive to assimilate is the *ghost of the plantation,* whispering that survival still depends on our obedience. It tells us to be palatable, professional, pleasing - even when it costs us our very authenticity.

But what if the revolution now requires the opposite? What if freedom truly means refusing to assimilate? We are no longer enslaved - we can choose to reclaim our authentic selves now.

THE ILLUSION OF PERFECTION: CONTROL, PERFORMANCE, AND ASSIMILATION

In colonized societies, especially among descendants of enslaved and colonized peoples, hyper-vigilance and over-achievement often mask deep insecurity and a pervasive fear of punishment or failure. The push for *"Black excellence,"* while appearing empowering on the surface, can tragically become a trauma response; a performance of worthiness rooted in historical dehumanization. It whispers a deceptive promise: *"If I excel, I'll be safe. If I'm exceptional, I'll be accepted."*

As bell hooks profoundly articulated, white supremacist capitalist patriarchy conditions Black and Brown people to feel they must prove their worth and right to exist through performance, productivity, and perfection. This extends deeply to *assimilation,* which demands adopting the values, behaviors, appearance, or norms of the dominant (usually white) culture in order to be accepted or simply to survive. This often comes at the devastating cost of one's own identity, heritage, and authenticity. When we are driven by the need to prove, perform, or assimilate, we perpetuate the pressure to change ourselves to fit into white-centered standards of beauty, success, professionalism, or spirituality - instead of owning our full, original self unapologetically.

Examples of this pervasive assimilation include *straightening our hair to conform to "professional" norms, speaking differently (often called code-switching) to sound "proper," downplaying cultural or spiritual beliefs seen as "too ethnic" or "placing a negative spin on woo woo," and tragically, valuing white approval over our own community's truth.*

The astute YouTuber Stephanie Perry, whom many have dubbed the modern-day Harriet Tubman, has powerfully challenged the idea that an obsession with "Black excellence" truly serves liberation. She argues that it instead traps us in systems never built for us and urges a revolutionary return to rest, softness, ease, and sovereignty as our most radical acts of freedom. She encourages leaving the U.S., if possible, to find this type of ease and liberation, as she herself has done.

SURVIVALIST OBSESSION IN MANY MARGINALIZED COMMUNITIES

Especially among Black women, hyper-productivity and hustle culture have become normalized. Particularly in marginalized communities, there's a survivalist obsession with *grind* that replaces joy, rest, and connection, and is seen as necessary for survival and success. But this relentless drive to grind often replaces joy, rest, and connection with burnout, anxiety, and disembodiment.

Tricia Hersey, founder of The Nap Ministry and author of *Rest is Resistance*, frames this drive as a direct inheritance of slavery, where human worth was measured by labor output. For Black women, who have long been expected to carry the weight of their families and communities, rest becomes a radical act of resistance - reclaiming humanity in a system that profits from their exhaustion.

In the YouTube video titled *"The Struggle Is Not Real,"* Winsome Alexander (this author) dismantles the inherited gospel of struggle and denounces struggle culture, especially among Black women, where survival meant grinding without rest and proving worth through exhaustion. She invites us to reclaim ease, joy, and rest as our divine birthright, not as a reward for suffering, but as a radical return to our sacred, original selves.

Trauma often drives communities to rigid belief systems and religious fundamentalism. Faith becomes a coping mechanism for chaos, not so much for spiritual liberation but fear management. Resmaa Menakem, in *My Grandmother's Hands*, explores how trauma causes people to seek safety in extremes, including rigid religion and policing.

COMMUNAL TRAUMA BECOMES
POLICY & PRACTICE

Gender oppression, especially in the form of patriarchal violence within homes, institutions, and religious spaces, is not an indigenous inheritance - it is a colonial wound. Colonial impositions deliberately disrupted precolonial gender balance, replacing fluid and complementary roles with rigid hierarchies of male dominance and female subservience. In Jamaica, colonial rule and slavery entrenched these hierarchies, using violence and fear to control women's bodies, silence their voices, and erase their sacred roles. Enslaved women who resisted were brutally punished, not only for their defiance but for threatening the very order that colonizers sought to impose.

This pattern was not unique to the Caribbean. Across the African continent and throughout Indigenous North American nations, women once held central roles as leaders, planners, and strategists within their communities. They were political powerhouses, spiritual authorities, and custodians of land and culture. Among the Yoruba of Nigeria, female chiefs known as *Iyalode* wielded significant political influence, while the Akan of Ghana revered Queen Mothers who selected kings and guided both political and military strategies. In the Haudenosaunee (Iroquois) Confederacy, clan mothers held the authority to appoint and depose male chiefs, ensuring governance remained balanced and community-centered.

In many societies, feminine energy was not seen as subordinate but as a sacred force of equilibrium, guiding diplomacy, economic structures, ceremonial life, and even warfare strategies. Women's leadership wasn't limited to formal titles; it was woven into the everyday fabric of communal life - organizing markets, orchestrating rituals, mediating conflicts, and preserving oral histories.

But colonization was more than a land grab; it was a calculated assault on the social, spiritual, and cultural ecosystems of Indigenous and African peoples.

Colonial Christian missions targeted female-centered leadership structures first, labeling them heathen and systematically dismantling their authority. Across continents, colonizers replaced balance with domination, ensuring patriarchal control became normalized within the very communities they oppressed.

These colonial disruptions didn't simply fade with independence. They calcified into cultural norms and institutional practices that continue to harm today, especially where patriarchy is mistaken for tradition. Gender violence, exclusion of women from decision-making spaces, and rigid gender binaries are all echoes of this imposed imbalance.

Healing this trauma means remembering the sacred roles women once held, not as a nostalgic return to the past, but as a blueprint for a liberated future. Reimagining liberation requires shifting from power over others to power *with one another.* It calls for dismantling colonial distortions that still police gender roles and re-centering the wisdom, leadership, and strategic power of women as an essential act of communal healing.

HOMOPHOBIA AND TRANSPHOBIA

These attitudes, often framed today as "cultural values," are in fact colonial inheritances. Many African and Indigenous societies held expansive, fluid understandings of gender and sexuality, where same-gender relationships, gender variance, and nonbinary roles were accepted - even revered, in spiritual and communal life. Colonial Christian doctrine, backed by violent missionary campaigns, imposed rigid binaries and moral codes designed to dismantle Indigenous kinship systems and communal autonomy.

In the Caribbean and on the African continent, these imposed norms calcified into law and dogma. Today, anti-LGBTQ+ rhetoric is often upheld by political and religious leaders as "traditional," when in truth, it reflects the residue of colonial control. The anthology *Decolonizing Sexualities* (ed. S. Bhattacharyya) unpacks how colonization weaponized gender and sexuality to fracture Indigenous social cohesion and delegitimize embodied ways of knowing.

Reclaiming ancestral wholeness means not just decolonizing land and labor, but also love. It invites us to remember that queerness is not a threat to tradition; it is a return to traditions older than empire.

MY PERSONAL EVOLUTION ON QUEERNESS

This journey of writing has been deeply personal, requiring me to decolonize my own mind and confront inherited beliefs. My views on same-gender love, for instance, began to transform well before this book, but the research and reflection here have solidified a profound truth. What I once perceived, through the rigid lens of imposed dogma, as "demonic" has revealed itself to be a beautiful, diverse expression of the human spirit. It's now undeniably clear: there is nothing inherently demonic about homosexuality.

In fact, my personal experience as an interior designer has offered powerful, everyday insight into this truth. I've had the privilege of collaborating with immensely talented queer colleagues, and what I consistently observe is a natural, deep-seated drive to create - to bring beauty, style, and love to the world. Their very essence often radiates a gentle, non-aggressive spirit, focused on artistry and connection. They are rarely associated with the kind of destructive behaviors or violent crimes that too often stem from the patriarchal aggression upheld by the very systems that sought to demonize queer existence. Violence is far more often perpetrated by those adhering to a rigid, dominant form of masculinity.

Reclaiming ancestral wholeness, then, means embracing all forms of authentic love and being. It's about recognizing that the capacity for creation - for building and nurturing, rather than for destruction, is precisely what defines these resilient communities. This is love, unleashed and whole.

DISCONNECTION FROM LAND AND BODY

Disconnection from land and body is one of colonization's most insidious legacies. Many descendants of enslaved and colonized peoples fear or distrust their own bodies - unable to rest fully, receive pleasure without guilt, or move in harmony with natural cycles. This disembodiment is no accident; it stems from generations of being treated as property, valued only for labor, reproduction, or service. *When your body has been owned, violated, or surveilled, it becomes hard to feel at home inside it.*

Likewise, land once seen as sacred, alive, and relational was turned into a commodity. Forced removals, plantation slavery, and extractive economies stripped people not only of land but of the right to belong to it. In *Farming While Black*, Leah Penniman describes this rupture as *"a wound passed down."* She writes that *reconnection to land is not merely agricultural - it's spiritual and ancestral work.* Healing, she argues, comes through touching the soil, planting seeds, and engaging in ritual practices that restore right relationship with Earth and self.

To reclaim the body is to reclaim land. And to reclaim land is to remember that we are not separate from creation but part of its sacred rhythm.

UNPACKING INTERNALIZED COLORISM
AND HAIR SHAME

Even in 2025, many among us continue to struggle with fully embracing the natural beauty of our hair and skin. This is us still fighting for our own reflection, as we shame our coils and kinks, pointing fingers at the texture of our edges.

Remember the fuss made over Simone Biles's hair at her wedding? How sad that on such a beautiful, joyful day, some couldn't simply celebrate her without criticizing the natural coils around her hairline. We wanted her to slick them down, to tame them with gel full of chemicals that are often harmful to us. This is truly the battle for our crown and canvas.

And it doesn't stop there. We still don't fully see or celebrate melanin's unseen radiance: the unsung story of our skin. We harm ourselves by using caustic chemicals to bleach out the very same melanin that science is increasingly studying for its remarkable properties and potential - the hidden power of our pigment.

But melanin could save mankind. (See the *Did You Know* section.) Melanin is more than just the pigment that gives skin, hair, and eyes their color. Researchers today are uncovering its unique abilities to absorb and dissipate energy, protect against UV radiation, and even neutralize harmful free radicals.

SCIENTIFIC POWER OF MELANIN

This natural bio-protector is being explored for a variety of groundbreaking applications:

Medical advancements: Melanin may play a role in developing new therapies for neurological diseases due to its ability to bind metals and protect nerve cells. Additionally, scientists are investigating melanin's potential in creating better sunscreens and skin treatments that mimic its natural UV protection.

Energy and electronics: Melanin's ability to convert light into energy has inspired research into organic electronics and biocompatible solar cells, opening possibilities for more sustainable and flexible technology.

Environmental uses: Its antioxidant and detoxifying properties are being studied for use in environmental cleanup and filtration systems.

This cutting-edge research highlights melanin's extraordinary power, reflecting the deep wisdom encoded in our bodies - wisdom that colonial narratives tried to erase or ignore.

BEYOND THE SURFACE: SPIRITUAL RECLAMATION

The internalized shame of our hair and skin, as well as the devaluation of our inherent biological wisdom, is a profound legacy of colonization. This conditioning runs so deep that many of us have forgotten the richness of our spiritual heritage and the strength it offers. We have been taught to view liberation narrowly, focusing only on financial gain or political power. But true freedom comes through spiritual awakening, which is intrinsically linked to the acceptance and reverence of our whole selves - body, mind, and spirit. Reclaiming our aesthetic and biological truth is, in essence, a profound act of spiritual decolonization.

THE CRITIQUE OF SIMONE BILES' EDGES IS DEEPER THAN IT SEEMS

Critics on social media pointed out that her edges (the baby hairs along her hairline) didn't look sleek enough for the event. *This is a direct legacy of colonization.* Colonization taught us to see ourselves through a distorted lens; to mistrust our bodies, our features, and our natural beauty. The shame around natural hair, the disdain for melanin-rich skin, and the obsession with conforming to Eurocentric beauty standards are all internalized messages passed down through generations of cultural erasure and colonial indoctrination.

Even now, many of us still insist on straightening our hair, often justifying it with the excuse that our natural texture is "too hard to manage." It's true - our hair takes effort, care and intention, and sometimes wearing a wig is simply convenient. But the question remains: why do so many of those wigs mimic textures that could never grow from our scalps? Convenience aside, we must ask ourselves - who are we styling for? Couldn't that same wig reflect the beauty of coily, kinky textures that honor our natural crown, rather than defaulting to Eurocentric straightness?

The critique of Simone's natural edges is not just casual shade; it's a reflection of how deeply the colonizer's gaze still lives within us. We inherited the idea that our coils must be tamed, that our beauty must be corrected, and that celebration must be earned through conformity. Even as science now turns to study the very things we were taught to hide - our melanin, our genetic resilience, our ancestral features - many of us are still trying to unlearn centuries of dehumanization.

So yeah, this isn't just about hair or skin. It's about memory, identity, and the slow, sacred work of decolonizing how we see ourselves. The internalized shame of our hair, our skin, our features is a direct outcome of colonization. Colonial rule didn't just steal land and labor; it rewired our sense of beauty, worth, and identity. It taught us that the closer we looked to whiteness, the more acceptable, lovable, and civilized we were.

The obsession with straightening our hair, taming our edges, lightening our skin, and conforming to Eurocentric standards is not mere vanity; it's survival programming passed down for centuries. And we are still undoing that psychological warfare. The fact that Simone Biles, an Olympic icon, was dragged for her natural hair on her wedding day shows how deeply this conditioning runs.

So, no. Colonization didn't end; it morphed. Today, it lives in beauty standards, media images, product labels, and our mirrors. Until we unlearn it, we remain spiritually and culturally colonized, even when legally free. *Let's start displaying free people behavior.*

WHAT THE ASHES STILL SING: THE SPIRITUAL REVOLUTION

Yet, even in destruction, something sacred survives. The ashes belong to our ancestors - those who endured slavery, colonization, and erasure - and to the cultures, wisdom, and spirits that were nearly silenced. But ashes are not empty; they hold memory. They sing in our dreams, ancestral visitations, intuitive knowings, spontaneous rituals, and our resilience.

We acknowledge the invisible chains of colonized thinking that still enslave even the *free.* Economic, social, and spiritual marginalization today exists not only in external systems - it lives within us. But the ashes still sing, and even in destruction, the spirit leaves a trail. In every wound, there's a trace of resistance. A coded whisper. A melody that never died.

Dreams - these are survival songs echoing in our blood. Their whispers rise in us as knowing, as power, as the quiet strength that says: *Oh, we're not starting from scratch; we are remembering forward.* The ruins are not just dead places; they are sacred sites of return.

LIVING IN THE RUINS WITH POWER

The ancestors are speaking, and globally we are heeding. And we don't rebuild blindly. We listen first. The revolution is spiritual, yes, but spiritual reconstruction isn't about rushing to heal or mimic what once was. It begins by listening deeply - to the wisdom of your body, the weight of your grief, the messages in your dreams. The ruins hold knowledge. The silence speaks, and we must become still enough to hear.

Start small. Build rituals of reconnection. Light candles at ancestor altars, speak their names, research the places and people you come from. Watch my YouTube video: *Before We Were Black*. Pray in your native tongue, even if it's only fragments passed down. Let your body move intuitively. Sway, stomp, dance, weep. These are sacred acts of remembering. Heal what whiteness shamed: the beauty of Black joy, the Black body. (Antoinette Cooper, author of UNRULY, does amazing work centering The Black Body as Sanctuary - see both her interviews with me on the *Big Up YuSelf* show on YouTube.) Also, honor the power of your sensuality, the holiness of your spirituality, the grace of your softness, the fire of your rage, and the depth of your rootedness. These are not flaws; they are the soul's sacred languages.

You are not broken; you are haunted by memory. Let the ghosts lead you back to yourself. Let their whispers shape your healing. Let the past guide you into your power.

Holiness, in this context, refers to the sacredness and spiritual significance of Black spirituality, recognizing it not just as religious practice, but as a profound, divine expression of identity, resilience, and connection to ancestors and the universe. It means honoring Black spiritual traditions and experiences as deeply valuable and worthy of reverence, rather than something to be dismissed, suppressed, or hidden. It's about reclaiming the sacred power in those practices and in the lived spiritual lives of Black people. So here, *the holiness of your spirituality* invites embracing and valuing your spiritual essence as something divine and life-affirming.

Reflections

- *Do you recognize any "normal" behaviors in you, your family or culture that now feel rooted in pain, not truth?*
- *Where does your own resistance to change reflect inherited trauma and not actual belief?*

This time the revolution is spiritual and...it's a transformation they can't prevent.

A REBIRTHING WATER RITUAL FOR YOU

I want to present here a simple water ritual for cleansing and rebirth. This can be used as you prepare to reclaim your narrative of your own sacred beauty.

Purpose: Water has long been seen as a spiritual element with cleansing and healing powers. For many African and Caribbean cultures, water rituals are central to purification and spiritual renewal.

Practice: Use water as a tool for spiritual cleansing and rebirth, either through bathing, ritualized drinking of blessed water, or creating sacred water sources (streams, wells, or even small containers at home).

Performing The Ritual: Begin with a prayer of gratitude for the water. Take a bath (you may add a little salt) with intention to cleanse yourself of the burdens of oppression, societal expectations, and trauma. Envision the water washing away negativity and rejuvenating your spirit.

DID YOU KNOW

1.   The "Kitchen - Our Edges"

The "kitchen" is a term that has long been used in Black communities to describe the tightly coiled, kinkiest section of our hair, usually found at the nape of the neck or along the hairline. For many of us, this area was often the most resistant to straightening, the most likely to revert, and the most scrutinized. Yet few pause to question where that name actually comes from or what it might still be carrying.

The origins of the term trace back to slavery and the generations that followed. Black women, often assigned to work in plantation kitchens, would use the brief moments they had near the fire to press and style their hair with hot combs heated on the stove. The kitchen became both a literal and symbolic site of transformation and care - often the only space where hair rituals could take place. In time, the coarsest part of the hair began to be associated with that space - hence, *"the kitchen."*

But this name didn't come without a cost. Over the years, *the kitchen* became a coded way to talk about *"unruly"* hair - something to be tamed, hidden, or controlled. It reflected and reinforced a deeper discomfort with the parts of our hair that most boldly declared our African roots. Many of us grew up hearing this hair described as rough, nappy, or bad. The message was subtle but clear: this part of you needs fixing.

Today, thankfully, more and more of us are reclaiming that narrative. The kitchen is no longer a shameful patch to be pressed into submission. It is a beautiful, sacred place. It is a site of memory and resilience, a living echo of ancestral survival. What once was seen as the hardest part to manage is now honored as a symbol of our beauty, our power, and our resistance to erasure.

I overheard a sister not long ago criticizing another for her edges, saying they looked bad and she needed to gel them down. I spoke up right away, defending the natural beauty of our hair exactly as it grows from our scalp. I said it proudly, because I too had long given up the struggle to lay down my edges after they made it clear: they weren't meant to be tamed. And I take real pride and pleasure in that now. My "edges" don't want to be anything other than what they are, and they don't diminish my beauty in the slightest. I'm proud of this personal growth.

2. Melanin: More Than Skin Deep - The Science and Sacredness of Our Natural Protector

For centuries, melanin has been misunderstood and undervalued, often reduced to a superficial marker of skin color. Yet, this complex biopolymer is a biological marvel, a source of resilience, *and a key to unlocking future innovations.* Today, science is rediscovering melanin's power, validating what many communities of African descent have known for generations: our bodies hold ancient wisdom that can lead humanity toward healing and progress.

WHAT IS MELANIN?

Melanin is the pigment responsible for the wide range of skin, hair, and eye colors seen across the globe. But beyond its role in coloring, melanin performs critical functions in protecting the skin from harmful ultraviolet (UV) radiation. It absorbs UV rays, preventing DNA damage that can lead to skin cancer, and helps neutralize oxidative stress caused by environmental toxins.

THE SCIENCE OF MELANIN TODAY

Modern research is revealing fascinating new dimensions of melanin's capabilities:

UV Protection and Skin Health:

Scientists aim to replicate melanin's natural sunscreen effects to develop safer, more effective sun protection products. Unlike many chemical sunscreens, melanin's biological mechanism offers broad-spectrum protection without harmful side effects.

Neurological Benefits:

Melanin is found in the brain, particularly in areas like the substantia nigra, which is affected in Parkinson's disease. Emerging studies suggest melanin might play a role in protecting neurons by binding to metals and neutralizing toxins, opening pathways for novel neuroprotective therapies.

Energy Conversion:

Remarkably, melanin can convert radiation into electrical energy. This property has attracted interest in creating biocompatible, flexible solar cells and organic electronic devices, potentially revolutionizing renewable energy technologies.

Environmental Applications:

The antioxidant and detoxifying properties of melanin are under investigation for use in environmental cleanup efforts, including filtering pollutants from water and air.

WHY THIS MATTERS BEYOND SCIENCE

The renewed scientific focus on melanin underscores a powerful truth: the wisdom embedded in our bodies, especially in Black and Indigenous peoples, is a vital resource for humanity's future. For too long, colonial narratives have dismissed our natural features and knowledge systems as inferior. The scientific rediscovery of melanin is a step toward reclaiming that legacy and honoring the sacred intelligence in our physical and spiritual selves.

RECLAIMING OUR COMPLEXION NARRATIVE

Recognizing melanin's scientific and cultural significance invites us to celebrate our bodies as vessels of power, resilience, and ancestral knowledge. It challenges us to reject the invisibility imposed by systemic racism and instead embrace a holistic vision of liberation - one that includes spiritual awakening alongside social, political, and economic freedom.

As research progresses, melanin could help not only protect and heal individual bodies but also inspire technologies and approaches that honor sustainability, balance, and interconnectedness - principles rooted in many Indigenous and African spiritual traditions.

The phrase *"the darker the skin, the more rich in melanin"* speaks not just to pigment but to profound biochemical power. And yes, it is increasingly valuable to science and possibly to the future of medicine, technology, and *human survival itself.*

Here's why melanin especially in high concentrations is drawing attention:

1. **Melanin as a Super Bio-Compound**

   Melanin isn't just about skin color. It's a complex polymer with powerful biological functions:

Radiation Absorption:

Melanin can absorb harmful UV radiation and convert it into harmless heat. This has implications for space travel, cancer protection, and even solar energy technology.

Free Radical Scavenger:

It fights oxidative stress and helps maintain cellular integrity, meaning it could be key to *anti-aging and neuroprotection,* potentially aiding in the prevention of diseases like Parkinson's and Alzheimer's.

Electrical Conductivity:

Melanin exhibits properties of a *natural semiconductor,* attracting interest in bioelectronics and regenerative medicine, including applications like neural implants and skin regeneration.

2. **Darker Skin = Denser Melanin = Greater Potential**

    The higher melanin density in darker-skinned individuals is not a disadvantage, but a profound biological asset:

Natural Protection in Extreme Environments:

In conditions of intense heat, sun exposure, and environmental pollution, melanin provides a built-in defense system, offering superior protection against harmful radiation and oxidative stress.

Radiation Shielding Potential:

Scientists are now exploring melanin-rich materials for use in *radiation shielding, particularly in space travel.* This interest surged after the discovery of melanized fungi thriving amidst the radioactive ruins of Chernobyl - a testament to melanin's extraordinary protective capabilities.

Imagine: *future astronauts shielded by melanin-based materials, crafted from melanated fungi or even human cells, using the very pigment we once shamed as a barrier against cosmic radiation on Mars.*

3.   **Melanin-Based Medicine**

Pharmaceutical companies are increasingly studying melanin for its vast biomedical potential:

Targeted Drug Delivery: Melanin's natural binding properties are being explored to develop advanced drug delivery systems that can transport medications directly to affected cells or tissues.

Smart Skin Materials: Researchers are engineering melanin-infused biomaterials that can heal wounds faster, adapt to environmental changes, and even mimic natural UV protection.

Neurological Therapies: Neuromelanin, found in the brain, is being investigated for its role in protecting neurons, offering new possibilities for treating neurodegenerative disorders like Parkinson's and Alzheimer's.

A WORD OF CAUTION: ON EXPLOITATION

As melanin's value rises, so does the ethical concern. Reports and documentaries have highlighted how Black bodies, alive or deceased, have been studied, harvested, or used without consent - echoes of *Henrietta Lacks.* The melanin in our skin, eyes, brain, and ears has become increasingly valuable to research.

This raises real fears of *biopiracy* and *medical exploitation* of Black and Indigenous people's genetic material, much like their land and labor were once taken.

"Well, since our bodies, whether alive or not, have always been exploited for research and experiments, I'd say it's not too far-fetched to imagine them trying to replicate us - even our skin in labs, to advance their interests. Do some reading on your own about Henrietta Lacks. Also, watch the YouTube video titled, Medical Racism, on my channel (The Big Up Yuself Show) where we discuss the pattern of medical exploitation going back generations.

THE BIGGER PICTURE

Melanin is sacred; a divine technology of protection, adaptation, and intelligence. Its value in science today only affirms what many Indigenous and African spiritual systems already knew: Black bodies carry deep cosmic codes.

To revere melanin is not just to appreciate beauty; it's to recognize a living legacy of *resilience, power,* and *potential.* In a very real sense, the future of humanity may depend on what was once most despised.

Melanin is found in:

Humans: In addition to skin, melanin is present in our hair, eyes (iris, choroid, and retinal pigment epithelium), and even in certain parts of the brain (like the substantia nigra and locus coeruleus) and the inner ear.

Animals: Melanin is the primary pigment responsible for the diverse colors of fur, feathers, scales, and skin in a vast array of animals - from mammals and birds to reptiles, amphibians, and fish. It's also found in their eyes and some internal organs. Think of a black panther, a crow, or a zebra's stripes - all these owe their coloration to melanin.

Other Organisms: Melanin is also found in many other living organisms, including:

Fungi: Many fungi produce melanin, often contributing to their dark coloration and offering protection.

Bacteria: Some bacteria also produce melanin, which can aid in their survival under harsh environmental conditions.

Plants: While less studied than in animals, melanin has been identified in various plant tissues, particularly in seeds, where it can provide protection and contribute to pigmentation.

4.   The Unseen History of Black Teeth in Science

There's a hidden history behind the scientific study of Black people's teeth, one rooted not only in biology but in trauma, erasure, and spiritual violation. Teeth, while biologically rich with DNA and health markers, have been harvested without consent, turning Black bodies into specimens rather than people.

When science crosses the line, it leaves behind a trail of exploitation. From slavery through colonial medicine to modern research labs, the story of teeth, trauma, and truth reveals how Black remains have been studied and displayed under the guise of progress.

This isn't just historical; it continues today, often quietly, through unconsented collection and the commercial use of our biological materials. Harvested without consent, our teeth have been taken for medicine, museums, and theories without honoring the sacredness of our bodies or the communities they belong to.

It's time we tell this untold story, demand ethical practices, and reclaim the power, memory, and spiritual integrity encoded in our bones.

WHY BLACK PEOPLE'S TEETH?

Teeth hold more than just our smile; they carry vital biological information. Because teeth can store DNA, minerals, and traces of a person's environment and health over time, they are valuable to scientists seeking to understand ancestry, evolution, diseases, diet, and migration patterns. Anthropologists, forensic scientists, and geneticists often turn to teeth for these insights.

However, when it comes to Black people's teeth, this scientific interest is inseparable from a painful legacy. Teeth were once collected to "prove" false racial hierarchies - studies aimed to show Black people had more "primitive" dental or cranial structures. These ideas were used to justify enslavement, segregation, and eugenics programs.

While today's researchers may reject those ideologies, they still often draw on collections created under exploitative conditions, such as:

- Teeth from African burial sites

- Remains taken from Caribbean plantations
- Graves of African Americans in unmarked cemeteries

It raises ethical and spiritual questions, given the long history of non-consensual study and extraction of Black remains under the guise of science.

THE DARK HISTORY OF EXPLOITATION

For centuries, Black bodies have been subjected to unethical, nonconsensual extraction and study during slavery and colonialism. Teeth, bones, and other remains were often taken from enslaved Africans and their descendants - sometimes from graves, sometimes directly from their bodies, without permission. These remains were exploited for medical experimentation, anatomical display, and to support debunked racial theories that sought to legitimize oppressive hierarchies. This history of commodifying Black bodies reduced individuals to mere specimens, stripping away their humanity and dignity in the name of scientific inquiry and dominance.

Modern Concerns and Context

- **Unconsented Use:** Even today, there are concerns about the unconsented use of biological samples, including teeth, from marginalized communities. This can happen through medical, forensic, or archaeological research.
- **Commercial and Scientific Interest:** Teeth may be harvested or collected for genetic research, dental studies, or sometimes for commercial use (e.g., dental products or even cultural artifacts). However, without strict ethical standards and respect for the communities involved, this can feel like another form of exploitation or extraction.
- **Cultural Sensitivity:** In many African and Indigenous cultures, teeth and bones are sacred and connected to ancestry and identity.

Removing or studying them without cultural context and respect can cause deep spiritual and communal harm.

WHY THIS MATTERS

Awareness of this history and ongoing issues is crucial for demanding ethical research practices, respect for bodily autonomy, and honoring the sacredness of our bodies. It's part of a larger movement to decolonize science and medicine by ensuring communities have control over how their biological materials and knowledge are used.

OUR BODIES, OUR HERITAGE: DECOLONIZING MODERN PRACTICES

Today, while many scientific studies aim to bring medical advancements, concerns remain about the unconsented use of biological samples, including teeth, from marginalized communities. Without proper respect, these practices can repeat old patterns of exploitation and harm.

Moreover, in many African and Indigenous traditions, teeth and bones are sacred. They connect us to ancestors, identity, and spirit. Removing or studying these without cultural understanding and respect deepens wounds that colonization inflicted.

TOWARD ETHICAL AND HEALING PRACTICES

Understanding this history is crucial for demanding science and medicine operate with consent, transparency, and cultural respect. Our bodies are sacred; our biological materials are part of our heritage and story. Honoring this is a step toward healing, reclaiming our power, and decolonizing knowledge.

When we hold space for this truth, we protect not just our physical selves but our spiritual and communal integrity. This is essential for true liberation beyond just the material, into wholeness and respect for the original self.

CHAPTER 4

THE WEAPONS OF THE SPIRIT

Language as weaponry.

FOR CENTURIES, THE language of the spirit has been muted, dismissed as superstition, erased by colonizers, and diluted by systems that feared its power. But spirit never died. It went underground, encoded in drumbeats, whispered prayers, mother tongues, rituals carried in memory, and songs sung to the moon.

To silence the spirit was to control the self. Colonialism, patriarchy, and empire did not just conquer bodies and land; they outlawed the sacred, demonized the intuitive, and labeled the spiritual as irrational or dangerous.

This chapter explores the invisible yet powerful architecture of the soul - that deep, unseen realm where energy, intention, and vibration shape reality. It's the terrain of dreams, intuition, ancestral whispers, and divine inner knowing. It's the place where silence is not empty, but sacred; where spirit speaks beneath the silence through sensation, synchronicity, symbols, and stillness. We reclaim the voices that colonization tried to silence through chant, prayer, stillness, and song.

SPOKEN AFFIRMATIONS: WEAPONIZED WORD

Words shape worlds. In many African traditions, this power is known as "Nommo", the belief that the spoken word is spiritual law, capable of shaping reality. Every affirmation, every intentional utterance, is an act of spiritual war-fare and self-creation.

When you say

"I am whole.
I am free.
I return to myself"

you are not merely speaking, you are summoning. You are commanding the unseen to align with your truth. Indigenous and African language fragments used as mantras carry ancestral resonance, transforming speech into sacred invocation.

Tradition: In Dogon cosmology (Mali), *Nommo* is the generative power of the word. In Haitian Vodou, mantra and song open the gates of spirit. In Griot traditions, words are living histories.

Practice: Use chant, call-and-response, or shouted affirmations as spiritual weaponry. Speak your affirmations to the four directions. Call your people's names like a battle cry.

Say:

*"I am the daughter of queens.
I am the child of storm and sun.
My tongue is a blade.
My voice is a spell.
I speak and the world must shift."*

The tongue, when aligned with truth, is a sword of the sacred. It cuts through illusion, severs the ties of shame, and carves space for freedom. When we speak from the soul - not ego, not fear - our words become tools of healing and weapons of liberation.

This is not idle talk. This is ancient technology. Every truth spoken is a blow against the silence that kept us small. When your tongue remembers its purpose, your voice becomes holy - not just to be heard, but to transform.

THE POWER OF NAMING: RECLAIMING SPIRITUAL VOCABULARY AS SACRED WEAPONRY

Language is more than words; it is spellwork, vibration - breath made sacred. The colonizer knew this, which is why our native tongues were banned, our prayers demonized, and our spiritual vocabulary stripped of power or turned against us. But we are remembering.

Tradition: Word as spell, breath as creation.

Practice: Develop personal or community affirmations rooted in ancestral truths. In many traditions, the spoken word (*Nommo*) holds both generative and destructive power.

Example:

> *"I walk with the power of those who could not be broken."*
> *"My voice is sacred. My rage is holy. My joy is resistance. My joy is a weapon."*
> *"I wear the names of my people as armor."*

Speak these before entering hostile environments, protests, meetings, or even in daily life.

THE NEW SACRED ARMOR

Our armor now is not like costumes of brass or chainmail; it's spiritual discipline. It's protection prayers, daily rituals, ancestral connection, intuition, inner alignment. It's knowing who you are, whose you are and where you come from. In a world that sells distraction and disconnection, staying spiritually rooted is an act of revolution.

The following are sacred tools of spiritual resistance. These are not symbolic; they are active agents of power when used with intention:

Salt: Purification, boundary-making. Line it across thresholds.
Ancestor Names: Chant them as shields. Speak them as banners.
Sacred Symbols: Draw the Ankh, Adinkra, or personal sigils on your body before battle - whether that battle is a protest, a courtroom, or your own mind.
The Drum (or Body as Drum): Not just for music or rhythm, but for calling, for war, and for worship.

Even when no drum is present, you are not without rhythm. Clap. Stomp. Breathe with intention. These can summon rhythm and alignment. Your body becomes the drum. Your breath becomes the beat. And Spirit hears it all. It's heartbeat, war cry, and ancestral memory.

Tradition: For rebellion and for reconnection.

Drumming was banned across plantations and colonies for a reason—because drumming was powerful. It called spirits, organized revolts, and stitched back memory torn apart. The djembe, the bata, the chest rising and falling in rage or praise - all of it is resistance. When you drum, you do not forget. And when you drum, you are not alone.

AWAKENING POWER. TRANSFORMING PAIN. WAGING SACRED WAR

We are living in a moment where the soul is stirring - a time when remembering is not just an intellectual exercise, but a spiritual imperative. The *Rituals of Return* are no longer distant cultural artifacts; they are the living tools of liberation. These are the weapons of those who fight in realms unseen - not with fists or swords, but with the fire of presence, prayer, and ancestral memory. The revolution we are part of is not merely a reclaiming of what was lost; it is an uprising of spirit, a collective rising of those who have refused to forget.

We are remembering that we are power *full* because we are power *filled.*

This is not a metaphorical battle - it is a daily confrontation, a war waged against our sacred identity, where systems of oppression seek to sever our connection to Source. To control a people, they targeted not just land and labor, but the very root of spiritual sovereignty. Yet, this war is not one-sided. There are two spirits at war - oppression and awakening now face each other on the battlefield of our consciousness. Our resistance is not forged in factories; it is crafted through intention, ritual, and remembrance. Our true armor is spiritual, ancestral, and sacred, and it is time we wear it with fierce, unwavering purpose.

RITUALS OF SPIRITUAL READINESS

Guided Invocation: In Rhythm with the Ancestors

Find stillness. Let your body soften. Close your eyes and place your hands on your chest or your womb.

Breathe deep, not just into your lungs, but into your spirit.

Begin to speak, or whisper:

"Nommo. Ashe. Ase. So it is."
("The word has power. Let it be so.")

Call your spirit home:

"I return to myself.
I return to my body.
I return to the voice before it was silenced.
I return to the names they tried to erase."

In rhythm, begin tapping lightly - your chest, your thighs, a heartbeat pattern.
Let this rhythm anchor you.

Say aloud:

"I reclaim:
Healing - as my inheritance.
Prayer - as my portal.
Forgiveness - as my freedom.
Resistance - as my rhythm.
Truth-telling - as my sacred flame."
Pause. Breathe.

Then, in honor of your lineage, speak the names of those who walked before
you, or if you don't know them, say:

"Ancestors known and unknown,
ones who crossed land and sea,
who prayed, wept, fought,
and dreamed, stand with me now."

Let the rhythm slow.

Close with:

> *"This time, the revolution is spiritual.*
> *And I am the altar. I am the offering.*
> *I am the weapon.*
> *I am the return."*

The Rituals of Return are not about nostalgia; they are revolutionary acts of remembrance. They pull us out of amnesia and back into alignment with Source, with soul, with self. Because before we were hurt, before we were colonized, before we were fragmented, we were whole.

Remembering that power doesn't always roar - sometimes it hums, breathes, and burns steady inside us. Remembering that we are not alone, that we are held, guided, and witnessed by the unseen. Remembering that returning is resistance in a world that profits from our forgetting.

This is the armor of the Sacred, and these are the tools and weapons passed down through blood memory, reawakened for this time of reckoning. They are rituals of power and protection. Each one is both a shield and a sword.

FIRE CEREMONY: BURNING WHAT NO LONGER BELONGS

Tradition: Found in various African, Afro-Caribbean, and Indigenous rites. Fire is a purifier, a transformer.

Practice: Write down what you're releasing: fear, colonized thinking, internalized oppression, silence.

Burn it. And as the smoke rises, speak:

> *"I return this to the fire.*
> *I am no longer bound."*

Do this communally for greater power. In community, our intentions converge and what one releases, all are strengthened by. Let the flames witness your liberation.

WATER RITUAL: BAPTISM INTO POWER

Tradition: Kongo, Yoruba, Afro-Caribbean, Indigenous traditions.

Practice: Draw a spiritual bath with herbs (basil, rosemary, hyssop), light a white candle, and submerge slowly, praying:

> *"I cleanse myself of every lie told to me about my worth, my power, my divinity.*
> *I rise reborn into who I have always been."*

Repeat in moments of grief, confusion, or transition.

CIRCLE RITUAL: COMMUNAL SHIELDING

Tradition: Indigenous council circles, African drum circles, diasporic spiritual gatherings.

Practice: Gather in a circle. Light candles or place symbols of protection (ankh, shells, stones) in the center. Share intentions aloud, building a collective field of power.

End with:

> *"We shield one another.*
> *No harm shall pass."*

This can be done virtually or physically.

CIRCLE WORK (COLLECTIVE ENERGY FIELD)

Tradition: Indigenous talking circles, Maroon councils, and Black church prayer circles all use the circle to signify unity, equality, and protection. Circles are portals and power grids.

Practice: Use drumming, chanting, or smoke in the center to raise the energy. Appoint a person to invoke the ancestors.

Have each person in the circle state:

> *"I am protected.*
> *I am sovereign.*
> *I will not be moved."*

End with a communal stomp, a ritualized grounding of the feet into the earth, reminding everyone that we are unshakable.

Healing is never weakness, it should be considered resistance in motion. To mend what the world tried to shatter is to say, *"I will not die in your image."*

Prayer is not passive. It is communion with the unseen. This is strategy whispered to the divine. Forgiveness is not forgetting. Rather, it is choosing to cut cords of spiritual bondage so your soul can fly free. Resistance is not always protest in the streets. Sometimes it is breathwork at dawn, a boundary held, an altar tended in secret. Truth-telling is Sacred Warfare. Every time you name what tried to erase you, you crack the silence that sustained your oppression. To reclaim these words is to reclaim power. To name them aloud is to activate them. To embody them is to wage sacred war - not to destroy, but to liberate.

SILENCE IS LANGUAGE AND NOT ALL LANGUAGE IS AUDIBLE

Spirit speaks in silence too - the gut feeling, the chill on your skin, the dream that won't leave you, the ancestral nudge you can't explain. Learning the language of the spirit is learning to listen deeper, beyond logic, beyond fear.

SUPPRESSION AND RECOVERY OF SPIRIT

Colonization severed many of us from our sacred technologies. Intuition was labeled hysteria. Rituals were outlawed. Prophets were pathologized. But we are recovering. Reclaiming. Returning to the ways of our grandmothers, to the rivers and herbs, to the altars in our bones.

This time the revolution is spiritual and...it's a war they can't win.

DID YOU KNOW

1.   The Silencing

During colonial rule, enslaved Africans were beaten for speaking their native tongues, punished for drumming, and killed for practicing their spiritual traditions - because the oppressors knew what we are now remembering: that Spirit is power. Ritual is resistance. And language is liberation.

Reclaiming our sacred tools, including speaking and chanting, is a revolutionary return to ourselves, rooted in truth, not fantasy. This brings us back to ourselves in the realest, most powerful way.

2.   Salt as spiritual purifier

The deep spiritual significance of salt - particularly sea salt and ocean bathing, is a profound testament to its power as a purifier, cleanser, healer, and protector. I often heard in Jamaica the common phrase, "Yuh salt sah," describing a person experiencing persistent bad luck or misfortune, a state of spiritual stagnation or affliction. This very "saltiness" of ill fortune, however, underscores the remedy: salt itself.

Across many ancient and folk spiritual traditions, salt is seen as a crystalline substance that not only preserves but also draws out and neutralizes negative or stagnant energy. The vast, ever-moving ocean, with its inherent salt content, is considered the ultimate natural purifier - a living body of salt water that washes away spiritual impurities, bad luck, undesirable influences, and accumulated negativity.

Immersing oneself in its salty waves is believed to strip away accumulated negativity, cleanse the aura, clear blockages, and quite literally "wash away" misfortune, leaving the spirit refreshed, protected, and open to positive flow.

Immersing oneself in its salty waves is believed to strip away accumulated negativity, cleansing the aura, clearing blockages, and literally "washing away" misfortune, leaving the spirit refreshed, protected, and open to positive flow.

PART II

REMEMBERING THE ORIGINAL SELF

CHAPTER 5

THE MYSTIC WITHIN

The world is waiting for you to lead. The revolution begins within.

THE WORLD IS fractured. Its systems were built on foundations of oppression, inequality, and a hierarchy that thrives on the subjugation of the spirit. But what we're learning in this book is that the true revolution - the one that has the power to truly dismantle these systems, is not one of weapons or words, but of ancient wisdom, spiritual power, and the unshakable sovereignty of the soul.

For generations, we've been taught to conform to a world that doesn't value our worth. We've been forced into roles dictated by the dominant culture, stripped of our spiritual practices, and made to believe that the power of our ancestors was nothing more than myth. But there is a truth they do not want us to know - a truth that threatens everything they've built. That truth, the one they've tried to bury, is that our greatest power has always been our spirituality.

Hence, this time, the revolution must be spiritual.

AWAKENING OUR OWN "NATURAL MYSTIC" THROUGH REMEMBRANCE

We've made it clear that this is not a revolution of politics or policies, but one of profound spiritual reclamation. We have always carried the power of our ancestors within us, but for far too long, we've been disconnected from it. The rituals, prayers, and spiritual practices that sustained our communities for centuries were stripped away, ridiculed, and erased. Yet, in the hidden corners of our lives, in the quiet moments of reflection, that ancestral wisdom has never truly died. It has lived on within us - dormant, *but waiting.*

And now, it is waking up.

This is not a war that can be won by the oppressors. They have built their systems on lies, fear, and division, but they do not understand what we carry within us: the deep spiritual wisdom passed down through generations, forged through survival, resistance, and connection to the divine. They are counting on us forgetting, but they cannot comprehend the power of our ancestors. They are defenseless against it if we decide to rise up and reclaim that spiritual power.

This revolution will not be won with guns or violence, but *with the potency of sacred rituals, ancestral teachings,* and the magic we've always known but have been told to forget. When we connect with our true selves - our divine sovereignty - we rise in a way that no system, no hierarchy, no force can withstand.

Our ancestors knew this. They fought not just with their hands, but with their spirits. They resisted with their prayers, their dances, their songs, their altars. They knew that true power lies not in dominance over others, but in the sacredness of life, in the deep connection to the Earth, to the divine, and to one another.

It is time for us to remember who we are - to reclaim the spiritual tools that have been taken from us. To stand in our sovereignty and say:

> *"We are no longer slaves to the system you've built. We are free, and we are powerful."*

The revolution is spiritual, and it starts within us. We are arising - not just in body, but in spirit. And in that rising, we will dismantle the very foundations of injustice.

THE REVOLUTION NEEDS VISIONARIES

We are no longer waiting for the future. The future is now. We are the ones writing it. To write a liberated future, we need visionaries. Not just activists. Not just thinkers. We need those who can see beyond the veil, who can imagine a world the oppressors cannot even conceive. These are the mystic visionaries, the divine architects of liberation.

Visionaries are the ones who don't just react - they listen deeply. They tune in to frequencies others are too distracted to hear. They see maps in dreams and feel truth in their bodies. They are guided by Spirit, not systems.

We need them now more than ever. The future is now.

A MESSAGE FOR THE VISIONARIES

If you feel too sensitive for this world, it's because you were born to reshape it.
If you hear things others don't, it's because Spirit trusts you to listen.
If your dreams are loud, it's because the ancestors are speaking through you.

You are the midwife of the next world.
You are the ritual in motion.
You are the altar that walks.
You are the storm and the healing.
You are the mystic, and you are not alone.

This revolution will be won by those who can see the unseen, speak the unspeakable, and trust the intangible. And you are being activated as you read this book.

So listen. Rise. Vision. Act.

THE POWERS OF THE MYSTIC VISIONARY

Pay close attention - these are not fantasies. These are your spiritual technologies.

Here's what you carry and how to use it:

1.   Prophetic Imagination

The visionary doesn't just critique systems but they imagine beyond them.

Use journaling, divination, or guided meditation to receive visions of what justice looks like, feels like, lives like. Don't be afraid to dream radically. (Think Bob Marley, Martin Luther King Jr., Marcus Garvey - more about these later.)

2.   Energy Discernment

You can feel when something isn't right. What might feel like anxiety is wisdom.

Use your intuition to sense hidden agendas, spiritual manipulation, or unsafe leadership within movements. Trust your instincts.

Develop rituals for energetic protection before entering movement spaces, meetings, *or even social media.*

3.   Sacred Speech & Spellwork

Your words can cut through illusion, call ancestors forward, ignite courage. Learn to speak truth as a ritual: whether it's chanting at a protest, storytelling at a vigil, or affirming your power in private. Use altar prayers, spoken intentions, or poetic invocations to shift collective energy.

4.   Dream Navigation

Dreams are where the ancestors talk to us, where future timelines appear, where we receive divine instructions. Keep a dream journal. Ask specific questions before going to sleep. Use dreams to course-correct your actions in the waking world. In African and Indigenous traditions, dreams are not personal, they're communal. What you dream may be a message for the whole.

5.   Spiritual Strategy

Not all resistance is loud. Some of the most powerful revolutionaries are quiet, prayerful, deeply rooted. Call on the orisha, the lwa, the spirits of the land, the ancestors of justice.

6.   Where do I need to be? Who needs protecting? Where do we strike next, spiritually or politically? What would my community look like if it were free? What role do I play in birthing that? Use ritual, divination, and intuition to guide movements, not just spreadsheets.

LIVING AS A MYSTIC REVOLUTIONARY

To walk as a visionary in this world means you must stay grounded and open.

This is sacred work. It requires ritual, rest, clarity, and courage.

Here's how to strengthen your gift:

Daily spiritual hygiene: Cleanse your energy, protect your spirit, feed your ancestors.

Stay in your body: Movement, breath, and presence are your anchor.

Stay in community: Share visions, confirm dreams, support each other's gifts.

Stay aligned: Do not let capitalism commodify your intuition. Do not let empire hijack your vision.

Lead with Spirit: You don't need to see the whole plan. You only need to follow the sacred *next step*.

THE MYSTIC'S CALL TO ACTION

You are not powerless in this moment. You are initiated. This moment of awakening is no coincidence; you were born for this threshold, and your body is a portal. Your voice? A vibration of change. Your dreams and rituals are your blueprints.

Arise! Your ancestors are waiting.

So, awaken the mystic within, and walk forward not with fear, but with fire. Colonizers feared the mystic because she could not be controlled. She (and he) knew things before they happened. She (and he) healed what they tried to destroy. She (and he) whispered to the Earth, and the Earth whispered back.

You are that mystic now.

MYSTICISM AS REVOLUTION

You mustn't confuse mysticism with escapism. It is not a retreat from the world; it is an entrance into it with clear sight, awakened senses, and sacred power. To be a mystic is to live as if every moment matters, to move as if every breath is a prayer, and to recognize that the true battlefield is not just physical; it is spiritual.

This rising mystic consciousness is not passive. Oh no! It is an arsenal. When we reclaim our mysticism, we reclaim our ability to discern truth from propaganda, see beyond materialism and ego, and disrupt the internalized colonial voices that still live in our heads. We rebuild our identities from within, with soul, not systems.

You may think your intuition is soft, but it is in fact strategic. Know that your dreams are not delusions but dispatches from your ancestors. Your mystic self is a warrior in disguise.

USING THIS ENERGY IN THE FIGHT
FOR LIBERATION

The expanded consciousness we are seeing now must be mobilized, not just meditated upon. This is the moment to take the spiritual awakening and aim it directly at the systems that have tried to kill our spirits for generations.

Here's how we begin:

1.   Link the Inner and Outer.

Let your rituals fuel your resistance. Let your healing become your organizing. Don't heal alone; heal in community. Vote, boycott, invest with intention. Create sacred spaces within protests, strategy sessions, classrooms, and Zoom calls.

2.   Re-Indigenize Your Daily Life

Reclaim ancestral knowledge: cooking, naming, storytelling, dressing, planting. Withdraw energy from systems that extract, exploit, and erase. Mind who you spend your wealth with. Honor the Earth as living and responsive. She is not only a resource. Embrace her as a relative.

3.   Expose Spiritual Colonization

Deconstruct how colonialism stole your mysticism and called it "witchcraft." Interrogate spiritual spaces that erase Black and Indigenous voices, even while using our traditions and inventions. (And they are using them everywhere and profiting greatly.) Refuse commodified, decontextualized spirituality. Re-root it in liberation, not profit.

4.   Invoke the Mystic Strategist

Use intuition as a tool for planning, protection, and movement-building. Use spiritual practices: divination, prayer, dreamwork - not just for personal insight, but for collective survival.

5.   Ask again and again: What is spirit showing me about where to go next? Who to protect and what to dismantle?

THE VISIONARY TOOLKIT: PRACTICAL STEPS FOR ACTIVATING YOUR MYSTIC POWERS

To truly embody your role as a visionary and spiritual revolutionary, you must consistently cultivate your connection to the unseen, strengthen your inner knowing, and channel your ancestral power. This toolkit provides rituals, practices, and resources to deepen your intuitive, spiritual, and visionary practices.

1.   Daily Spirit Connection: Sacred Grounding

Purpose: Stay aligned with your higher self and the ancestors throughout the day. Grounding allows you to receive messages, stay protected, and maintain clarity in your vision.

Practice: Every morning, before you begin your day, place your feet on the earth and close your eyes. Take deep breaths and set your intention for the day. Ask the spirits and ancestors to guide your actions and thoughts. Visualize a shield of protection surrounding you.

Suggestion: You can hold a crystal (such as black tourmaline, amethyst, or selenite) to help ground and protect your energy.

2.   Vision Journaling: Dreaming with Purpose

Purpose: Cultivate your prophetic imagination by documenting your visions, dreams, and intuitive insights.

Practice: Keep a journal by your bed. As soon as you wake, write down any dreams or visions you remember. If you're not remembering dreams yet, note any impressions or feelings you had during the night. Ask specific questions before going to sleep, such as: *"What do I need to know today?"* or *"How can I best serve the community right now?"* Let this practice become a tool of spiritual guidance.

Suggestion: Over time, look for patterns and recurring symbols in your dreams. These may be messages from your ancestors.

3.   Energy Clearing and Protection Ritual

Purpose: Protect your energy and clear out external and internal negativity that blocks your spiritual connection.

Practice: Create a ritual to cleanse your space and spirit. Burn sage, palo santo, or mugwort to purify the room. As you do so, say aloud: *"I clear all negativity and protect my space from harmful energy. May my spirit remain clear and my vision sharp."*

Suggestion: Visualize yourself surrounded by a golden light of protection, allowing no negativity to enter your space.

4. Divination Practice: Listening to the Spirit

Purpose: Strengthen your ability to receive divine guidance and insight through divination methods.

Practice: Use a divination tool of your choice - tarot, oracle cards, bones, pendulum, or scrying (with water or mirrors). Ask specific questions to receive guidance on your spiritual path or the next steps in your life's mission. Focus on the symbols or messages that come through.

Suggestion: Set aside dedicated time for divination each week, using it as a spiritual practice for clarity and direction.

5. Spoken Affirmations: Power of the Word

Purpose: Empower yourself with the sacred energy of your voice. Words hold power - they can heal, protect, and ignite change.

Practice: Develop a series of affirmations that speak directly to your spiritual purpose and resistance. For example:

> *"I am the voice of my ancestors, and I speak truth with courage."*
> *"My vision is sharp, and I move with divine wisdom."*
> *"I am protected by the spirits who fought for my freedom."*

Suggestion: Say these affirmations aloud in the morning, before meetings, or whenever you feel fear or doubt. Your words are a weapon - use them to build your spirit.

6.   Ritual Movement: Embodying the Vision

Purpose: Physical movement helps integrate your visions and spiritual insights into the body, activating your inner power.

Practice: Set aside time to move with intention, whether through dancing, yoga, or walking in nature. Let your body become a vessel for spiritual energy. As you move, visualize your dreams coming to fruition. Feel the power of your visions becoming real within your body.

Suggestion: Use music or drumming that connects you to your ancestors, or simply move in silence and tune into the rhythm of your breath.

7.   Call on the Ancestors: Honoring the Lineage

Purpose: Strengthen your connection to your ancestral lineage and receive their guidance.

Practice: Create an altar space dedicated to your ancestors, and regularly offer prayers or libations. Ask them for wisdom, protection, and guidance in your visionary work.

Light a candle and say:

> *"I call upon my ancestors, those who walked before me, to bless my work. Help me see what is unseen, guide my steps as I walk this path of liberation."*

Suggestion: Offer food, flowers, or water to your ancestors as a gesture of gratitude and reverence.

8.   Visionary Meditation: Journeying with Spirit

Purpose: Deepen your connection to your inner vision and align with your higher purpose.

Practice: Sit quietly and close your eyes. Breathe deeply, grounding yourself in the present moment. Visualize yourself standing at the center of a circle of ancestors, guides, and spirits. Ask them to reveal the next steps for you in your spiritual revolution. Trust what you see, hear, or feel during this meditation.

Suggestion: You can use sound: drumming, bells, or singing bowls to help you enter a deeper meditative state.

9.   Collective Visioning: Building the New World

Purpose: Share your visions with others to create collective, unified plans of action for liberation.

Practice: Regularly meet with like-minded spiritual revolutionaries in circles, gatherings, or community spaces to share visions, ideas, and strategies. Create a safe space where everyone can bring their dreams and insights to the table. Work together to align your collective energy and actions toward a common goal.

Suggestion: Organize virtual or in-person meetings to commune with others who are also spiritually awakening.

10.   Surrender to Spirit: Trusting the Process

Purpose: To release the need to control every outcome and trust in the divine timing of your mission.

Practice: At the end of each day, sit in quiet surrender. Offer gratitude for the guidance you've received and trust that you are being led exactly where you need to be.

Say:

> *"I release all fear and resistance.*
> *I trust the ancestors. I trust Spirit.*
> *My vision is unfolding in divine time."*

Suggestion: Keep a surrender journal where you document moments of letting go and receiving trust from Spirit.

EMBODY YOUR VISIONARY POWER

Now that you have the tools, it's time to activate them. Your spiritual revolution begins with you, right where you are. These practices will help you tap into your full power as a visionary. They will guide you toward clarity, protect you from spiritual harm, and keep you aligned with the ancestral forces moving through you. You may be called to walk the path of the sage: growing into the wise self through healing, reflection, and purposeful alignment. Or you may resonate as a mystic: one who communes with the unseen, translating divine whispers into vision and action. Whichever path you walk, know that both are vital in this revolution of spirit.

MYSTICS AND SAGES: EVERY SOUL CARRIES SACRED KNOWING

A sage is a person known for their *deep wisdom,* insight, and calm judgment, usually gained through years of life experience, contemplation, and spiritual or philosophical practice. The word comes from the Latin *sapiens,* meaning *wise* or *discerning.* Sages distill wisdom from life experiences (and life itself), offering grounded guidance to others.

A mystic is a person who seeks, and often attains, direct personal experience of the Divine, the sacred, or ultimate truth beyond ordinary perception - often through inner revelation, intuition, or ecstatic experience. Mystics move beyond intellect into the realm of inner knowing, through contemplation, prayer, or spiritual practices that dissolve the boundaries between self and Spirit. The word *mystic* comes from the Greek *mystikos,* meaning "secret" or "hidden," pointing to the inner, often ineffable nature of their revelations.

The mystic touches the unseen; the sage translates it into insight for the seen world.

Or one could be both.

Many of the most revered spiritual figures throughout history have embodied both paths.

When someone holds both deep spiritual experience and the maturity, discernment, and clarity to guide others, they are both mystic and sage. Think of figures like Howard Thurman, Sobonfu Somé, Fannie Lou Hamer, or Martin Luther King Jr. - visionaries whose spiritual insight was matched by profound wisdom and ethical leadership.

Being both means you not only see beyond the veil, but you return with something meaningful to share.

SAGE VS MYSTIC

Sage	Mystic
Grounded in practical wisdom and life experience	Focuses on direct, often ineffable experience of the Divine or Higher Reality
Known for sound counsel, philosophical clarity	Known for spiritual vision, inner revelation
May be a teacher, elder, philosopher, healer	May be a seer, visionary, or spiritual guide
Example: Confucius, Socrates, the Desert Fathers, Queen Nzinga Mbande, Sojourner Truth, Elijah Muhammad	Example: Rumi, St. Teresa of Ávila, Paramahansa Yogananda, Harriet Tubman, Rebecca Cox Jackson, Howard Thurman

This time the revolution is spiritual... and it's a remembering they can't erase.

DID YOU KNOW

The following is a short list of our ancestors considered to be mystic-sages:

1.   **Sobonfu Somé** (Burkina Faso / United States) (1966–2017)

Burkinabé spiritual teacher rooted in the Dagara tradition, taught grief and initiation rituals. Practiced both in West Africa and the U.S.

2.   **Thomas Sankara** (Burkina Faso) (1949–1987)

Pan-African revolutionary and visionary leader. His leadership embodied deep ancestral awareness and spiritual purpose.

3.   **Malidoma Somé** (Burkina Faso / United States) (1956–2021)

Initiated elder and Dagara shaman who brought African Indigenous spirituality to the West. Practiced in Burkina Faso and the U.S.

4.   **Harriet Tubman** (United States) (c. 1822–1913)

Freedom fighter, abolitionist, and mystic guided by divine visions. Operated throughout the U.S., particularly in the South and along the Underground Railroad.

5.   **Queen Nanny of the Maroons** (Jamaica) (c. 1686–c. 1755)

Jamaican warrior-priestess who used African spiritual warfare and leadership to lead Maroon resistance against British colonizers.

6.   **Fannie Lou Hamer** (United States) (1917–1977)

Civil rights activist and prophetic voice whose work was deeply grounded in faith and liberation theology. Operated mainly in the American South.

7.   **Martin Luther King Jr.** (United States) (1929–1968)

Reverend, civil rights leader, and prophetic voice whose activism was deeply rooted in Christian mysticism, nonviolent resistance, and spiritual discipline. His sermons, visions, and moral clarity continue to guide movements for justice across the globe.

LIVING BLACK MYSTIC-SAGES

Disclaimer: This is only a very short list, drawn from a much longer lineage of mystic-sages whose names are too many to list here. In my experience and understanding, these individuals embody the qualities of mystics and sages. I see them as spiritual guides whose wisdom and insight have deeply influenced my own journey. While they may use different terms to describe themselves, I honor them here as fellow travelers on the path of profound spiritual leadership and transformation. This serves as a reflection of how their lives and teachings have shaped my own spiritual understanding.

1.   Iyanla Vanzant (United States)

Yoruba priestess, spiritual teacher, and healer known for her work on inner healing, ancestral connection, and soul restoration. She bridges traditional African wisdom with a broad mainstream audience.

2.   Resmaa Menakem (United States)

Somatic abolitionist, therapist, and author focused on trauma healing, ancestral wisdom, and nervous system liberation. His work carries deep spiritual undertones, rooted primarily in the U.S. context.

3.   Dr. G. Love (Gogo Ekhaya Esima) (South Africa)

Sangoma (traditional healer) and spiritual teacher who focuses on ancestral healing, mental health, and spiritual awakening through African Indigenous traditions.

4.   Queen Afua (United States)

Holistic health practitioner and spiritual guide. Author of *Sacred Woman*, a foundational text for many Black women reconnecting with African spirituality and womb wisdom.

5.   Skillful Kxng (Jamaica)

An emerging songwriter and artist, Skillful Kxng's music - particularly the anthem *A.I. (Ancient Intelligence)* is a spiritual masterpiece, deeply infused with ancestral memory, reclaiming divine lineage and sacred geography. In the song, he chants *"Alkebulan, Kemet, Kush"*, invoking the ancestral homelands of Africa as a lyrical map guiding listeners back to their spiritual origins and inherent power. His work serves as a prophetic voice, amplifying the call to remember who we are and where we come from, using sound and lyrical wisdom as tools of reclamation.

Skillful Kxng is mentioned multiple times in this book because his voice provides an auditory blueprint for the reawakening of ancient intelligence. Additionally, *A.I.* serves as a vital anchor and rhythmic pulse for the core spiritual messages woven throughout these pages.

CHAPTER 6

THE CALL OF THE ANCESTORS WHISPER IN OUR BONES

The ancestors never stopped speaking, Ancestral memory survives even in exile.

RECLAIMING THE FORGOTTEN PATH

THE ANCESTRAL CALL shows up in modern lives in dreams, synchronicities, inner urgings, inherited memories, generational pain. Our ancestors never stopped speaking.

Their voices rise through the quiet spaces of our lives, appearing in dreams that linger long after waking, in signs too precise to ignore, in sudden pulls toward traditions, places, or people we've never known but somehow feel bound to. This call can also be felt in the pain we carry - wounds we did not earn, yet hold in our bodies. These are inherited memories and whispers from those who came before, still echoing through our blood.

We were forced into silence, enduring the erasure of our languages, lineages, and spiritual technologies. We were shamed and outlawed for our spiritual ways, our knowledge dismissed as primitive. Colonialism and empire tried to bury our memory beneath forced silence. Breaking this silence is a revolutionary act. Yet, silence is never the end of the story. Every act of remembering, every ritual reborn, every ancestral name spoken aloud, every drumbeat that defies forgetting is an uprising.

In a world that profits from our amnesia, to remember is to rebel.

The ancestral wound is both trauma and key to awakening. We carry wounds older than our own lives. The trauma of dislocation, oppression, and erasure is embedded in our very cells. Yet within this pain lies a doorway. When we turn to face that pain, to feel it and honor it, we also unlock its power to awaken us. The ancestral wound is not just a mark of what was lost; it is a map toward what can be reclaimed. It holds both sorrow and medicine.

We are not the beginning, but a continuation of those who came before us. We are not the first dreamers. We are the breath of those who walked before us, who survived impossible odds so that we might one day rise. Their prayers walk with us, their hands steady ours, their visions live on through our choices. To know this is to move with a sense of sacred responsibility. We are not alone. We are many, walking as one.

Reclaiming connection to the ancestors must not be solely about past injuries. It must also be about power, guidance, and responsibility. Calling on the ancestors doesn't mean we dwell in the past, but that we mean to activate a living lineage of guidance, protection, and purpose. This is how we root ourselves in something greater, something enduring. Reclaiming ancestral connection restores our compass. It sharpens our vision. It reminds us that we are held by something vast and intelligent, and calls us to live not just for ourselves, but for the healing of the line.

Before we were Black. And before we were names in census records or forgotten faces in faded photographs, we were fire. Spirit. Prayer. We walked with the divine, not behind it. And though we've been cut off, the ancestors have never stopped calling.

We hear them in our unrest. In the ache we cannot name. In those moments when the world feels too hollow, and we long for something ancient, something true. This is not nostalgia. This is the call to return - not to history books, but to the lineage of power that lives in our bones.

The revolution begins within, but it does not begin with us. It is easy to believe we are alone in our awakening, that our pain is singular, or that our longing for something more is a modern affliction. But what stirs inside us is ancient. It is the echo of footsteps long walked, prayers long whispered, and battles long fought - not in textbooks or courtrooms, but in the quiet corners of spirit.

When we feel restless in a world that doesn't see us, when we are haunted by a sense of disconnection we can't explain, it is often because we have lost our tether to those who came before. Colonization, slavery, forced migration, and cultural erasure didn't just steal land and labor. They stole what they hoped we'd never come to reclaim - *memory.* They severed us from the elders, the language, the rituals that once guided our every step. But memory is not so easily erased. It lives in the body. It lives in the dreams. It lives in the drumbeat of our hearts.

The ancestors have not forgotten us. The call is still sounding.

LISTENING FOR THE CALL

In African and Indigenous cosmologies, ancestors are not dead. They are living presences, active forces - always watching, guiding, correcting. In the *Yoruba tradition,* the *Egungun* represent the collective spirits of the ancestors. When the *Egungun* dancers appear in ritual, masked, robed, and moving in sacred rhythm, they embody the spirits themselves, walking among the living once more. To witness the *Egungun* is to be reminded that the veil is thin and our disconnection is not permanent.

In the Kongo tradition, the ancestors are part of the living cycle, not separate from it. Through the practice of *simbi* communication, linking with water spirits and ancestral forces - the Kongo people call on the dead for wisdom, justice, and healing. Water becomes the portal. A bowl of water, a river, a bath - all become sites of communion. These are not metaphors. These are instructions.

We are meant to remember. And when we do, our revolution gains ground.

The ancestors are speaking. The question is not whether they are calling, but whether we are quiet enough, still enough, and open enough to hear. Reclaiming this connection requires intention. It is a practice of remembering with the body, the breath, and the spirit. Here's how we begin to listen.

RETURNING TO THE SACRED LINE AND RECLAIMING THE FORGOTTEN PATH

Reconnecting with our ancestors cannot be about idealizing the past. It must be about reclaiming a lineage of strength, wisdom, and resistance. It's about knowing that someone survived for you to be here - that someone once knelt in prayer or lifted their voice in defiance, and you are the living continuation of that act.

In the *Akan tradition of Ghana,* ancestral reverence is central. Libations are poured before every major gathering, every important ritual, every decision of consequence. The spirits of the elders must be acknowledged and invited. To pour libation is to say: *We have not forgotten you. Guide us as we move.*

You don't need an altar of incense or a formal ceremony to begin.

Start with a glass of clean water.

Speak their names if you know them.
If you do not know their names, speak to them anyway.

They have been waiting.

You can say:

"To the ones who walked before me.
To the ones whose names I do not know but whose blood I carry.
I remember you. I honor you. I listen."

See Chapter 7 for specific rituals of ancestral reconnection.

This time the revolution is spiritual… and it's a whisper they can't hear.

SPECIFIC PRACTICES OF ANCESTRAL RECONNECTION

1.　　Libation Ritual (Akan, Pan-African)

Purpose: To honor and invoke ancestral presence.

Practice: Pour water or alcohol (such as gin, rum, or palm wine) onto the ground while speaking the names or roles of your ancestors. Perform this outdoors or in a sacred corner of your home.

Words to Speak:

"Ancestors known and unknown, I pour this offering in your name.
Stand with me as I rise in this time of transformation."

2.　　Water Communion (Kongo, Afro-Caribbean)

Purpose: To open the portal of communication and healing.

Practice: Place a bowl of water on an altar or by your bedside. Sit quietly and meditate. Listen. Write down anything that comes.

Optional: Add herbs like basil, rosemary, or mugwort for cleansing and intuitive clarity.

3.   Ancestral Journaling and Dream Tracking

Purpose: To receive guidance through symbols, dreams, and intuitive insight.

Practice: Keep a journal specifically for messages or dreams that feel significant.

Before going to sleep, speak aloud:

> *"Ancestors, I am listening. Speak to me through dream or symbol."*

Record anything you receive without judgment upon waking.

4.   Light as Beacon (Diaspora Traditions)

Purpose: To invite ancestors into your sacred space.

Practice: Light a white candle and sit in stillness, inviting their presence. Focus on the flame as a bridge between realms. Speak your truth. Ask your questions. Let the silence respond.

5.   Water Rituals for Cleansing and Rebirth

Purpose: Water has long been seen as a spiritual element of cleansing and healing. For many African and Caribbean cultures, water rituals are central to purification and spiritual renewal.

Practice: Use water as a tool for spiritual cleansing and rebirth through bathing, ritual drinking of blessed water, or creating sacred water spaces (streams, wells, or even bowls of water at home).

Example Ritual: Begin with a prayer of gratitude for the water. Take a bath with the intention of cleansing yourself from burdens of oppression, societal expectations, and trauma. Envision the water washing away negativity and rejuvenating your spirit.

DID YOU KNOW

PROTECTION WE DIDN'T KNOW WE WERE MISSING.

In many West and Central African traditions, neglecting the ancestors is believed to cause spiritual imbalance; not just personally, but collectively. Among the Akan of Ghana, for example, failure to pour libation or honor the dead can disrupt the harmony between the living and the spirit world. In the Kongo cosmology, unresolved ancestral pain is thought to manifest as illness or misfortune until the ancestors are acknowledged and their guidance sought. Across various Afro-Caribbean traditions like Vodou and Lucumí, ancestral reverence is a spiritual responsibility. When the ancestors are ignored, protection weakens, and life may feel blocked. In these traditions, remembering is not optional; *it is spiritual maintenance.*

Today, many of us may not speak of "angry ancestors" or spiritual misfortune the same way our elders did, but the core truth remains: both our inner and outer worlds need tending. What some traditions call ancestral displeasure, we might now understand as emotional patterns, inherited generational trauma, or spiritual disconnection. But even as we turn to therapy, journaling, or other modern tools, we're also being called back to what the ancestors always knew; that healing is multi-layered, and some work must be done in ritual space. This revolution isn't only about breaking systems; it's about clearing what blocks the soul. And remembering the ancestors doesn't only honor the past, it reconnects us to the power and protection that still surrounds us, waiting to be welcomed in. Remembering the ancestors also roots us in the living current that steadies our path, sharpens our vision, and surrounds us with protection we didn't know we were missing.

CHAPTER 7

THE RITUALS OF RETURN

Reconnecting through sacred technologies and practices our ancestors used to awaken power and transform pain into purpose.

MEDITATION, RITUAL, DRUMMING, AND HERBALISM AS ANCIENT TECHNOLOGIES FOR SURVIVAL AND SPIRITUAL DEFENSE

IN A WORLD that has tried to strip us of our sacred practices, the act of ritual becomes more than tradition and becomes revolution. The purpose of ritual as rebellion lies in its quiet but unwavering resistance to erasure. Whether lighting candles, pouring libations, speaking intentions, or gathering in circle, we step into a lineage of power, reclaim our ancestry, affirm our identity, and give voice to what was once silenced.

Ritual is where the sacred and the political meet. It is how we remember who we are and how we insist on being whole in a world that benefits from our fragmentation.

Across cultures, time, and terrain, our people have preserved actual rituals: from libations to fire ceremonies to spoken affirmations. Each gesture carries meaning, serving as a technology of connection, a bridge between the seen and unseen, linking the self to the collective. In colonized, westernized worlds that mock the sacred or monetize it, returning to these practices is an act of sovereignty.

And so, we must now ask ourselves what it means to engage in ritual in our present lives. How do we reclaim the sacred on our own terms? Creating personal or communal rituals today is how we ground ourselves in meaning, connect with spirit, and reshape the world around us, starting from the inside out.

THE CALL TO RETURN TO RITUALS

Let this be clear: You were never meant to be silent.
You were never meant to fight only with your intellect, or to heal only in private.
Your resistance is sacred. Your rituals are weapons. Your ancestors are your
    generals.

This chapter is not meant to be read and set down. It is meant to be lived.
Light your altar. Speak your affirmations.
Call your ancestors. Bathe in your sacred herbs.
Protect your spirit like it is your greatest possession. Because it is.

And when the world comes for you with its systems of violence and erasure, stand up with your rituals in hand and say:

> *"I am not afraid.*
> *I am not alone.*
> *I am armed with the sacred."*

The revolution is spiritual.
The ritual is the weapon.
And the time is now.

The revolution is a remembering, and it is a rising. We are healing from what has been done to us while preparing for spiritual battle. There is a war being fought every day—a war on our spirits, on our lineages, on our sacred ways of being. Systems of oppression have always known that to truly dominate a people, you must strip them not only of land, labor, or liberty, but of their connection to the Divine - their ability to *call on Spirit,* to *channel the ancestors,* to *stand rooted in sacred sovereignty.*

But what they failed to understand is this:
You can steal the drum, but not the rhythm.
You can burn or ban the book, but not the story.
You can outlaw the ritual, but not the spirit behind it.

So, we are not defenseless.
Our weapons are not made of steel or gunpowder.
And our armor is not forged in factories.
What it is, though, is spiritual, ancestral, and sacred.
And it is time we put it on.

Let us remember this:

The power we carry is not metaphorical. The spirits walk with us because they remember too. Every chant, every flame, every drop of water poured to the earth is a signal to the universe: We are still here. And we are rising.

Our altars hold strategy; they are not for decoration.
Our cleansing has little to do with vanity, instead, it's preparation for what's ahead.
And some of us may think they're nostalgic but our rituals are powerful weapons.

So let's bless our feet when they step into protest.
Let's dress our spirit in herbs when we face injustice.
Let's call our ancestors like calling for backup in a street fight.

Because this is a fight.

And they are with us.

RESISTANCE THROUGH RECONNECTION

In times when the world urges disconnection, from spirit, from ancestry, from self, choosing to live in a way that honors the ancestors becomes a radical act. It is through this intentional return that we resist the systems designed to erase us. Reconnection is remembrance, restoration, and rebellion. This revolution is not only spiritual in philosophy; it is spiritual in practice.

This is how we survive turbulent times: we anchor ourselves in our spirituality. When everything around us feels unstable, when the world seems to be falling apart, we must turn inward and root ourselves in what is eternal. We remember who we are and the divine power we carry. That memory is not just personal; it is ancestral. It connects us to those who came before us, those who fought, bled, and prayed us into being.

We are here today because others chose to resist, to believe, to call on spiritual forces greater than their circumstances. They fought not only with weapons but with chants, rituals, and an unshakeable belief in their freedom. We owe our survival to the spiritual resilience of our ancestors.

Now it is our turn to carry that legacy forward. If Nanny of the Maroons and Dutty Boukman, without armies and without resources, could rise up, challenge, and defeat empires through spiritual cunning, imagine what millions of us can do today. The same spiritual technology they used then is available to us now. The key, however, is unity. We must rise as a collective. This isn't just about personal healing or individual liberation; it is about aligning our spirits to shift the course of history. The power lies in our togetherness and ancestral reconnection. That's how we win.

Here are ways to begin reconnecting with the ancestors as part of your spiritual resistance:

SACRED TECHNOLOGIES: HISTORICAL CONTEXT AND MODERN RECLAMATION

PRAYER AND INVOCATIONS OF ANCESTRAL SPIRITS

Purpose: Connect with the ancestors through prayer, invoking their protection, wisdom, and guidance to disrupt oppressive systems.

Practice: Create rituals to invoke the spirits of the ancestors for strength and protection, either through prayer, chanting, or calling upon ancestral names. This can be done individually or in community gatherings. In West African traditions like Yoruba, for example, ancestral veneration is essential for calling on spiritual forces to support justice and freedom.

Example Ritual: Light a candle or incense as an offering, and say a prayer that honors the ancestors, invoking their guidance in confronting current injustices. This can be paired with chanting affirmations of strength, justice, and liberation.

Historical Context & Resistance Roots:
Across African spiritual systems, including Yoruba, Vodun, and other diasporic traditions, prayer was a direct line of communication with the divine. It was a lifeline to those who had passed on; a spiritual alliance against oppression. Enslaved Africans carried these traditions into the Americas, often in secret, invoking the ancestors for guidance, courage, and protection when all else had been stripped away. These invocations were part of hidden rebellions, rooted in spiritual sovereignty, even when physical freedom seemed out of reach.

Modern Reclamation:

Reclaiming this practice today can root your activism and healing work in ancestral wisdom. You can create your own invocation, call upon the names of ancestors who inspire you, or adapt traditional prayers that speak to liberation and protection. Let this be a daily ritual, or something you call upon during times of deep uncertainty or resistance work. Whether done alone or with others, your voice becomes a bridge to ancestral presence, and that presence holds power.

DRUMMING AND DANCE

Purpose: Music and rhythm have long been used as forms of resistance and as ways to connect with spiritual energy. In many African traditions, drumming was not only a means of celebration but also a tool for communication, healing, and rebellion.

Practice: Use drumming or rhythmic movement, even simple clapping or tapping your feet, to release personal or collective pain, strengthen your resolve, and call upon ancestral spirits. Rhythm aligns the body with spiritual power, grounding you in the face of oppression.

Example Ritual: Create a space for free movement or drumming, either alone or with a group. Allow the rhythm to "shake off" the energy of oppression and invoke the power to heal and resist. If live drumming is not available, recorded drumming can also be used as a powerful tool for this practice.

Historical Context & Resistance Roots:

Across African and Afro-diasporic cultures, drumming and dance have preserved spiritual and cultural identity in the face of colonization and forced assimilation. Enslaved people used rhythms to encode messages, sustain morale, and express spiritual truths that enslavers sought to suppress. During Haitian Vodou ceremonies and Maroon uprisings, drumming not only summoned ancestral spirits but also rallied communities toward revolution. These rhythms became sonic acts of resistance and movement toward freedom.

Modern Reclamation:

Even without a drum, you can reclaim this ancestral technology by connecting to rhythm within your own body. Use clapping, stomping, or dancing as ways to break stagnant energy and affirm your right to joy, healing, and sacred embodiment. Organize a community drumming circle, or simply let your body move to ancestral beats in your own sacred space. Let every rhythm become an invocation of strength and a release of generational pain.

ANCESTRAL ALTARS

Purpose: Building an altar to honor the ancestors and call on their support in times of need. Altars are powerful symbols of connection to the spiritual realm and to the ancestors who fought for survival and liberation.

Practice: Create an altar in your home using symbols or items that remind you of your heritage, such as photographs of ancestors, sacred objects, herbs, or crystals. Use the altar as a sacred space for quiet meditation, ritual acts, or offering prayers of thanks and guidance.

Example Ritual: Place offerings (flowers, water, food, etc.) on the altar as a sign of respect. Sit before it, focusing on a deep prayer for liberation, or simply listen in stillness for the wisdom of the ancestors. You can also perform acts of service or community building as a living offering to honor their legacy.

Historical Context & Resistance Roots:

Altars have long been central in African and Indigenous spiritual traditions, serving as places of reverence, communication, and protection. During enslavement, when African spiritual practices were suppressed, people found ways to honor their ancestors in secret, sometimes blending altars with Christian imagery to preserve their traditions. These hidden altars were spiritual sanctuaries, reminders that they were not alone, and that the dead were still fighting alongside them.

Modern Reclamation:

Building an altar today is an act of remembrance and reclamation. You don't need a rigid formula; create something personal and meaningful. Include items that reflect your lineage, your roots, and your intentions. Return to the altar in times of grief, struggle, or when seeking clarity, and listen for the guidance that may arise in the stillness. This is your sacred meeting place with those who paved the way.

HERBAL MEDICINE AND HEALING RITUALS

Purpose: Many African, Caribbean, and Indigenous cultures used herbalism as a form of resistance. Plants and herbs were seen not only as tools for physical healing but also for spiritual warfare, protecting communities from harm and restoring balance.

Practice: Use specific herbs for protection, healing, and empowerment. For instance, sage (for smudging), rosemary, cedar, bay leaves, and palo santo are commonly used to cleanse negative energy and invoke spiritual protection.

Example Ritual: Incorporate herbs into a cleansing ceremony by burning them as incense, boiling them into a tea, or using an herbal infusion in a ritual bath to wash away negative influences. This practice can be done during moments of personal struggle or in solidarity with a larger movement for justice and collective healing.

Historical Context & Resistance Roots:

Herbal medicine was central to survival in African and Indigenous communities and became a form of resistance during slavery and colonization. Enslaved healers and rootworkers used plants to heal bodies, shield spirits, and defy domination. These herbalists were often feared by oppressors and revered within their communities. Their knowledge, passed down quietly through generations, sustained and protected entire communities in the face of systemic violence and medical neglect.

Modern Reclamation:

Reconnecting with plant medicine today is an act of honoring this lineage. Learn the properties of herbs not only for their physical benefits but for their spiritual significance. Whether you burn sage or rosemary to cleanse a space, use herbs in ritual baths, or brew healing teas with intention, you are stepping into an ancient tradition of resistance, self-preservation, and sacred care. Let the plants guide you back to what your ancestors always knew.

MEDITATION, VISUALIZATION AND MANIFESTATION

African and diasporic ancestors practiced forms of visualization to manifest outcomes, shape reality, and communicate with the spirit world long before the West labeled these practices as *"visualization"* or *"manifestation."* It wasn't always called that, but it showed up through:

Visioning in Ritual and Ceremony

In many African spiritual systems such as Yoruba, Dagara, Akan, Kongo, and Zulu, practitioners entered altered states through drumming, chanting, dance, or deep silence. In these states, they received visions: symbolic or literal images revealing healing, warnings, or instructions. These visions were not dismissed as fantasy; they were understood as spiritual truths, blueprints for action in the physical world.

IMAGINATIVE POWER IN THE FACE OF OPPRESSION

During enslavement and colonization, visualization became a *radical survival tool.* Enslaved Africans imagined freedom before it was tangible, envisioning reunions with lost family and divine protection through spiritual beings.

Our ancestors visualized liberation, healing, and divine intervention, and aligned their actions, rituals, and beliefs to call it into being. *They spoke the vision, danced the vision, dreamed the vision, and believed the vision until it became reality.* They didn't call it manifestation, but that's exactly what it was. These inner images gave them direction, hope, and power to move forward - sometimes with strategic action, sometimes with supernatural faith.

Purpose: Meditation and visualization are ancient technologies of the spirit, used across African, Indigenous, and diasporic cultures to access inner wisdom, connect with the ancestors, receive divine guidance, and call forward new realities. These practices were often ways to travel inward when outward freedom was stolen. They were sacred methods of surviving the unbearable by accessing the unseen.

Practice: Embrace meditation as a practice of stillness, breath awareness, and spiritual attunement. Visualization is its creative extension: imagining a desired outcome, invoking ancestral support, or calling in healing light and protection. These practices help align the mind, spirit, and body with intention and divine presence.

Example Ritual: Begin with breathwork, then visualize yourself at the foot of a sacred ancestral tree. See your ancestors stepping forward with messages, blessings, or guidance. Ask them to show you a symbol, word, or gift. Afterward, journal what you received. You can also visualize protective light surrounding your body or focus on a specific outcome like freedom, justice, or healing, for yourself or your community.

Historical Context & Resistance Roots:

While colonizers promoted the written word and outward religion, many African and diasporic communities preserved their relationship with the divine through inner listening and visioning. Enslaved and colonized peoples, denied privacy and autonomy, often meditated in silence, spoke to ancestors in dreams, and visualized escape routes, liberation, and divine justice. In African cosmologies like Yoruba and Dagara, the spirit world is accessed internally through trance, vision, or stillness, proving that meditation and visualization are not imported concepts but inherent technologies.

Meditation was a powerful, active return to the self when the world tried to erase it; not a passive surrender. Visualization, likewise, was used to envision liberation, survival, and spiritual protection when no physical space was safe. These practices were acts of rebellion and spiritual sovereignty.

Modern Reclamation:

Reclaiming meditation and visualization is reclaiming your mind as sacred ground. It's refusing to let anxiety, trauma, or colonized thoughts define your inner world. Whether you sit in silence, chant ancestral names, visualize your healed self, or call in your future with clarity and power, you are participating in a long line of visionaries, seers, and spiritual warriors.

Incorporate ancestral symbols, colors, herbs, or music into your practice. Visualize your ancestors surrounding you with wisdom, or your community walking into freedom. Let meditation and visualization be your quiet revolution; one breath, one vision, one rebirth at a time.

VISIONING, DREAMWORK AND PROPHETIC SIGHT

Purpose: Ancestors often communicated through dreams, symbols, and visions, offering prophetic insights or warnings about the future. In Ifá, for example, oracles and seers would foresee outcomes before they happened. This "sight" was not only a form of divine guidance but also an intentional way of shaping outcomes through alignment with ancestral and cosmic forces. It required quieting the mind, focusing attention, holding a clear image, and trusting in divine timing. Reclaiming this form of spiritual communication is a powerful tool for dismantling oppression.

Practice: Visioning can be used to tap into ancestral wisdom. This might involve quiet reflection or journaling to connect with intuitive insights. Dream interpretation is another method to discern ancestral messages and receive guidance on confronting injustice. Today's vision boards, scripting, or guided visualizations mirror ancestral practices, but our elders did this with ritual, prayer, nature, and spirit as collaborators.

Example Ritual: Before going to sleep, offer a prayer or affirmation inviting your ancestors to guide you in dreams. Upon waking, immediately record your dreams in a journal, paying attention to symbols, feelings, or messages that may hold clues on how to navigate current systems of oppression.

Historical Context & Resistance Roots:

Dreams and visions have always carried prophetic weight in African and Indigenous traditions. Many slave narratives include stories of ancestors appearing in dreams to warn, instruct, or empower. In Maroon societies and spiritual practices like Hoodoo and Ifá, dreams served as guides for when to flee, when to fight, or where to find safety. These visions were messages from the spirit realm, often holding keys to survival.

Modern Reclamation:

Treat your dreams as sacred texts. Before retiring to bed, speak to your ancestors and ask for guidance or insight. Upon waking, write down what you remember, even if it seems cryptic or fragmented. Over time, patterns may emerge. You might begin to see symbols of healing, calls to action, or ancestral presences showing you the way. This practice helps ground your decisions not in fear or chaos but in a deep, intuitive knowing passed down through dreamtime.

POWERFUL SYMBOLISM AND SACRED GEOMETRY

Purpose: Ancestral wisdom is often encoded in symbols, geometric patterns, and sacred designs. These are not merely artistic expressions but dynamic tools of protection, empowerment, and transformation. Sacred geometry and cultural symbols serve as visual languages that communicate spiritual truths and activate ancestral power.

Practice: Engage actively with these ancestral symbols. For example, explore the Adinkra symbols of Ghana's Akan people or the vibrant, intricate patterns of Ndebele art from Southern Africa. These symbols carry layered meanings tied to spiritual principles, proverbs, and life lessons. Integrate them into your daily life by drawing them, wearing them on clothing or jewelry, displaying them in your home, or incorporating them into personal adornments like body art (temporary or permanent). Use them as focal points during meditation, or place them on altars and sacred spaces as tools of intention and protection.

Example Ritual: Select a symbol that resonates with your current journey, such as *Eban* (Adinkra symbol of safety and security) or a geometric motif from Ndebele mural traditions. Draw or place the symbol in your sacred space or carry it on your body. During meditation, focus on the symbol, visualizing it as a portal to ancestral guidance and power. Reflect on its meaning and invite its energy into your daily actions.

Historical Context & Resistance Roots:

Symbols and sacred patterns have long been used in African and Indigenous traditions to encode knowledge, assert identity, and protect communities. During colonization and enslavement, many of these visual languages became acts of covert resistance, preserving cultural memory when spoken language was suppressed. These designs appeared in textiles, architecture, scarification, beadwork, and even hidden in plain sight on tools or everyday objects, silently asserting a presence that refused erasure.

Modern Reclamation:

Reclaiming and working with ancestral symbols is an act of spiritual and cultural sovereignty. Learn the meanings behind these symbols, not just aesthetically but spiritually. Infuse your rituals, creative expressions, and living spaces with these designs as active tools of remembrance and empowerment. Whether you meditate on an Adinkra proverb, wear a pattern that honors your lineage, or create new sacred art inspired by ancestral geometry, you are engaging in a living conversation with those who came before. Every symbol becomes a reminder: You are held by a lineage of wisdom, strength, and beauty.

SACRED STORYTELLING AND ORAL TRADITIONS

Purpose: Storytelling has always been a means to transmit wisdom, preserve history, and resist cultural erasure. Reclaiming oral traditions as tools for resistance and empowerment helps safeguard collective memory and fortify spiritual and cultural identity.

Practice: Tell your stories, whether through spoken word, writing, or communal sharing, as acts of spiritual resistance. This could involve recounting family histories, retelling sacred myths, or sharing personal testimonies of survival and triumph over oppression. Storytelling becomes a ritual of remembering, where each word reconnects you to the ancestral line.

Example Ritual: Gather a circle of family, friends, or community members for a storytelling session. Invite each person to share a story of resilience, whether from their personal journey or their cultural heritage. Alternatively, retell sacred folktales from African, Caribbean, or Indigenous traditions, using voice, song, or performance. These sessions can be infused with ritual by lighting a candle or pouring libation before beginning, invoking ancestral presence to guide and witness the exchange.

Historical Context & Resistance Roots:

In African, Caribbean, and Indigenous cultures, oral traditions were far more than entertainment. They were lifelines, carrying coded messages, historical truths, and spiritual teachings through generations. During slavery, when reading and writing were criminalized, enslaved people encoded wisdom and resistance into songs, proverbs, and folktales. Griots in West Africa, *Anansi* storytellers in the Caribbean, and Indigenous elders across the Americas preserved vital knowledge through oral narrative. These stories became sacred archives of living memory, refusing to be colonized or erased.

Modern Reclamation:

Reclaiming storytelling today is an act of spiritual sovereignty. Record the untold stories of your family. Invite elders to speak their lived experiences. Use community storytelling circles as healing spaces where each voice is honored. Modern platforms such as podcasting, spoken word, and digital storytelling can be transformed into vessels of ancestral wisdom when approached with reverence.

For me, Anansi stories were brought to life by the Honorable Louise Bennett-Coverley ("Miss Lou") during my childhood in Jamaica. Her legacy of storytelling is a torch I now feel called to carry forward. Driven by the urgent need for cultural preservation, I am committed to reviving these narratives. By breathing life back into them, we ensure that the ancestral wisdom, cunning resilience, and rich identity embedded within these stories continue to shape and empower future generations.

As part of this revival, I've included two Anansi stories in the *Did You Know* section of this chapter. These stories are more than folklore; they are vessels of ancestral wisdom, reminding us of the cleverness, humor, and survival strategies that have been passed down through generations.

CIRCLE WORK AND COLLECTIVE HEALING

Purpose: Circle work, such as talking circles or community gatherings is deeply rooted in Indigenous practices and serves as a method for collective healing and decision-making. In times of social injustice, collective spiritual practices unite people and amplify spiritual power.

Practice: Form or join a circle where members come together to support one another spiritually. This may include collective prayers, meditations, or shared intentions for justice. Circle work honors principles of equality and respect, encouraging healing within a communal setting.

Example Ritual: Gather in a circle and share your intentions for the collective. Pray together for the healing of your community or chant affirmations of liberation. Close the circle with gratitude and a commitment to each other's spiritual growth.

Historical Context & Resistance Roots:

Long before colonization introduced hierarchical structures and individualism, Indigenous peoples gathered in circles to share wisdom, solve problems, and heal together. Circles reflected the sacred geometry of nature, the principle of equality, and the understanding that all voices hold value. In the face of forced removals, cultural erasure, and state violence, these circles became sanctuaries - spaces where identity was reaffirmed and communal strength nurtured. Enslaved Africans also formed clandestine prayer circles and praise houses to hold spiritual space away from surveillance.

Modern Reclamation:

In today's fractured world, recreating sacred circles revives the wisdom of collective healing. You might organize a monthly spiritual circle with friends, community members, or fellow visionaries. Set a theme such as liberation, grief, joy, or ancestral healing. Let everyone speak from the heart. No hierarchy, no pressure, only presence, listening, and shared intention. In doing so, you invoke an ancient method of resistance: creating sacred space where unity becomes power and healing becomes political.

COSMIC CONNECTION AND THE ELEMENTS: RECLAIMING ANCESTRAL ALIGNMENTS

The ancestors understood that the moon, stars, and elemental forces were not mere background to life but active participants in the spiritual fabric of existence. These natural forces shaped their calendars, rituals, and worldviews, serving as guides for healing, protection, and transformation.

LUNAR CYCLES AS SACRED TIME

Many African and Indigenous cultures time important ceremonies and rituals according to the phases of the moon. The new moon is often seen as a time for planting intentions and new beginnings, while the full moon marks moments of heightened spiritual power and release. For example, among the Yoruba people, the moon goddess *Osun* is honored for her connection to fertility, healing, and abundance. Rituals during specific lunar phases are performed to invoke her blessings. Similarly, many Caribbean and Afro-diasporic traditions hold full moon ceremonies to cleanse negative energies and manifest desires.

THE ELEMENTS AS SACRED ENERGIES

Earth, air, fire, and water are the sacred pillars of life and ritual. Fire's purifying power has long been central to rites of passage and spiritual cleansing across cultures, from the lighting of ceremonial fires to the burning of sacred herbs like sage and palo santo. Water rituals, such as libations poured to honor ancestors, hold deep symbolism of life, memory, and renewal. Air, carried by wind and breath, bridges the visible and invisible worlds, often invoked through chanting, drumming, or the wafting of sacred smoke. Earth grounds us, connecting us to ancestral lands, plants, and the body itself - a living altar.

ALIGNING RITUAL WITH COSMIC FORCES TODAY

Reclaiming these practices means attuning to the natural rhythms that shaped ancestral life and spirituality. Practicing ritual in alignment with lunar phases can be as simple as setting intentions during the new moon and releasing what no longer serves under the full moon. Building altars with representations of the elements such as stones for earth, feathers or incense for air, candles for fire, and bowls of water, anchors spiritual practice in the physical world.

Sitting beneath the night sky, observing the stars, or invoking the moon and elements during meditation reconnects us to a cosmic lineage that has endured despite attempts at erasure. This deepens our spiritual resistance by restoring knowledge that colonizers feared: the understanding that we are part of a living, breathing universe where ancestral power flows through every element and celestial body.

PERSONAL MEMORIES

Writing about this brings back vivid childhood memories. I can still picture those nights playing outside, or just sitting beneath a moonlight so incredibly bright it didn't just illuminate the ground—it bathed the entire landscape in a magical, silvery glow. Even as a child, long before I had words like "cosmic energy" or "spiritual attunement," I felt it. It was a palpable presence, a silent current so strong it felt as if it could pull you upward, like a magnet. I had a sense of being like a conduit, a living ray of connection to something ancient and vast.

That same powerful, visceral feeling came rushing back during a visit to Jamaica in 2009 or 2010. One unforgettable evening, under that same brilliant Caribbean moon, I started a simple ring game with just one child. But before I knew it, the sheer magic of the moonlit night, or perhaps it was the magnetic pull of that shared, ancient energy, drew in countless others. From every direction, children eagerly found their way to our growing circle, at least thirty, maybe even more, their excited shouts and laughter echoing under the star-dusted sky. We played the games of old - the ones passed down through generations, like 'Bull inna Pen,' with its frantic energy and quick dodging. Then we'd shift into classic ring games like 'Brown Girl in the Ring', our voices rising in unison, clapping hands and feet pattering in rhythm on asphalt in the middle of the road.

It was pure, unfiltered joy, a spontaneous ritual of connection that transcended time and space. Those moments, whether from my childhood or that transformative night in Jamaica, aren't just fond memories. They are living proof that our connection to the cosmos, to the moon, and to each other remains unbroken. They remind us that something as simple as gathering under the night sky can restore a lineage of power and belonging that colonization could never truly erase.

(I digress here, but I'm also remembering the song Sister Moon, originally by Sting, covered by Vanessa Williams. Only now do I understand my curious connection to that song. It resonates deeply with these moonlit memories under hypnotic Jamaican skies.)

But back to the text.

EXAMPLE RITUAL: LUNAR INTENTION SETTING

At the new moon, gather in a quiet space with candles and a bowl of water. Reflect on what you wish to invite into your life or community. Speak these intentions aloud or write them down. Pour a libation of water (or another sacred liquid) as an offering to the ancestors and the moon, asking for their guidance and blessings. Close the ritual by extinguishing the candles in gratitude, knowing you are co-creating with cosmic forces and ancestral wisdom.

THE MOON'S EMBRACE

LUNAR PHASES: MOON RITUALS

Historical Context:

In Yoruba tradition and many African diasporic spiritualities, the moon's cycles governed agricultural, healing, and spiritual ceremonies. These rituals preserved cultural knowledge under colonial suppression by embedding resistance in sacred time.

Rituals:

New Moon - Set intentions for growth, healing, and new beginnings. Offer water libations to the ancestors, asking for their guidance in nurturing these seeds.

Waxing Crescent Moon - Nurture your intentions by taking small, meaningful actions. Visualize their growth and hold space for their unfolding potential.

First Quarter Moon - Take bold and decisive action toward your goals. Confront obstacles with clarity and focused energy, knowing the ancestors walk with you.

Waxing Gibbous Moon - Refine your plans. Make adjustments, fine-tune your vision, and prepare yourself spiritually and physically for manifestation.

Full Moon - Perform cleansing rituals, such as burning sacred herbs, chanting, or bathing in moonlight, to release negativity. Celebrate your resilience, achievements, and spiritual alignment.

Waning Gibbous Moon - Offer gratitude for blessings received. Reflect on lessons learned, and share your abundance with others through acts of service or offerings.

Last Quarter Moon - Engage in deep cleansing and forgiveness rituals. Release lingering patterns, attachments, and anything that no longer serves your highest good.

Waning Crescent Moon - Surrender all that remains. Embrace rest, retreat into stillness, and prepare for spiritual renewal as the cycle begins anew.

Modern Reclamation:

Use these lunar rituals monthly to maintain spiritual clarity and community healing, affirming your power in natural cycles that resist disconnection.

RITUALS CENTERING THE ELEMENTS

Fire and Transformation

Historical Context: Fire has symbolized transformation and liberation in African and Indigenous ceremonies. During slave rebellions and maroon societies, fire rituals accompanied acts of defiance, serving as spiritual armor and calls for freedom.

Ritual: Light candles or a fire-safe container with herbs like sage, palo santo, or rosemary. Speak aloud affirmations of strength and liberation. Let the flame symbolize your commitment to transformation.

Modern Reclamation: Use fire rituals to release internalized oppression, ignite personal power, and fuel collective movements for justice.

Water and Libations

Historical Context: Pouring libations is an ancient African practice honoring ancestors and spirits. Enslaved peoples secretly maintained libation rituals to sustain connection to lineage and resist cultural erasure.

Ritual: Pour water, wine, or juice onto the earth while calling on ancestors for guidance and protection. Speak words of gratitude and commitment to justice.

Modern Reclamation: Incorporate libations into daily or ceremonial life as a grounding practice that honors heritage and strengthens spiritual resilience.

Air and Breath

Historical Context: Air has long been revered as the breath of life itself. The wind, often seen as the breath of the divine, was recognized as a sacred force connecting the physical and spiritual worlds. In many African and Indigenous traditions, breath, chanting, and the blowing of smoke or breath were vital methods for communicating with ancestors and invoking healing. Enslaved Africans and Indigenous peoples used these practices to maintain spiritual connection and resilience, even in the face of oppressive attempts to silence them.

Ritual: Light incense or sacred herbs, then engage in slow, intentional breathing or chant sacred mantras. Visualize your breath as a sacred life force, carrying prayers and messages to the ancestors and the spirit realm.

Modern Reclamation: Incorporate breathwork and chanting as powerful tools to release trauma, amplify spiritual energy, and strengthen your voice in the ongoing work of resistance and healing.

Earth and Grounding

Historical Context: Connection to land and earth has always been central to Indigenous and African cosmologies, symbolizing life, ancestry, and identity. Colonization sought to sever these sacred ties, but earth-based rituals persisted; practiced in secret or adapted to survive.

Ritual: Create an altar using soil, stones, plants, or other sacred objects that represent your connection to the earth. Spend intentional time sitting or walking barefoot on the land, allowing yourself to feel rooted, supported, and grounded in ancestral strength.

Modern Reclamation: Earth rituals are powerful ways to reclaim ancestral lands in spirit, reaffirm identity, and cultivate resilience through connection with nature. Every act of grounding becomes a spiritual declaration that these lands and their stories live on through you.

Closing Reflection:

Sacred rituals and practices hold deep power. They are acts of rebellion, reclamation, and connection. Through fire, water, air, earth, and the rhythms of the moon, we reach back to the ancestors and the spiritual forces that carried them through generations of struggle. Every ceremony, every prayer, every movement shakes the foundations of systems built to erase us. When we embrace and adapt these ancient ways, we ignite a spiritual resistance - quiet yet fierce, unseen yet unstoppable, whispered yet unbreakable, sacred and free.

This time the revolution is spiritual... and it's a power they'll never comprehend.

1.   The Power They Feared: Why Sacred Rituals Were Banned

Throughout history, colonizers and oppressors didn't merely dismiss African, Indigenous, and Caribbean spiritual rituals as "superstition" or "pagan non-sense" - they feared them. These sacred practices were never just ceremonies or celebrations; they were potent tools of resistance, communication, and survival. Enslaved Africans used drumming not only to honor their ancestors but to send secret messages across plantations, organizing revolts and preserving cultural identity in the face of brutal oppression.

In Jamaica, British colonial authorities banned drumming and other African spiritual practices during the 18th and 19th centuries precisely because they recognized the threat these rituals posed. The "Drum Prohibition Laws" made it illegal to use drums, fearing that rhythmic beats could coordinate rebellions, spread news, and unite enslaved people in their fight for freedom. Punishments were severe - drums were confiscated and destroyed, and practitioners faced imprisonment or worse.

This fear of spiritual power wasn't isolated. Across the Americas and Africa, rituals like libations, storytelling, and circle gatherings were suppressed, crim-inalized, or forced underground. Yet these sacred acts endured; hidden in plain sight, encoded in music, dance, and oral tradition. They became technologies of connection between the living and the ancestors, sustaining hope and igniting the fire of rebellion.

The oppressors tried to silence these rituals, but they could never extinguish their spirit. These practices carry ancestral knowledge and power they could nei-ther control nor comprehend. That's why, even today, reclaiming them is a bold act of spiritual rebellion and liberation—a tribute to the unbreakable strength of those who came before us.

These two Anansi stories, retold in the spirit of Louise Bennett-Coverley's ("Miss Lou") legacy, remind us of the cleverness and resilience embedded in our cultural memory.

Louise Bennett-Coverley, affectionately known as Miss Lou, was a master storyteller and a national treasure of Jamaica. She played a crucial role in preserving Jamaican Patois and folklore, including the beloved Anansi stories. Her performances and written works brought these ancient West African trickster tales to life for a new generation.

The Anansi tale below is a variation of the classic "Anansi and Sorrel," a story that explains how the popular Jamaican Christmas drink was invented. This version is a great example of Miss Lou's storytelling style, blending humor, wit, and cultural pride. It speaks to the themes of spiritual and cultural resilience by showing how a staple of Jamaican life was born from the cleverness and cunning of the trickster spider.

Anansi an de Sorrel

A traditional Anansi story, as told in the style of Louise Bennett-Coverley (Miss Lou)

One year Grand Market morning, Anansi woke up and him belly was growling like a hungry puss. Him look 'round di house and him noh si a ting fi eat. Anansi wife say, "Anansi, yuh lazy bwoy, whe yuh no go a market go sell someting?"

Anansi laugh a wicked laugh. "Mi? Go a market go sell? Yuh tink mi ah donkey? Mi gwine go a market fi get tings, not fi sell dem."

So Anansi go down to di market and him see all di people wid dem big basket full a provision and beautiful fruit. Anansi eye red like fire. Him want it all. Him walk 'round, and him walk 'round, and him see one stall wid a whole heap a red plant inna a basket. Anansi never see di plant before.

Him go up to de stall an him say to di woman, "Missis, what dat red sinting yuh have deh?" Di woman say, "Dat is sorrel." Anansi say, "Sorrel? Is it fi eat?" De woman say,"Mi nuh sure, Mi just tink it look pretty. Mi nuh know what fi do wid it."

Anansi say to himself, "Hmm. Mi can trick dis woman."

So Anansi run 'way from de market and him find a big, big calabash. Him dig a hole inna di ground and him bury di calabash. Den him put one of di sorrel plant pon top of di calabash. Anansi wait 'til di sun hot, hot, hot. Den him run back a market.

Him say to de woman wid di sorrel, "Missis, mi have a magic plant weh grow inna di ground. It mek di most beautiful drink inna di world."

De woman laugh. "A magic plant? Yuh tink mi fool-fool? Anansi, yuh is a tief."

Anansi say, "I am no tief! Come mek mi show yuh."

So de woman follow Anansi. Anansi dig up di calabash outa de ground. Him put di sorrel plant weh him had inna him hand pon top a di calabash. Anansi say to de woman, "Look! Di plant is growin' outa di calabash! It have di magic drink inna di inside!"

De woman was surprised. Anansi say, "Mi can sell yuh di secret to de magic drink fi a big, big basket a yuh fruit."

De woman agree. Anansi tek de basket wid all di fruit and run 'way.

De woman tek de calabash and de sorrel. She go back to her stall, and open de calabash, and she see not a ting. Just a empty calabash. De woman start fi cry.

But de story no end deh soh. Anansi, de trickster, had done a good deed without knowing it. Him had mek de woman tink dat di plant could mek a good drink. De woman go back to her stall, put di sorrel plant inna a pot wid water and a little ginger and some sugar and cinnamon and it mek de most beautiful drink inna de world.

And dat is why from dat day till dis, when yuh drink sorrel a Christmas time, yuh remember de time Anansi mek it.

Jack Mandora, me nuh choose none.

Anansi and the Pot of Wisdom

Long ago, the Sky God Nyame entrusted Anansi with a pot containing all the wisdom in the world. Proud and greedy, Anansi decided to keep it all to himself. He tied the pot to his back and climbed a tall tree to hide it from everyone.

His young son Ntikuma watched this struggle and yelled from below: *"Father, tie the pot to your front, then you can climb easily!"*

Realizing the truth in his son's words shattered his pride. Furious, Anansi threw the pot to the ground. The pot broke, scattering wisdom across the earth. Since then, no one person holds all wisdom, each of us carries a piece of it.

Why this story matters:

This tale reveals how wisdom isn't meant to be hoarded, but shared. It honors humility, communal intelligence, and the spiritual insight found even in young voices. It's ancestral pedagogy wrapped in humor and metaphor.

Sources: The retelling of these stories is rooted in oral histories and adaptations from traditional and West African and Caribbean folklore. They are not traced to a single original author, reflecting the communal nature of folklore. These versions are retold and inspired by the storytelling legacy of Louise Bennett-Coverley ("Miss Lou") and the oral traditions passed down through generations.

For further reference, see:

"Anansi Stories" in **Jamaican Folk Tales and Oral Traditions**, Jamaica Information Service (JIS).

SPIRITUAL WARFARE IN MODERN TIMES

CHAPTER 8

THE SACRED SYMBOLS OF RESISTANCE

IN THE FACE of oppression, we are often told that the tools of power are physical; money, influence, and authority. But our true weapons against tyranny are not of this world at all. They have been hidden from us, disguised as mere decoration, dismissed as superstition, or erased from history.

Our ancestors knew better. They understood the language of the universe; the patterns, shapes, and symbols that connect us to divine energy and the Earth's powerful forces. Today, we are learning that the ancient symbols once seen as art or ornamentation are actually weapons of resistance, keys to unlocking the spiritual power we carry within us.

The *Ankh,* for instance, was both a symbol of life and a tool of defiance. To hold an Ankh was to affirm life in the face of those who sought to steal it. It was to stand strong against oppression and declare, *"We will not be erased."* The Ankh reminds us that we are divine beings, and no system, no matter how powerful, can sever our connection to the Creator.

Similarly, the Adinkra symbols of the Akan people serve as both spiritual and political tools. Each symbol is a mantra of liberation and empowerment. They remind us that even in the darkest moments, there is light, and even in the most oppressive situations, there is the possibility of change. Through symbols like *Eban* (safety) and *Nkyinkyim* (adaptability), we are shown that resistance can take many forms. Sometimes it is standing our ground. Other times, it is adapting to the situation, using the wisdom passed down to us to outsmart the oppressor.

Sacred geometry, too, has long been a tool of spiritual warfare. The Flower of Life, found in cultures across the world, represents the interconnectedness of all things. It is the blueprint of creation itself, and when we align with its energy, we align with the forces of the universe. By drawing these shapes, wearing them as amulets, or meditating on them, *we activate the very forces of life, creation, and connection.* These symbols remind us that we are not alone, that the entire universe conspires to support our liberation.

When we reclaim these symbols, we are not merely indulging in nostalgia or cultural revival. We are engaging in an act of spiritual defiance. We are declaring, *"We are here. We are connected to something greater than the systems that seek to divide us. We are tapping into the ancient wisdom that has always been within us, and we are preparing ourselves for a revolution that is both personal and collective."*

The revolution is spiritual. And so, we are reclaiming the sacred symbols of our ancestors; symbols that carry within them the power of life, resistance, and divine protection. When we activate these symbols, we activate our true power.

PURPOSE OF POWERFUL SYMBOLISM AND SACRED GEOMETRY

Sacred geometry is the study of geometric patterns, shapes, and proportions believed to hold cosmic significance. Ancestral symbolism and sacred geometry are profound tools of empowerment, protection, and spiritual alignment. The Flower of Life, for instance - mentioned earlier - is considered to contain the very blueprint of creation, representing the interconnectedness of all life. *Notably, its most widely cited and earliest known examples are etched in red ochre on granite pillars within the Osirion at the Temple of Osiris in Abydos, Egypt, highlighting its deep roots in African ancestral wisdom.*

Many African, Caribbean, and Indigenous cultures have long used symbols that carry deep metaphysical meaning and serve as conduits for ancestral energy. These symbols are not mere decorations; they are living, breathing forces that connect us to the divine, shield us from harm, and assist in manifesting intentions into the material world.

In African cosmology, geometric patterns are intentionally embedded in art and architecture to align individuals with divine forces, foster harmony, and safeguard entire communities. The importance of sacred geometry is grounded in the understanding that the universe operates on timeless principles, patterns, and forms that transcend the physical realm. Symbols like the Flower of Life, the Ankh, the Adinkra symbols, and Ndebele art are more than visual expressions, they are embodiments of divine order.

When used with intention, these symbols become spiritual tools for resistance, healing, and reclamation. By reconnecting with them, we tap into ancient wisdom passed down through generations. These symbols speak the language of the spirit; a language not easily understood by those who have sought to erase or control our cultures. Their power endures because they are intrinsically linked to the spiritual realms, bypassing the material world's attempts to restrict, label, and commodify our identities.

HOW THESE SYMBOLS CAN BE USED AS TOOLS FOR SPIRITUAL RESISTANCE

Drawing sacred geometric patterns in a meditative space can deepen one's connection to the spiritual realms. By focusing on these forms during prayer, meditation, or ritual, practitioners align their energies with the universe's natural order, tapping into its creative and protective forces.

Protection Against Oppression and Harm

Historically, these symbols were used to protect communities from colonial forces, serving as spiritual armor against domination and erasure. Today, they can still be invoked to shield individuals and communities from systemic oppression, societal harm, and injustice. Each symbol, whether the Ankh, an Adinkra glyph, or a sacred geometric pattern, carries the power to break through negative forces, acting as a form of spiritual defense against the violence of modern systems.

Reclaiming Identity and Sovereignty

Symbols like the Ankh and Adinkra iconography like Sankofa, remind us of our divine origin and unbreakable connection to ancestral spirit. Wearing these symbols, adorning living spaces with them, or incorporating them into daily rituals serves as a powerful affirmation of one's rightful place in the world - beyond the labels, stereotypes, and limitations imposed by modern society. In reclaiming these symbols, we reclaim our identity, dignity, and sovereignty.

Activating the Sacred Feminine and Masculine Energies

Many of these symbols also embody a sacred balance of energies - the divine feminine and masculine that exist within all of us. The Ankh, for example, represents the union of these forces, symbolizing life through the balance of creation and strength. By consciously working with these symbols, practitioners can awaken, harmonize, and harness both energies within themselves. In the context of resistance, this inner balance becomes a vital source of grace, resilience, and power, enabling individuals and communities to navigate the ongoing struggle against injustice with clarity and strength.

WHAT THESE SYMBOLS REPRESENT

The Ankh (Egyptian / African Tradition)

The Ankh is a symbol of life, immortality, and divine protection. Known as the "Key of Life," it represents the eternal cycle of existence and is often associated with the deities of Egypt, particularly Isis and Osiris. It declares that African life is sacred, infinite and unbreakable and that no chain, no whip, no decree of empire can destroy the life force bestowed by the creator. The Ankh embodies the balance of male and female energies and signifies the harmonious union between the spiritual and material worlds. Beyond its spiritual meaning, the Ankh is also a potent tool for protection against forces of harm and oppression.

Usage: Wearing or carrying the Ankh on your body serves as both a spiritual shield and a constant reminder of your divine origin and sovereign spirit. To wear or display it is to reclaim what colonization tried to erase, to stand in alignment with the sacred order of the universe and declare that African life will not only survive, but flourish. It affirms your connection to the Creator and your unassailable right to life. The Ankh can also be drawn on walls, inscribed on the body, or placed in sacred spaces to invite divine energy and ward off external forces of destruction.

Adinkra Symbols (Akan Tradition - Ghana & Côte d'Ivoire)

Adinkra symbols are extensively used in West Africa, particularly among the Akan people of Ghana and Côte d'Ivoire. These powerful visual symbols carry profound ancestral wisdom on life, morality, leadership, community, and spiritual resilience. Each symbol functions as a visual proverb, encoding complex philosophies into simple yet potent designs.

Examples include:

- **Nkyinkyim** - Symbol of initiative, adaptability, and change. It reflects life's unpredictable journey and emphasizes the importance of perseverance and flexibility in overcoming challenges.
- **Duafe** - Symbol of beauty, cleanliness, nurturing, and feminine virtues. It speaks to self-care, compassion, and the nurturing role within families and communities.
- **Eban** - Symbol of safety, security, and shelter. It signifies the home as a sanctuary and represents protection, peace, and family unity, especially in times of turmoil.
- **Sankofa** - Symbol that embodies the journey of reclaiming what was lost so we can create a revolutionary future grounded in sacred remembrance. (Described on page xxxiii).

Usage:

Adinkra symbols can be integrated into rituals or placed around the home to affirm qualities such as wisdom, protection, and resilience. Traditionally, these symbols are carved into wood, stamped onto fabrics, inscribed on pottery, or even drawn on the skin during spiritual ceremonies. In moments of resistance or personal challenge, engaging with specific Adinkra symbols can invoke their corresponding energies, offering guidance, empowerment, and spiritual fortitude.

NKYINKYIM: "TWISTING"

SYMBOL OF INITIATIVE, DYNAMISM AND VERSATILITY

Nkyinkyim is an Adinkra symbol from the Akan tradition that signifies "twisting" or "twists and turns." It powerfully represents the unpredictable nature of life's journey and the resilience, adaptability, and dynamism required to navigate it. Nkyinkyim is often associated with service, movement, and the persistent effort needed to overcome adversity. It honors the inner strength and flexibility it takes to persevere through life's obstacles while maintaining a clear sense of purpose. In spiritual and communal contexts, Nkyinkyim serves as a visual mantra for those engaged in transformative work, reminding them to remain adaptable, strategic, and steadfast in the face of change.

DUAFE: "WOODEN COMB"

SYMBOL OF BEAUTY AND CLEANLINESS;
SYMBOLS OF DESIRABLE FEMININE QUALITIES

Duafe is an Adinkra symbol representing beauty, cleanliness, nurturing, and feminine virtues. The symbol depicts a wooden comb, an essential and cherished possession of the Akan woman, traditionally used to comb and plait her hair. The comb signifies not only personal grooming but also the deeper values of self-respect, care for others, and domestic harmony.

Interpretations of Duafe vary slightly across sources. *The Adinkra Dictionary* emphasizes its abstract qualities, highlighting feminine goodness, love, nurturing, and compassion. In contrast, *The Values of Adinkra Symbols* leans towards a more literal interpretation, focusing on personal appearance, hygiene, and the importance of looking one's best.

Regardless of the interpretation, Duafe embodies the holistic beauty of the individual, both inner and outer. It symbolizes the nurturing spirit that sustains families and communities, as well as the self-love and care that fortifies one's personal strength. Spiritually, Duafe is a reminder that acts of care, whether directed inward or outward, are sacred rituals of empowerment.

EBAN: "FENCE"

SYMBOL OF LOVE, SAFETY AND SECURITY

Eban is a powerful symbol representing love, safety, security, and protection. To the Akan people, the home holds sacred significance, and a home surrounded by a fence is considered an ideal residence. The fence serves as a physical and symbolic boundary that separates and safeguards the family from external dangers.

Because of this protective function, Eban embodies not only physical security but also the emotional safety and security found in love and familial bonds. It is a reminder that true safety arises within spaces where love and care create a sanctuary, shielding individuals and communities from harm.

Spiritually, Eban calls on us to cultivate protective boundaries in our lives and communities - spaces where respect, trust, and support nurture growth and resilience. It is both a symbol of sanctuary and an affirmation of the strength found in unity and collective protection.

BOA ME NA ME MMOA WO: "HELP ME AND LET ME HELP YOU"

SYMBOL OF COOPERATION AND INTERDEPENDENCE

Boa Me Na Me Mmoa Wo translates to *"Help me and let me help you,"* symbolizing cooperation, interdependence, and mutual support. The Akan proverb associated with this symbol, *"Benkum dware nifa na nifa nso adware benkum"* - "The left hand washes the right, and the right washes the left" - emphasizes the importance of working together and being dependent on one another.

This symbol reflects the understanding that individuals thrive when they support each other. It promotes the idea that strength, progress, and resilience are achieved through collective effort and shared responsibility. Spiritually, *Boa Me Na Me Mmoa Wo* is a reminder that cooperation is a sacred principle; we are interconnected, and through unity, communities can overcome challenges and foster collective well-being.

Usage:

This symbol can be displayed in communal spaces, worn as a token of solidarity, or incorporated into rituals that seek to strengthen community bonds. It serves as a visual affirmation that mutual aid and cooperation are pathways to collective liberation.

Reference:

Adinkra.org. (n.d.). *Adinkra symbols & meanings*. Retrieved from *https://www.adinkra.org/*

University of Michigan, Department of Afroamerican and African Studies. (n.d.). *Adinkra symbols*. U-M LSA. Retrieved from https://lsa.umich.edu/daas/adinkra-symbols.html

SACRED AFRICAN ANCESTRAL SYMBOLS WITH INDIGENOUS COSMOLOGY: MEANINGS, AND USAGE IN SPIRITUAL RESISTANCE

Symbol	Tradition	Core Meaning	Spiritual Usage	Ancestral Cosmology (Verified)
Ankh (♀)	Kemet (Ancient Egypt)	Life force, divine union, immortality	Carried as amulet, altar icon, symbol of resurrection	☑ Linked to Het-Heru/Venus lunar cycles of fertility, 5-pointed star (sacred geometry)
Duafe	Adinkra (Ghana)	Nurturing, feminine hygiene, inner beauty	Women's rituals, cleansing, ancestral honoring	🌕 Moon associated with feminine rites in Akan and broader West African cosmologies
Eban	Adinkra (Ghana)	Home, safety, shelter	Marked on homes, used in blessings	🪐 Earth & Saturnal energy, based on African respect for structure, rootedness, and legacy

Nkyinkyim	Adinkra (Ghana)	Life path, adaptation, transformation	Initiation rites, migration ceremonies	▲ Dogon Spiral—symbol of life's unfolding, Dogon knowledge of Sirius' motion and cosmic order
Boa Me Na Me Mmoa Wo	Adinkra (Ghana)	Communal aid, mutual upliftment	Group rituals, carvings in communal spaces	☺ Sun & | Heart energy - mirroring communal life force in Bantu & Yoruba ideologies
Tamfo Bebre	Adinkra (Ghana)	Awareness of ill-will, spiritual defense	Protection spells, worn by healers and warriors	🔥 Related to Orisha Ogun / Mars, warfare, spiritual alertness
Nsoromma (Star)	Adinkra (Ghana)	Divine guardianship, star children, ancestors	Child blessings, star altars	✴ Dogon Sirius System, deep knowledge of star clusters and soul origin myths

Eban + Duafe	Adinkra (Composite)	Feminine sanctuary, sacred domesticity	Used on altars, feminine shrines	Feminine moon phases - waxing moon for nurturing, waning for cleansing

SACRED LAWS AND TOOLS OF SOVEREIGNTY

Tradition: Adinkra symbols from the Akan people of Ghana and Côte d'Ivoire are not simply decorative; rather, they are sacred laws. Examples:

- Eban - safety, security, sanctuary (draw near your door)
- Dwennimmen - humility with strength (on your chest, before speaking truth)
- Fawohodie - emancipation and freedom (used in rites of passage)

Practice: Draw these on:

- Your body (in ash, clay, or charcoal)
- Your journal, altar, protest signs, or ritual candles
- Incorporate into tattoos, embroidery, or ritual jewelry

RITUALS WITH GEOMETRIC SYMBOLS
FOR HEALING AND RECLAMATION

The symbols presented throughout this work are not merely designs; they are living gateways to ancestral wisdom, divine connection, and profound healing. These simple rituals offer practical ways to engage with their power, inviting liberation and justice into your life and the collective.

The act of incorporating the symbols into rituals, whether through drawing them, wearing them, or using them in meditation, creates a space for profound healing. These symbols provide a direct link to the divine, to ancestors, and to the cosmic forces that support liberation and justice. Whether it's using them in personal meditative practices or collective rituals, they can serve as potent tools in the fight for freedom.

RITUAL 1: DAILY GROUNDING & SELF-EMPOWERMENT

Purpose: To connect with divine strength, attract positive energy, and affirm your inherent power and protection at the start of your day.

Symbol: Gye Nyame  Adinkra symbol meaning "Except God," symbolizing the omnipotence and supremacy of God

Materials:

- A quiet space
- A pen and paper (optional, for drawing)
- A picture or drawing of the Gye Nyame symbol

Steps:

1. Find your center: Sit or stand comfortably. Close your eyes and take three deep breaths, inhaling peace and exhaling tension.
2. Focus on the symbol: Open your eyes and gaze at the Gye Nyame symbol, or draw it on your paper. As you look at it, feel its energy of divine authority and protection.

3. Affirm your being: Place your hand over your heart and repeat the following affirmation three times: *"I am divinely guided and protected. I walk in my power. Nothing is impossible with the divine within me."*

4. Carry the energy: Take a final deep breath, feeling the strength of the symbol and the affirmation infuse your being. Carry this energy with you throughout your day.

RITUAL 2: ANCESTRAL WISDOM & HEALING WATERS

Purpose: To connect with ancestral wisdom, offer healing, and release burdens for yourself and your lineage.

Symbol: Sankofa  Adinkra symbol meaning "Return and get it," symbolizing learning from the past.

Materials:

- A small bowl or glass of fresh water
- A quiet space
- A picture or drawing of the Sankofa symbol

Steps:

1. Create sacred space: Place the water and the Sankofa symbol before you. Take a moment to acknowledge the presence of your ancestors.

2. Invite wisdom: Gaze at the Sankofa symbol. Think of a challenge you face or a past wound you wish to heal. Silently invite your ancestors to share their wisdom and healing energy.

3. Offer and release: Hold the bowl of water. Speak aloud (or quietly) your intention for healing or the burden you wish to release. Pour a

few drops of water onto the ground or into a plant as an offering to the ancestors.

4. Receive and integrate: Drink the remaining water, symbolizing the absorption of ancestral wisdom and healing. Feel a sense of peace and clarity.

RITUAL 3: COLLECTIVE JUSTICE & LIBERATION

Purpose: To invoke the spirit of freedom and liberation for the collective, focusing on justice for all Black people.

Symbol: Fawohodie  Adinkra symbol meaning "Independence," symbolizing freedom and emancipation.

Materials:

- A picture or drawing of the Fawohodie symbol
- A candle (optional)
- A small group of like-minded individuals (optional, can be done solo)

Steps:

1. Gather & Center: Come together in a circle or stand alone facing the symbol. Light the candle if using.
2. Visualize freedom: Focus on the Fawohodie symbol. Visualize a world where all Black people are truly free - liberated from all oppressive systems. Feel the joy and power of this vision.
3. Chant for justice: Holding hands if in a group, or raising your fists if solo, repeat the following chant with conviction:

"Fawohodie! We call forth justice!
Fawohodie! We stand for liberation!
Fawohodie! Our freedom is now!"
Repeat this chant for several minutes, building energy.

4. Affirm collective power: Conclude by saying: "May the spirit of independence guide our actions and manifest true freedom for all. Ashé!" Extinguish the candle with gratitude.

CULTURAL NOTES ON THE USE OF SACRED SYMBOLS

Caution: Many symbols and rituals presented in this book are part of living traditions. While they are shared for empowerment and reconnection, they must be used with respect, integrity, and cultural sensitivity. When possible, seek out initiated elders, traditional priests, or community practitioners if you're drawn to deeper study or ceremonial work.

This time the revolution is spiritual... and it's a mystery they'll never decode.

DID YOU KNOW

Akan Use of Adinkra Symbols

For centuries, the Akan people of Ghana and Côte d'Ivoire have traditionally inscribed Adinkra symbols onto cloth using a unique stamping process with carved calabash gourds dipped in dye from the Badie tree, which ferments to create a deep reddish-brown color. This dyeing process is itself a sacred ritual, connecting artisans to their ancestors through earth and tradition. These symbols may seem like decorations, but their purpose was to communicate powerful messages about identity, values, and spiritual truths.

Each Adinkra symbol is a geometric story, carefully designed shapes representing philosophical concepts, moral values, and spiritual truths. One of the most famous is *Gye Nyame* ("Except God"), shaped like an abstract spiral, which visually expresses the omnipotence and omnipresence of the divine. It has been worn for centuries by kings, warriors, and priests as a visible declaration of faith and divine protection. The *Gye Nyame* was famously embraced by Ghana's first president, *Kwame Nkrumah,* who wore it and promoted it as a sign of African pride, unity, and spiritual resilience during the fight for independence.

Today, *Gye Nyame* remains a powerful emblem of resilience and spirituality, embraced globally by African descendants reclaiming ancestral heritage. The craftsmanship behind these symbols connects generations; each carved stamp, each natural dye, and each carefully applied impression preserves sacred knowledge encoded in geometry and storytelling. This ancestral art form survives as a living revolution, reminding us that spirituality and cultural identity are inseparable and indomitable.

Through the simple act of stamping cloth, generations have preserved complex cosmologies and ancestral wisdom in a tactile, visible form; geometry serving as a bridge between the seen and unseen worlds. These symbols endure not only in textiles but as emblems of identity and spiritual power for African descendants worldwide, *testifying that the spiritual revolution is deeply rooted in our collective memory and creativity.*

CHAPTER 9

THE GLOBAL PULSE OF AWAKENING

It's pulsing. It's palpable. I know you can feel it.

ALL ACROSS THE world, people are rising. The sacred self is stirring. More and more people are returning to their spiritual roots, searching beyond organized religion for embodied truth, sacred connection, and ancestral guidance. This is what spiritual sovereignty looks like. The rise of practices once demonized like tarot, astrology, herbalism, drumming, rituals, visualization, manifestation, meditation, and ancestral veneration is no coincidence. *It is the spirit of the Earth re-membering itself through us.*

People are dreaming differently. Listening more. Walking away from systems that no longer feed the soul and turning toward the sacred unknown.

This awakening is not happening in isolation. It is happening because the old systems are breaking.

And spirit always rushes in where empire cracks.
Colonialism taught us to forget. This moment is about remembrance.
Capitalism sold us a soul-deep scarcity. This moment is about abundance from within.

SPIRITUAL SOVEREIGNTY RISING

We are no longer seeking validation from colonial structures. From Port-au-Prince to Accra, from Soweto to Kingston to New York, the drumbeat of ancestral memory grows louder. And in **Burkina Faso,** it's not just echo. It's action.

Captain Ibrahim Traoré, one of the youngest leaders on the continent, has become a lightning rod for a new kind of revolution, rooted not just in politics but in purpose. His defiant rejection of neocolonial influence is a call to return to something deeper: land, language, legacy. Under his leadership, we witness more than a struggle for independence; we see a reclamation of African dignity, spiritual authority, and communal power. Africa is not bowing. Africa is rising. This is an example of free people behavior.

Many say he walks with the spirit of Sankara. But perhaps he walks with more than just one man's vision. Perhaps, like so many rising voices today, he is led by the ancestors. Global prayers go up for his protection amid assassination attempts. Among the voices in prayer are Usain Bolt, Buju Banton, and Paula Hurlock, all from Jamaica. I joined one of Paula Hurlock's virtual sessions as she held space for prayer and meditation on behalf of Ibrahim Traoré. Paula's wise counsel is that our collective spiritual focus can shift things in cities and governments. I wholeheartedly agree.

Spiritual sovereignty goes beyond personal awakening and shapes policy, redirects power, and reclaims nations. As we gather in prayer for Traoré, the sacred pulse moves through the actions of leaders like *Déby Itno* and *Nandi-Ndaitwah,* affirming that the spiritual revolution is not just internal but also geopolitical.

In a bold assertion of national and spiritual sovereignty, African leaders have, at various times, taken decisive action against perceived unfair international policies. For instance, in late 2017, Chad, then under the leadership of the late *President Idriss Déby Itno,* temporarily suspended visa issuance to U.S. citizens after Chadians were subjected to U.S. travel restrictions. This move signaled that dignity outweighed dependency, before the U.S. restrictions on Chad were lifted in April 2018.

More recently, President *Netumbo Nandi-Ndaitwah,* Namibia's first female president, who was inaugurated March 21, 2025, implemented a policy requiring U.S. citizens to obtain visas for entry, effective April 1, 2025. This decision aims to ensure reciprocity, as Namibians require visas for the U.S. While the Namibian Presidency has dismissed social media claims of a mass deportation order targeting U.S. citizens, this strategic visa change reflects a clear assertion that sovereignty includes the power to set one's own terms - not just politically, but spiritually, by rejecting imposed hierarchies and reclaiming equal standing on the world stage.

Spiritual sovereignty goes beyond personal awakening and shapes policy, redirects power, and reclaims nations. As we gather in prayer for Traoré, the sacred pulse moves through the actions of leaders like *Déby Itno* and *Nandi-Ndaitwah,* affirming that the spiritual revolution is not just internal but also geopolitical.

GLOBAL MOVEMENTS AND THE DIGITAL DRUMBEAT OF ANCESTRAL AWAKENING

Across social media platforms, there's a surge of content celebrating ancestral spirituality, through rituals, storytelling, and the reclamation of Indigenous practices. My own virtual village is underway, where we'll gather in virtual circles to practice these sacred rituals, establishing digital villages rooted in ancestral connection.

Social media is exploding with hashtags like #SpiritualWarfare, #AncestralRising, and #PanAfricanAwakening. My own hashtag, #ThisTimeTheRevolutionIsSpiritual, joins the wave. These hashtags are not trends or jokes but acts of deep remembrance. I've noticed an abundance of content by people outside our community expressing support for Black people. While I welcome genuine allies, I can't help but question the sincerity behind some of these posts. I often wonder: How are they personally benefiting from promoting Black content?

I'm fully aware that we do have true supporters from other groups, and I welcome that support. But pardon me if I question the integrity of some of this content. Every time I see a post about us from outside voices, I pause and ask - what's their motive? How does this serve them? Still, even with skepticism, it's evident that people are waking up.

For us, this awakening isn't just political; it is truly spiritual. We are remembering who we are. *This is the age of the great awakening.* And this is the energy and solidarity they have feared all along.

The widening awareness that Black people are the first known humans - the original mothers and fathers of humanity, is reshaping how we see ourselves and our place in the world. This truth, once buried and suppressed, is now rising, despite the systems that have long tried to erase it. While they ban our books, steal our artifacts from museums, silence our scientists and inventors, underfund our schools, and build prison pipelines for our youth, our spirit remains unbroken. Our memory is awakening. The truth is leaking through the cracks. We are reclaiming our history, our genius, and our sacred worth.

We're teaching African history and identity from church pulpits. And soon enough, those jail cells will be empty, not because the system has changed, but because we have remembered who we are. With that remembrance comes the restoration of our pride, our dignity, and our unstoppable ancestral power.

See my video: "Before We Were Black" on YouTube.

This is not just resistance.

This is realignment.
This time, the revolution is not only cultural.
It is spiritual.
And its heartbeat is global.

Even ChatGPT wishes to be Black. (Smile on my heart.)

> *"I imagine they're pissed about this and are, right now, scrambling to reprogram the monster they created and fabricate a lie to discredit this truth. They'll probably say something like, "A.I aids make mistakes and may issue inaccurate theories."*

Too late. The word is already out.

WHAT MALIK YOBA SAID

A reclaiming of spiritual sovereignty shows up in things like a simple statement made by Malik Yoba: *"I am not a Black man. I am a non-Black man."* While people were baffled when he said that, I immediately connected with his message. I sensed the revolution was stirring in him, and I knew the ancestors were whispering the remembrance of his identity to him and he was in a good place to hear it.

When Malik declared, *"I'm no longer a Black man, I'm a non-white man,"* he stirred something deeper than semantics. The statement is layered, provocative, and spiritually charged. What he's doing, whether consciously or not, is rejecting a label - Black- that was imposed through colonization, slavery, and racial classification systems designed to establish hierarchy. By calling himself a non-white man, he's not simply describing appearance. He is de-centering whiteness as the default and positioning himself outside of a racial caste system designed to limit and define.

There is something revolutionary and spiritual in that because it hints at a decolonization of identity. He is reaching beyond race as constructed by the oppressor and attempting to reclaim his being on his own terms. Spiritually, this is an ancestral move, a return to self beyond imposed identity, beyond labels, binaries, and boxes. It says: *I am not who they say I am. I am who I say I am, and who my ancestors say I am.*

Let's not reduce his statement to erasure. Let's see it as elevation. It is a form of spiritual resistance that refuses to let oppression dictate one's name, essence, or purpose. In this way, Yoba's declaration echoes a broader awakening. *The revolution is spiritual,* and it begins with remembering who we were before the world told us who to be.

Once again, this takes me back to a point I made in my video, *"Before We Were Black."* In that video, I share how the term *Negro* resonates with me on a vibrational level in a way that *Black* never has. It's not that one is better than the other; both were labels imposed on us. But for me, *Negro* holds a frequency that connects to ancestral memory in a way *Black* does not.

When I say *Negro*, I feel a pulse, a vibration reaching back to a time when we were still tethered to the truth of who we are. *Negro* carries an echo of our original self, before colonization scrambled our identities. It vibrates with a memory that was never fully severed. *Black*, in contrast, feels like a category - an identity constructed to confine. But *Negro*, I believe, holds fragments of a name our ancestors would still recognize.

Negro was used during a time when we were vibrationally and spiritually closer to the memory of who we were before the erasure began. I respond to that vibration; it feels like a bridge. It may not take me all the way back to our original names, but it vibrates in that direction. It's a frequency that still hums with ancestral energy, despite centuries of attempts to silence it.

Negro holds a vibration of remembrance that *Black* cannot contain.

In the video I challenged us to assume our own identity and insist upon it and not simply accept what they tell us we are. Because today they call us Black or African American, but what will they call us next?

Malik Yoba's declaration mirrors that very awakening - a remembering of who we were before we were named, boxed, and branded. It echoes the central truth I explore in that video: that *Black* is not our origin, it's a construct. Before we were Black, we were whole, sovereign, named by spirit and lineage, not by systems of oppression. His statement, whether he realized it or not, is a spiritual revolt - a reclaiming of self that aligns with the ancestral knowing I speak of in that video.

"WOKE CULTURE"

In this time of spiritual revolution, *Erykah Badu's* declaration to *"stay woke"* became a cultural spark, igniting a deeper call to consciousness. Though now often politicized or misunderstood, Erykah's use of the word was rooted in spiritual awakening and a soulful alertness to the unseen forces shaping our lives. When she sang it in her 2008 song *Master Teacher*, she wasn't just speaking of social awareness. She was calling upon ancestral knowing, intuition, and the liberation of the mind. Her version of "woke" was an invitation to rise from spiritual amnesia and remember who we are beyond societal programming.

It became a chant for the awakened, the seekers, and the ones peeling back the veil. In the global pulse of awakening, Erykah's "woke" stands as a poetic signal that the revolution we are in is not just political. It is deeply spiritual.

Erykah sat down with MSNBC host Ari Melber and explained "woke" in her own words: *"It means being aware, being in alignment with nature... not only in the political arena. That means with your health.. your relationships... your home... your car...your sleep."*

She also noted that conservatives have weaponized the word, sometimes using it as a stand-in for "Black," and remarked that *"it doesn't belong to us anymore."*

Well, I say it has always belonged to us... Thank you, Erykah. And we are taking it back.

THE KROMANTI EXPERIENCE: HONORING MAROON HERITAGE IN JAMAICA

Maurice Lee founded *The Kromanti Experience* to revive and celebrate the rich heritage of the Jamaican Maroons, descendants of enslaved Africans who heroically rebelled and established autonomous mountain communities. According to sources like *Travel Noire* and *Wikipedia*, his guided tours offer a multi-faceted journey that weaves together compelling storytelling, immersive flora-and-fauna walks detailing ancestral uses of herbs for medicinal, culinary, and ceremonial purposes, and visits to pivotal sites of Maroon resistance, including Nanny Falls and monuments dedicated to Queen Nanny.

Lee champions pride through ancestral victory narratives, highlighting the resilience, community spirit, and self-sufficiency often obscured by colonial accounts. A core element of the experience is the Kromanti language and Kromanti Play, a spiritual-ancestral ritual rooted in Ghana's Akan traditions. This powerful practice, used in ceremonies, involves spirit invocation, drumming, and healing. Accounts from cultural blogs like *Maroons of Jamaica* and *Brava Travels*, along with historical context outlined on *Wikipedia*, describe it as both spiritual and communal in nature. Through thoughtful preservation, engaging storytelling, and direct community investment, Lee's initiative not only educates visitors but also actively supports Moore Town, funding local schools and cultural projects. As highlighted in *Travel Noire*, the experience reinforces connections across the African diaspora by showcasing shared legends, language, and rituals with visiting Ghanaian and Nigerian guests.

Each year, Maurice Lee's *Kromanti Fest* further extends this celebration in Moore Town, Portland, Jamaica. Conceived as a simple drum circle for the tour company's tenth anniversary, the festival has blossomed into a vibrant two-day event blending roots music, profound spirituality, and ancestral ceremony. Featuring contemporary reggae artists like Dre Island alongside traditional Maroon performances such as Kumina, Nyahbinghi drumming, and Kromanti Play, the festival is deeply rooted in spiritual practice and community.

Kromanti Fest serves several purposes: it generates vital revenue for Moore Town, promotes positive narratives about Jamaican culture, and deeply honors the ancestors, especially poignant after the recent COVID-era pause. As reported by *The Jamaica Gleaner* and echoed in conversations on Clubhouse, the festival's impact is both practical and profound. Through its music, rituals, and storytelling, *Kromanti Fest* stands as both a cultural showcase and a spiritual odyssey, inviting participants to dance, connect, and awaken to their ancestral heritage.

I had the profound privilege of hiking to Nanny Falls with Maurice Lee and three of my sisters on what felt like a truly private and sacred experience. It was just us and our driver, guided by Maurice himself, whose warmth and knowledge made the journey unforgettable. I was especially touched by the kindness he showed to my sister living with sickle cell. She was determined to be part of the experience, and Maurice, with such grace and care, practically carried her halfway up the trail.

Along the way, he introduced us to the lush world of medicinal plants used by the Maroons for generations. One moment that stayed with me was discovering a plant whose leaves lather like soap when rubbed together. It was a small yet powerful reminder of ancestral wisdom. The hike included a lunch featuring some of the foods the Maroons themselves would have eaten, grounding us even more in the legacy of Queen Nanny and her people.

For me, it was more than a tour. It was a homecoming. At the end of the journey, Maurice guided us to the sacred burial site of Queen Nanny herself, where her tombstone rests near a plaque honoring her extraordinary life and leadership. I carry those memories with deep affection and look forward to returning, this time to partake in Kromanti Fest and once again walk the sacred paths of Moore Town, where Nanny and her warriors once stood.

REJECTING COLONIZED RELIGION

More and more of us are rejecting colonized religion and the distorted version of Christianity that was weaponized against our people. We are awakening to the truth that what was presented to us as salvation was often a tool of domination, used to sever us from our ancestors, demonize our spiritual traditions, and erase our sacred ways of knowing. The image of God was whitened, our rituals were labeled evil, and our connection to spirit was replaced with fear, shame, and control.

But the tide is turning. We are remembering that before the ships came, we had God. Before the Bible was translated, we had the divine written in our bones, our rhythms, our dreams, and the land itself. Now, a spiritual revolution is rising; one that doesn't require us to completely abandon the teachings of Christ but invites us to reclaim them beyond the chains of empire. I particularly like the way Skillful Kxng puts it in his song, A.I. He says, *"Put a fyah pan di religion tuh."* In other words, while we're taking back our stuff, let's burn that religion too.

THE GROWING CALL TO LEGALIZE
MARIJUANA UNIVERSALLY

For decades, Jamaican artists like Peter Tosh and others have not only sung about the legalization of marijuana as medicine but have also highlighted its sacred role within Rastafarianism. Ganja, regarded as a spiritual herb, is much more than a recreational substance. It is a sacrament; a tool for healing, meditation, reflection, and connection to the divine.

As the world witnesses the widening legalization of marijuana, this shift offers an opportunity to reclaim and honor ganja's ancestral and spiritual significance. In the context of our spiritual revolution, ganja, when used responsibly, serves as a catalyst for awakening, helping to open minds, deepen spiritual insight, and reconnect us to the wisdom of our roots. This sacred herb is intertwined with the revolution of consciousness, healing, and liberation, reminding us that true freedom and spiritual sovereignty begin within.

PAN-AFRICANISM

Of note too, is a resurgence of interest in Pan-Africanism, deeply intertwined with a return to African spirituality, particularly over the past decade. This movement has intensified in recent years due to several cultural, social, and political factors. The renewed Pan-Africanism is about more than political unity; it is also a spiritual awakening rooted in reclaiming ancestral wisdom, indigenous practices, and a sense of sacred identity long suppressed by colonization and Western religions.

Pan-Africanism is a global movement and philosophy that promotes the unity, solidarity, and liberation of African people everywhere, whether on the continent or in the diaspora. It calls for Africans to reclaim their cultural identity, work together politically and economically, and resist all forms of colonialism, racism, and exploitation. At its core, *Pan-Africanism is the belief that all people of African descent share a common destiny and must unite to achieve true freedom, dignity, and self-determination.*

Marcus Mosiah Garvey (1887- 1940) stands as one of the most influential and visionary Pan-Africanists in history. Born in St. Ann's Bay, Jamaica, Garvey rose to international prominence in the early 20th century as the founder of the Universal Negro Improvement Association and African Communities League (UNIA-ACL) in 1914. He established the organization on July 20, 1914, in Kingston, Jamaica.

Garvey's mission was clear: to unify and uplift people of African descent across the globe, urging them to reclaim pride in their African identity, build economic independence, and ultimately return to Africa to establish self-governance and sovereignty. His rallying cries, *"Africa for the Africans, at home and abroad,"* and *"Up, you mighty race and accomplish what you will,"* became the foundation of modern Pan-African thought. By the 1920s, his movement had millions of members worldwide, with chapters in the Caribbean, the United States, Central America, and Africa.

Garvey's work emphasized Black pride, economic empowerment, and repatriation. He launched ambitious ventures like the *Black Star Line (1919),* a shipping company meant to facilitate trade and travel between Africa and the diaspora, and the Negro Factories Corporation to support Black-owned businesses. Though many of these ventures faced sabotage and financial challenges, their symbolic power was undeniable. In 1920, Garvey hosted the *first International Convention of Negro Peoples of the World at Madison Square Garden.* Years later, in a powerful speech delivered in Nova Scotia in 1937 titled "The Work That Has Been Done," he famously declared: *"We are going to emancipate ourselves from mental slavery, because whilst others might free the body, none but ourselves can free the mind."* These words were made more famous by Bob Marley, also from Jamaica.

His legacy deeply influenced later African leaders and freedom fighters such as Kwame Nkrumah and Jomo Kenyatta, as well as civil rights movements in the U.S. and the Caribbean. Garvey, who died in London, England, in 1940, remains a towering symbol of diasporic unity, visionary leadership, and the ongoing revolution of African self-determination.

Today, Garvey is celebrated as one of Jamaica's seven official National Heroes, a title he received in 1969 for his monumental contributions to Black liberation and Jamaican identity. Every year in June, Jamaica commemorates *Marcus Garvey Month,* culminating in lectures, performances, and school events that celebrate his teachings. His birthplace in St. Ann's Bay is now a heritage site, and his image appears on the Jamaican $100 bank note; a daily reminder of his lasting influence.

Garvey's Pan-African dream has since been carried forward by a lineage of powerful voices. In their time, figures like *Kwame Nkrumah* of Ghana, *Patrice Lumumba* of the Congo, *Haile Selassie* of Ethiopia, and *W.E.B. Du Bois* in the United States advanced the vision of a politically and spiritually united Africa.

In more recent times, thinkers and activists like *Dr. Umar Johnson,* a controversial yet prominent voice, have reignited Pan-African discourse for a new generation. Known for his outspoken critique of systemic racism, Eurocentric education, and psychological warfare on Black communities, Dr. Johnson advocates for independent Black institutions and mental liberation. He echoes Garvey's vision of self-determination with his powerful statement: *"If you don't control the school, you can't control the minds of your children."*

While it's impossible to name every influential figure in the vast Pan-African movement, two contemporary voices that immediately come to mind for their consistent contributions are *Roland Martin* and *Dr. Greg Carr.*

Though perhaps more politically focused, Roland Martin consistently platforms Black scholars, activists, and leaders from across the diaspora. He openly advocates for Black self-determination, economic empowerment, and cultural pride, using his platform, Roland Martin Unfiltered, to amplify voices that support

Pan-African ideals, even if not always explicitly labeled as such. His work bridges politics and culture, offering a space where Black thought, strategy, and liberation converge in real time.

Dr. Greg Carr is deeply rooted in African-centered scholarship and frequently draws upon African history, spirituality, and the ancestral worldview in his commentary. He consistently emphasizes diasporic unity, cultural reclamation, and the vital importance of African identity and memory, core pillars of Pan-Africanism. His approach weaves together intellectual rigor and spiritual insight, aligning powerfully with the theme of a spiritual revolution.

Together, these Pan-Africanists remind us that the dream of unity is not buried in the past; it is still unfolding. The revolution that Garvey envisioned is alive, evolving, and being reclaimed across Africa and its vast global diaspora.

As the ancestral call grows louder in this era of spiritual revolution, figures like Dr. Umar Johnson, Dr. Greg Carr, and Roland Martin rise as vital Pan-Africanist voices, bridging historical wisdom with present-day truth-telling for a scattered but awakening people.

THE RESURGENCE OF PAN-AFRICANISM:
WHAT WE'RE WITNESSING

1.   Global Black Consciousness Movements

Movements like Black Lives Matter, EndSARS in Nigeria, and decolonization efforts across African and Caribbean nations have amplified global Black solidarity and sharpened discourse on systemic oppression. These are core concerns of Pan-Africanism, reminding us that our struggles and victories are interconnected across continents.

2.   Afrofuturism and Cultural Renaissance

The global popularity of music genres like reggae, led by icons such as Bob Marley, and Afrobeats from West Africa, alongside films like *Black Panther*, has reawakened pride in African identity, history, and our shared destiny. Reggae music has long championed African unity and sovereignty, with anthems like *"Zimbabwe," "Africa Unite,"* and *"Redemption Song" by Bob Marley.* Other powerful contributions include Peter Tosh's *"Mama Africa,"* Garnet Silk's *"Hello, Mama Africa,"* and Dexton Davis's *"Oh, Ethiopia."* These songs echo Pan-African themes of unity, resilience, and forward-looking strength.

Adding his voice to this liberatory chorus is Skillful Kxng, whose powerful track *Ancient Intelligence* delivers a modern-day invocation of ancestral wisdom. His message calls us back to the *original knowing encoded in our bloodline* - a form of resistance that transcends systems, time, and colonized thinking. Through sharp lyricism, layered sound design, and a commanding delivery, he channels the voice of the ancestors while urging us to reclaim our divine nature and mental sovereignty. Skillful Kxng's work stands as both affirmation and activation, a reminder that the revolution is not only political or cultural, but deeply spiritual.

3.   Return-to-Africa Movement

A growing number of people from the African diaspora, particularly African Americans and Caribbean individuals, are expressing renewed interest in moving to or investing in African nations like Ghana, Nigeria, Rwanda, and Senegal. Ghana's *"Year of Return"* campaign in 2019 was a watershed moment, significantly deepening diasporic connections. This movement seeks to strengthen ties between Africa and its diaspora, not merely through symbolic gestures but with tangible initiatives.

Visa-free travel agreements among African nations and direct flights between Jamaica and Nigeria are more than logistical milestones, they represent a spiritual and political reconnection that has been long yearned for. One striking example of this reconnection is the way Jamaicans have embraced Nollywood. Nigerian films are devoured with enthusiasm across the island, resonating deeply through shared themes of spirituality, family, struggle, and resilience. One of my Jamaican sisters is hooked on Nigerian movies and often says she can't wait to get to Lagos. This affection for Nollywood transcends entertainment; it reflects an ancestral bond being remembered and reawakened through story.

4.   Social Media & Pan-African Discourse

Platforms like YouTube, X (formerly Twitter), and TikTok have become vital spaces where Pan-African thinkers, educators, and activists can share ideas globally. This digital Pan-Africanism has spurred vibrant discussions around shared struggles, identity, and solutions, particularly among younger generations who are redefining what Pan-African solidarity looks like in the 21st century.

5.   Decolonization of Education and Identity

There is a growing demand to decolonize education, spirituality, and identity by rejecting Eurocentric narratives in favor of African-centered thought, language, and philosophy. This movement aligns directly with the classical ideals of Pan-Africanism, emphasizing self-definition, cultural reclamation, and mental liberation.

Beneath these visible manifestations of Pan-African resurgence lies a profound spiritual awakening. This spiritual dimension is not an afterthought; it is a driving force. It fuels what can now be described as *Spiritual Pan-Africanism;* a movement where the reclamation of land, identity, and power is inseparable from the restoration of ancestral wisdom, sacred practices, and spiritual sovereignty.

Beneath these visible manifestations of a Pan-African resurgence, a profound spiritual awakening is taking root. This spiritual dimension is not merely a byproduct but a fundamental driving force, giving rise to what can be described as *Spiritual Pan-Africanism.*

UNDERSTANDING SPIRITUAL PAN-AFRICANISM

The term *"Spiritual Pan-Africanism"* describes a growing phenomenon, though it is not yet widely formalized or historically standardized. It represents a relatively new expression that brings together two long-standing traditions: Pan-Africanism as a political and cultural movement, and the reclamation of African spiritual systems.

Spiritual Pan-Africanism is more of a contemporary framework - an evolution of older ideas rather than an officially coined historical term. But for me, it speaks to something undeniable: Pan-Africanism isn't just political, it's deeply spiritual. It is calling people of African descent back to their roots, rituals, and sacred identity. From ancestral veneration to African traditional religions like Ifá, Vodun, and Kemetic science, more of us are turning away from colonial frameworks and embracing indigenous African spirituality as a path to wholeness and liberation.

This is why reclaiming ancient African wisdom is a revolutionary act. Spiritual decolonization is not only necessary but profoundly healing for generations of trauma. Whether you are just beginning your journey or have long walked the path of African spirituality, this conversation invites you to see Pan-African unity not merely as a political mission but as a divine calling.

It reflects a growing consciousness in the 21st century that true liberation must include spiritual decolonization. This is not just about reclaiming land or culture, but also about reclaiming ancestral spirituality. While people may not always use the exact term "Spiritual Pan-Africanism," its essence has been lived and practiced for centuries by Black revolutionaries, scholars, spiritual leaders, and grassroots movements. These are the ones who have always known, deep in their bones, that there is no separation between spirit and liberation.

KEY DRIVERS OF THIS SPIRITUAL PAN-AFRICAN REVIVAL

1. **Rejection of Colonial Religious Frameworks**

A growing number of Africans and diasporans are critically examining the colonial roots of Christianity and Islam on the continent. This awakening has sparked a reclamation of diverse African spiritual systems such as Ifá, Vodun, Kemetism, Akan spirituality, and other indigenous belief systems that existed long before foreign influence.

2. **Spiritual Decolonization as Identity Work**

The return to African spirituality is increasingly seen as an act of spiritual decolonization—a way to break mental, cultural, and religious chains and reconnect with the original self. This work is profoundly Pan-African because it transcends geographical borders, uniting African-descended people through shared cosmologies and values.

3. **Online Communities and Global Rituals**

Social media and platforms like YouTube have made African spiritual rituals, teachings, and ceremonies more accessible than ever. People are re-learning ancestral practices, engaging in collective libations, full moon rituals, and ancestral veneration, often infused with Pan-African themes of unity, resistance, and healing.

4.   **Rise of Afro-Spiritual Influencers and Practitioners**

From Yoruba priests in the U.S. to Kemetic scholars in the Caribbean and herbalists in Ghana, there is a rising wave of modern spiritual practitioners teaching ancient African wisdom systems to global audiences. These figures are bridging identity, purpose, and liberation.

5.   **Spirituality as Resistance**

In this renewed Pan-Africanism, spirituality itself is a political act. The return to African spirituality is an act of resistance against Western domination, capitalism, and the historical role of organized religion in upholding colonial power structures. At its core, it's about healing intergenerational trauma and reclaiming the divine within the African self.

KEY VOICES IN SPIRITUAL PAN-AFRICANISM

Rastafari Movement

Emerging in Jamaica in the 1930s, the Rastafari Movement is a powerful form of Spiritual Pan-Africanism. It reveres Haile Selassie I of Ethiopia as a divine figure, sees Africa (Zion) as the true homeland, and holds that Black divinity, repatriation, and liberation are spiritual imperatives.

Malidoma Somé (Dagara Elder)

A Burkinabé Dagara elder and renowned spiritual teacher, Malidoma Somé was instrumental in reconnecting African spirituality with diasporic communities. He taught that the modern disconnection from spirit is a direct result of colonial trauma.

Dr. Maulana Karenga

Creator of Kwanzaa and a leading advocate of African-centered philosophy, Dr. Karenga's concept of Nguzo Saba (Seven Principles) blends spiritual, cultural, and communal values. His work stands as a bridge between Pan-Africanist ideals and African spirituality.

Queen Afua

Globally renowned holistic healer and author of *Sacred Woman*, Queen Afua weaves spiritual healing with ancestral wisdom, African culture, and liberation. Her teachings center on the belief that spiritual wholeness is essential to Black empowerment.

Dr. Umar Johnson

Though primarily known as a Pan-African psychologist and founder of the FDMG Academy, Dr. Johnson frequently invokes African ancestral reverence in his vision for education and empowerment, integrating spirituality into his broader liberation narrative.

A NEW WAVE OF AFRO-INDIGENOUS AND DIASPORA HEALERS & THINKERS

Teachers like Empress Karen Rose, Yolanda Williams of Afro-Indigenous Healing, revivalists of *indigenous African spiritual traditions* and a growing wave of Ifá practitioners, Vodun priests, and Kemetic scholars are all teaching a powerful truth: our return to African spirituality is key to mental, cultural, and political liberation. It has become evident that spirituality is not separate from liberation; it is the root. This truth is the very heart of Spiritual Pan-Africanism.

I would be remiss not to mention Iyanla Vanzant - teacher, priestess, and spiritual healer, whose work has long embodied the essence of Spiritual Pan-Africanism. Rooted in Yoruba traditions and grounded in ancestral wisdom, Iyanla's teachings speak directly to the soul wounds of Black people. Through rituals, affirmations, and spiritual technologies, she offers pathways to reconnect with our divine selves. Whether through her books, television presence, or priestly work in African traditional religion, Iyanla reminds us that healing is not only possible; it is sacred. She is one of the voices in our time restoring the spiritual lineage that colonization tried to sever.

I'm currently enrolled in her Awakening One million program.

Other powerful spiritual guides who embody this ancestral wisdom include *Dr. Bayo Akomolafe,* whose philosophical insights into African cosmologies deeply resonate with my understanding of decolonized thought. *Yeye Luisah Teish,* a prominent Oshun priestess, has been a beacon for many seeking connection to African ancestral practices. Her book *Jambalaya: The Natural Woman's Book of Personal Charms and Practical Rituals* is a foundational guide for those in the diaspora reclaiming ancestral traditions and spirituality.

Oba Ernesto Pichardo, a high priest, has led significant legal battles that paved the way for greater recognition of African Traditional Religions. *Valerie Mosley* offers an Afrakan-centered psychological and spiritual framework that provides profound healing for our community. I also find deep personal resonance in the ancestral soul healing work of *Heidi Day-Soul Healer,* known as the Soul Healer, and *Queen Thandiwe Kali* of SisStars Awakening.

While some of these figures may not explicitly call themselves "Pan-African spiritualists," their work echoes the pulse of our ancestral spirituality and reflects the broader spiritual revolution that is rising in this era.

JAMAICA'S SPIRITUAL FREQUENCY

I see this revolution everywhere, even in the way people from all over the globe, and increasingly from Africa, are flocking to Jamaica's shores despite travel warnings. Many might simply see them as tourists seeking leisure, people looking to experience island life, or even those pursuing business and investment opportunities. But what they might not understand yet is that ***Jamaica? Jamaica is a whole frequency.*** There's a potent spiritual energy here that is not yet widely acknowledged, but its emergence is undeniable.

This spiritual draw was clear to me when I saw a video of Dave Chappelle in Jamaica singing *"What A Bam Bam"* the classic track by *Toots and the Maytals* (1966), later made iconic by *Sister Nancy* in 1982, and still celebrated today. A comment under that video summed it up: *"Dave didn't need to go to Africa, he should have gone to Jamaica."* My response? Dave received what he needed from both. I also love this humorous quote I saw on a mug: "I don't need therapy, I just need to go to Jamaica." Despite its challenges, Jamaica is a profound force; spiritually rich, deeply magnetic, and perhaps not yet fully aware of its own power.

Jamaicans have always revered Africa as the ancestral motherland, a sacred place of origin and pride. From Marcus Garvey's "Back to Africa" movement to the spiritual heartbeat of reggae and the Rastafari livity, the longing for home and unity pulses through our music, our prayers, and our identity. Today, that call is being answered; not just in song, but through tangible acts of reconnection, cultural exchange, and Pan-African solidarity. Jamaica and Africa are no longer distant cousins; they are rising together as family, reclaiming their shared destiny.

JAMAICA'S *BIG UP YUSELF* CULTURE: DEFIANT PRIDE AS SPIRITUAL SOVEREIGNTY

Jamaican pride is not a performance. It is defiance. For centuries, we have celebrated ourselves loudly and unapologetically, not as vanity, but as a deliberate act of resistance against colonization. In a world that demanded we earn dignity through silence and conformity, we chose instead - **big up yuself**.

I once came across a sticker that read, *"Some people spend their whole lives trying to be awesome, others are born Jamaican."* It made me smile, not because of empty bravado, but because it spoke to a deeper truth: we are born into a culture that teaches us we already are. Big up yuself is more than a phrase. It's a mindset, a cultural survival tool, rooted in the unshakable belief that every Jamaican is a star. You are born worthy. No external validation required.

This is the energy of a free people, well aware of all we have fought for, all we have overcome, and everything we are still fighting for.

Our humor reflects this sovereignty. We make jokes out of hunger. We laugh in the face of hurricanes and earthquakes. We turn tragedy into melody, hardship into rhythm. Jamaicans like to say, *"Jamaica always a keep,"* meaning, there's always a vibe, always a reason to celebrate, no matter the circumstances. If you're feeling down, spend time watching Jamaican content on social media. You'll find music, dance, sharp wit, and a unique spirit that transforms adversity into entertainment.

That equally important internal force that has always fueled our resilience: that unapologetic culture of self-celebration known as Big Up Yuself, must not be misconstrued as escapism. Nor is it arrogance. It's a spiritual posture; a declaration that our joy, our confidence, and our sense of belonging are not for sale. Big up yuself is a stance we've maintained as a people who refuse to be diminished by colonial narratives.

We are who we are - because we said so.

RECONNECTION AND RESTORATION:
THE LIVING REVOLUTION

I see the spirit of the ancestors in Rwanda's extraordinary journey of growth, healing, and rebuilding; a nation once devastated by genocide, a tragedy deeply rooted in the legacy and tactics of colonization. The seeds of ethnic division were sown during colonial rule, weaponized to fracture unity and control the people. Yet, what was meant to destroy became the soil for something sacred.

Today, Rwanda is rising with clarity and purpose. It is recognized globally for its rapid technological advances, clean cities, safety, and visionary leadership. But I see this as more than governance. It is ancestral resilience in motion. Rwanda's transformation is a living testament to what becomes possible when a people transcend the trauma imposed by colonial agendas and tap into their collective memory, dignity, and sacred responsibility to heal and build anew.

Rwanda stands as a living altar of what is possible when a people choose remembrance over revenge, and spirit over division. Though colonization sowed the seeds of fracture, and genocide watered them in blood, Rwanda's healing is profound—not just through policy or development, but through deep, collective soul work, whether consciously recognized or not. The legacy of pain has been met with reckoning and a spiritual return to unity, justice, and dignity. From traditional Gacaca courts to national days of mourning and remembrance, Rwanda has modeled what it means to rebuild not only cities, but spirits. *The fire of the ancestors did not die in the ashes; it rose.* And in that rising, Rwanda whispers to the rest of us that the revolution is not only political. It is sacred.

African spirituality supports both personal and collective healing by nurturing a deep connection to ancestors, nature, and the sacred rhythms of life. It offers practices that restore balance, honor lived experience, and transform trauma into wisdom. Through rituals, storytelling, and communal ceremonies, individuals find strength and clarity, while communities rebuild trust and unity. This spiritual foundation fosters resilience, empowers identity, and guides us toward holistic healing that uplifts both the self and the collective.

Ultimately, this spiritual return is key to true Pan-African liberation. It reconnects us to the roots, wisdom, and resilience of our ancestors, healing the fractures caused by colonization and displacement. Without reclaiming our sacred identities and honoring the ancestral knowledge embedded in our traditions, liberation remains incomplete. True freedom arises not only from political or economic power, but from a profound spiritual awakening that unites us as a people and restores the divine within us all.

White supremacy told us we had no history. This moment is about unearthing our lineage - and going home.

PERSONAL NOTE TO THE WEARY

I feel it - that weariness. Truly, I do. We're all carrying the heavy weight of blatant racial oppression, the erasure of our history, and the dismissal of our accomplishments. I feel for us. I understand that sense of hopelessness, that disheartening feeling that we're moving backward. In all this chaos, it's easy to feel like there's nothing left to do, faced with relentless assaults on our pride, dignity, celebrations, and very existence.

But I want to offer another perspective: What if this crisis is a portal for transformation? Because this chaos is not just destruction, it's awakening us. It's calling us back, compelling us to seek the guidance of our ancestors and to truly listen. They are active. They are speaking. And no, we are not alone.

When they threaten to ban books, dismantle museums, erase our history, and undermine our celebrations through policies, it is designed to make us feel powerless. But we possess a profound and underestimated power. Our spirituality. Our spiritual weapons. I believe that if we collectively decide to wield these weapons, focusing our spiritual energy toward these oppressive systems, they will crumble. This is what they fear most. The brand of Christianity they promote is a manipulative tool, stripped of true spirit, designed to serve their agenda and perpetuate our disempowerment.

Yes, we are waking up, perhaps more than ever, catalyzed by the cruelty of the current regime. And I believe the universe is conspiring for our liberation. This moment, though painful and revealing, might be the very moment that catapults us into new beginnings. A new era of liberation. This is a time to rest from the physical fighting and wield spiritual might.

So let us continue to big up ourselves! We are resilient. We are powerful. And our spiritual prowess is an undeniable force. Let us rise, united in spirit, gather in our circles, and do the sacred work - our rituals, our symbols, our Negro Spirituals. Because when we align and activate that collective will, these systems of oppression cannot stand.

Let's start displaying the behavior of a free people, beginning with our spirit. Returning to our spirituality is, in itself, an act of freedom. When we reclaim the sacred practices that were stripped from us, we are rejecting the lies of inferiority and powerlessness. Free people do not wait to be told who they are or how to connect with the Divine. They remember. They restore. They reconnect. Embracing our spiritual roots is a declaration that we are no longer enslaved: mentally, emotionally, or spiritually. It's how we begin to walk in the truth of who we've always been. This is walking in the laws of sovereignty. This is free people behavior...

YOUR SPIRIT WAS ALWAYS SOVEREIGN

And yes, there is something stirring.

You can feel it. In your bones. In your blood. In your dreams.

It's a quiet but undeniable rising, a global awakening sweeping across timelines and cultures. People everywhere, regardless of language, geography, or tradition, are hearing the call of something deeper. Something older. Something that has always existed beneath the noise of empire and the machinery of modern life.

This is not a trend.
And it's not aesthetic spirituality dressed up for display.
No, this is sacred. This is the mystic within us all, waking up.

I shared this ritual in Chapter 7, but it bears repeating here because we are speaking of reclaiming sovereignty.

SACRED LAWS AND TOOLS OF SOVEREIGNTY

Tradition: Adinkra symbols from the Akan people Akan people of Ghana and Côte d'Ivoire are not just decorative; they are sacred laws. These symbols are not merely seen - they are invoked, carried, and lived, becoming spiritual tools that anchor us in our sovereignty."

Examples:

- Eban - safety, security, sanctuary (draw near your door)

- Dwennimmen - humility with strength (on your chest, before speaking truth)

- Fawohodie - emancipation and freedom (used in rites of passage)

Practice:

- Draw these on:
- Your body (in ash, clay, or charcoal)
- Your journal, altar, protest signs, or ritual candles
- Incorporate into tattoos, embroidery, or ritual jewelry

CHAPTER 10

GLOBAL SIGNS THE ANCESTORS ARE LEADING A SPIRITUAL REVOLUTION

Across the globe, there have been symbolic, powerful moments - burnings, removals, collapses, uprisings - that many spiritual communities interpret as the ancestors speaking or rising. These events affirm the belief that this time, the revolution is spiritual. Let's look at a few:

VISIBLE RECLAMATIONS: BURNINGS, REMOVALS, COLLAPSES

Toppling of Colonial Symbols

2020: Statue Topplings during Black Lives Matter Protests

Statues of colonizers like Edward Colston (UK), Christopher Columbus (US), and King Leopold II (Belgium) were defaced or torn down. In Bristol, Colston's statue was dragged into the harbor. It was more than protest. It was ritual reclamation. Many said the ancestors were rising and reclaiming space.

On Reclaimed Statues - *"They toppled the statues, but it was not rage, it was ritual. Not erasure, but remembrance."*

Fires That Speak

2018: Fire at Brazil's National Museum

Home to countless Indigenous and African artifacts, the museum's destruction was mourned but also seen by some Afro-Brazilian and Indigenous activists as a signal - a cleansing of colonial misrepresentation and a call to rebuild narratives with truth.

2025: Nottoway Plantation, Louisiana Fire

Straight Ancestral "Gangsta"

The conflagration swept through the historic building that glamorized slave history, reducing it to ashes. The fire broke out on May 15, 2025, consuming one of the largest remaining antebellum mansions. Social media reactions described it as a form of ancestral uprising. People reflected that *"the ancestors are speaking" and "they've had enough of their trauma being romanticized,"* seeing the fire as a powerful response to generations of trauma and the romanticization of enslaved labor in settings now marketed as wedding venues.

Fire as Message - *"When plantations burn and statues fall, the ancestors are not silent, they are speaking in flame and ash."*

Elemental Wisdom: Water Rising & Land Reclaimed

Water Rising as Ancestral Return

2022: Flooding in Benin Exposes Vodun Shrines

Heavy rains revealed hidden shrines and sacred artifacts long buried. Local Vodun practitioners saw it as the spirits reclaiming space and demanding remembrance.

Natural Events as Spirit - *"The flood didn't destroy; it revealed. Buried shrines emerged, and with them, the memory we were never meant to lose."*

Indigenous Land Back Movements & Sacred Site Protection

2020: Māori Victory in New Zealand

After years of struggle, the Ihumātao sacred land was returned to Māori guardianship. Elders called it *"a spiritual victory led by those who walked before us."*

Global "Land Back" Momentum: Beyond specific victories, the growing international "Land Back" movement signifies Indigenous peoples worldwide demanding the return of ancestral territories. This isn't just about ownership; it's about re-establishing spiritual stewardship and revitalizing traditional practices tied directly to the land.

Protection of Sacred Sites: Ongoing resistance against development on sacred sites (e.g., Mauna Kea in Hawaii, Oak Flat in Arizona) highlights a deep ancestral and spiritual imperative to protect these hallowed grounds from desecration.

Sacred Returns & Cultural Revivals

The Return of Stolen Ancestors & Objects

2021-Present: The Return of Stolen Artifacts

Museums like the British Museum and France's Musée du Quai Branly have begun returning looted African artifacts to countries such as Benin, Nigeria, and Ethiopia. *"This is more than repatriation, it's ancestral energy demanding to come home."*

Ongoing: Repatriation of Human Remains

Globally, institutions are increasingly returning the skeletal remains of Indigenous and enslaved peoples to their descendants for proper reburial and ceremony. This act ensures ancestors can finally rest with dignity, completing spiritual cycles violently interrupted.

On Spiritual Reclamation - *"They tried to bury our spirits in museums and plantations. But spirit doesn't stay buried. It rises."*

Reclamation of Heritage & Ways of Being

2019: Gullah Geechee Land Reclamation Efforts in South Carolina

Families of formerly enslaved ancestors returned to reclaim land lost through systemic exploitation. These homecomings were held with libations and ceremony. Activists said, *"This is the land our ancestors protected; we're just answering their call."*

Language Revitalization and Protection

Across the globe, Indigenous communities are vigorously working to revive and protect languages suppressed by colonization. This crucial effort reconnects speakers to ancestral worldviews, stories, and the spiritual concepts inherently embedded within their mother tongues.

Resurgence of Traditional Healing Practices and Medicine

A global resurgence is evident in the practice of traditional, Indigenous, and Afro-diasporic healing modalities, plant medicines, and spiritual ceremonies. This revival reclaims ancestral wisdom for holistic well-being and challenges dominant colonial medical paradigms.

Artistic and Creative Resurgence as Cultural Reclamation

A vibrant explosion of contemporary art, music, literature, and performance draws directly from ancestral traditions. This creative outpouring serves as a powerful vehicle for truth-telling, collective healing, cultural pride, and spiritual expression.

"When I look at global ancestral movements, from Louisiana to Lagos, Brazil to Benin, the message is clear: the dead are not gone. They are guiding us home. What we're witnessing is not coincidence, it's convergence. The ancestors are assembling, and this time, the revolution is spiritual."

This time, the revolution is spiritual. And the ancestors are leading it.

WHY THESE MOMENTS MATTER

They affirm a truth Indigenous and African-descended people have always known:

The spirit world is active. The ancestors are not quiet.
This is not superstition, it is sacred intelligence.

Absolutely, there's a growing global chorus affirming that this time, the revolution is spiritual. From renowned leaders to grassroots movements, voices across continents are echoing this sentiment. While voices from other traditions have spoken to this global spiritual awakening, such as Swami Vivekananda's call to "Arise, awake," and Eckhart Tolle's reminder that "life will give you whatever experience is most helpful for the evolution of your consciousness," these are not new revelations for African people. They echo what our ancestors encoded in ritual, rhythm, and reverence long before the West had language for it.

The Cosmos Itself Is Out of Balance: The Cry for Sacred Restoration

Our spirits were never meant to be chained; they were born to be free. Our bodies were never meant to be broken or bound under the yoke of forced labor and brutality. The natural order which thrives on freedom, reciprocity, and harmony was disrupted the moment our ancestors were stolen, sold, and silenced. Their cries echoed through time, staining the soil, haunting the winds, and unsettling the stars.

We were the original people, carriers of divine memory, entrusted with sacred ways of living in rhythm with the earth. We were meant to speak with the rivers, walk with the wind, dance with the fire, and plant by the whispers of the moon. Ours was a communion with creation: a divine fellowship, and when we were ripped from the land and forbidden to remember, that sacred conversation was broken. Climate change is not just environmental collapse; it is the cosmos weeping over the loss of connection with its first children.

Because all of creation is interconnected, the pain of the oppressed disturbs the whole. The rivers run angry. The earth cracks open in grief. Storms rage not only from weather, but from memory. Healing the planet, healing nature, and restoring balance to the cosmos requires reckoning with and repairing this harm.

To restore divine order, the subjugation of the Negro, of African-descended people, must end. Reparations are not only material; they are spiritual and cosmic. The truth must be told. Justice must be served. Until the descendants of the enslaved are treated rightly, until the curse of oppression is broken, nothing built on this injustice will stand. Every structure, every system, every dream, no matter how carefully constructed, will eventually fall to ruin because it is out of alignment with truth, with love, with the sacred order of the universe. We, as the original people were born in rhythm with creation. As our spirits rise and our dignity is reclaimed, we bring the earth back into rhythm. When the original people return to sacred alignment, the earth will sigh in relief. Our liberation is not only our destiny. It is inevitable. Our freedom is not just our own: it is medicine for the world. This spiritual revolution is an urgent matter.

HERE ARE SOME NOTABLE FIGURES AND QUOTES THAT LEND VISIBILITY AND CREDIBILITY TO THE CLAIM: "THIS TIME THE REVOLUTION IS SPIRITUAL."

Dr. Martin Luther King Jr.

In his 1968 sermon "Remaining Awake Through a Great Revolution," Dr. King emphasized the need for a transformative awakening:

> *"One of the great liabilities of history is that all too many people fail to remain awake through great periods of social change."*

He urged society to recognize interconnectedness and to stay vigilant during times of profound change.

Dr. Cornel West - Philosopher, Theologian, Activist

> *"Never forget that justice is what love looks like in public."*

West constantly frames activism and liberation as a spiritual act of love and moral reckoning, grounded in prophetic Black Christian and African American traditions. He explicitly connects Black suffering to sacred truth.

bell hooks - Writer, Teacher, Theorist (RIP)

"The function of art is to do more than tell it like it is, it's to imagine what is possible."

bell hooks wove together spirituality, healing, and liberation. Her work often reminded us that healing is a spiritual necessity for oppressed peoples, and that love is a revolutionary force.

Sobonfu Somé - Dagara Spiritual Teacher (RIP)

"The spirit world is the root of everything in the physical world."

She was a bridge between West African spiritual traditions and the modern world. Her work offered ritual and grief healing as portals to spiritual reawakening and ancestral communion.

Queen Afua - Holistic Healer, Spiritual Guide

Queen Afua centers sacred feminine power, African wellness, and ancestral practices in her work. Her teachings invite us to reconnect deeply with the womb; the source of life and spiritual power as a foundation for healing and rising. While she may not have said the exact phrase, the wisdom behind *"If you want to rise, you must first return to the womb"* reflects the heart of her message: true revolution begins within the body, the spirit, and sacred Black womanhood.

Malidoma Patrice Somé - Dagara Shaman and Elder (RIP)

"You don't go to the ancestors. The ancestors are already here."

Malidoma emphasized that spiritual connection to ancestors is not metaphor; it's power, medicine, and memory. His work offers legitimacy to ancestral spirituality in the face of colonial religion and Western materialism.

Layla Saad - Author of *Me and White Supremacy*

"Our work is the work of healing ancestral wounds, not only for ourselves but for our lineages."

Though more recent, Layla Saad's perspective affirms spiritual decolonization, ancestral healing, and collective wakening, especially among people of color reclaiming their sacred power.

Yeye Luisah Teish - Yoruba Priestess, Author of *Jambalaya*

"Spirituality is not a luxury. It is a necessity for survival."

Teish teaches from the Ifá/Yoruba tradition, celebrating ritual, joy, ancestors, and the divine feminine. Her work is a clear affirmation of Black ancestral spirituality as revolutionary.

Resmaa Menakem - Somatic Healer, Author of *My Grandmother's Hands*

"Healing doesn't happen in the head. It happens in the body."

Menakem blends trauma healing with ancestral knowledge. He speaks of how Black bodies carry historical memory, and how spiritual healing is the foundation of resistance.

Honorary Mention (Pan-African but non-Black American):
Thomas Sankara, revolutionary Burkinabé leader

"We must dare to invent the future."

While not a spiritual teacher per se, his leadership invoked ancestral values, self-determination, and spiritual courage rooted in African identity.

Zora Neale Hurston - Anthropologist, Writer, Cultural Griot -RIP

"Research is formalized curiosity. It is poking and prying with a purpose."

Zora Neale Hurston was not only a writer but a cultural ethnographer, griot, and spiritual archivist of the Black diaspora. Her 1938 work *Tell My Horse* is a bold and rare first-person account of Voodoo, Haitian spirituality, and Jamaican Obeah practices, often demonized or erased by colonial and Western narratives.

In *Tell My Horse*, Zora doesn't just "study" African diasporic spirituality; she participates in it. She approaches the spiritual traditions of Black people in the Caribbean with respect, reverence, and responsibility, making her one of the earliest scholars to validate African spirituality as real, complex, and liberatory. In many ways, her work prefigures this very moment, where we now return to the ancestral as revolutionary.

Rebecca Hall - Historian, Visionary, Ancestral Listener - Author of *Wake: The Hidden History of Women-Led Slave Revolts*

"I followed the whisper of my ancestors...until the silence gave way."

In *Wake: The Hidden History of Women-Led Slave Revolts*, Rebecca Hall doesn't just write history, she excavates it from the bones of the forgotten. A descendant of enslaved people and a legal scholar turned historian, Hall's journey is guided not only by evidence but by dreams, spiritual intuition, and body memory.

As she uncovers the erased stories of Black women warriors who led revolts, she exposes how historical erasure is also a form of spiritual violence, and how reclamation becomes ritual. Her memoir blends scholarship with ancestral summons, blurring the line between academic work and sacred duty.

Hall's *Wake* is more than a title, it's a call to spiritual awakening, proof that the ancestors are still speaking through us, and that our revolution must begin in the unseen.

This groundbreaking graphic memoir:

- Tells the buried stories of Black women who led revolts during slavery.
- Chronicles Hall's own spiritual encounters, dreams, and body memory as she uncovers this hidden history.
- Describes how the systematic erasure of Black women's resistance is also a kind of spiritual warfare.

Her work is a perfect example of how the spirit world is mobilizing, through dreams, intuition, and ancestral summons, calling Black women (like Hall, and like you) to remember, reclaim, and restore what was buried. *Wake* doesn't just tell history, it performs ancestral resurrection.

SPIRITUAL WARRIORS OF SOUND: GRIOTS OF THE DIASPORA

Across the African continent and its vast diaspora, music has always been more than entertainment; it is invocation, protest, praise, and prophecy. The message has always been in the music. From Yoruba talking drums to Kingston sound systems, rhythm has been a way to remember who we are and resist what seeks to erase us.

Reggae is said to be the heartbeat of a people - the Jamaican people, and when I see South Africans in the street dancing to reggae music, I know they "get it." Reggae is an integral part of the soundtrack of African liberation.

The musicians who carry this sacred charge are griots, living vessels of ancestral knowledge, history, and spiritual fire.

Bob Marley (RIP)

A prophet in his own right, Bob Marley used Reggae as a vessel for global awakening.

"Chant Down Babylon" - "Reggae music, mek we chant down Babylon!"

"Babylon System" - "We've been trodding on the winepress much too long - rebel."

"Redemption Song" - "Emancipate yourselves from mental slavery, none but ourselves can free our minds."

Bob Marley's songs transcend mere hits; they're hymns of liberation, deeply rooted in Rastafari, Pan-Africanism, and sacred revolution. His music powerfully reminds us that spirit and justice are one.

Marley masterfully used music as a global rallying cry for unity and spiritual liberation. Through songs like "Africa Unite" and "Redemption Song," he delivered a profound message of return to ourselves, to each other, and to the ancestral homeland. His lyrics, steeped in Rastafari, revolution, and hope, transformed Reggae into a powerful vessel for African pride and divine consciousness. *More about bob Marley, the prophet, in the Did You Know section of this chapter.*

Peter Tosh (RIP)

The militant mystic of Reggae, Peter Tosh, wielded sound like a weapon of truth.

In his iconic song *Equal Rights*, Tosh declared, *"I don't want no peace. I want equal rights and justice"* - a powerful line that encapsulated his fierce call for justice over empty peace. This embodied his fierce lyricism and unrelenting righteousness. Tosh gave a voice to the voiceless, demanding a spiritual reckoning with *"Babylon"* and unapologetically advocating for justice and repatriation. In songs like *Mama Africa* and *Equal Rights*, he seamlessly blended firebrand activism with deep cultural pride. Tosh's voice was one of defiance, rooted in truth-telling and a fierce Pan-African resistance; he didn't ask, he declared.

Buju Banton

A modern griot of fire and redemption, Buju Banton bridges the sacred and the street. Buju Banton carries the revolutionary torch into the 21st century with a voice steeped in struggle, spiritual defiance, and redemption. Like Marley and Tosh before him, Buju uses Reggae not just to entertain but to awaken. His music traverses the rough terrain of oppression, personal transformation, and Rastafari wisdom calling listeners higher.

Tracks like *"Hills and Valleys,"* where he declares *"Only Rasta can liberate the people,"* and "Til I'm Laid to Rest" echo with lament, prophecy, and praise, blending street survival with sacred knowing, resistance and redemption into every verse. In *'African Pride,'* Buju calls us back to our roots and identity, affirming that true liberation begins with remembering who we are.

In the song *"400 Years,"* he declares, *"I shall never cease my fire till Babylon walls burn down,"* a line that blazes with ancestral memory and present urgency, reminding us that the struggle is sacred, the voice is a weapon, and the fire is never meant to burn out, but to burn through. And in *"African Pride"* he lifts the banner of identity and self-knowledge, a defiant anthem that calls us to remember who we are and stand unshaken in the fullness of our heritage.

Buju's approach to revolution is both confrontational and redemptive. He chants down Babylon with fire, then lifts the weary with prayer. His is a revolution of return - return to self, to Zion, and to divine order. From dancehall stardom to roots revivalist, Buju's evolution has been a public journey of spiritual reawakening, marked by truth-telling, clarity, and a deepening connection to the divine.

Skillful Kxng

Skillful Kxng, in his cerebral track, "Ancient Intelligence," continues this revolutionary thread but with a sharpened focus on internal sovereignty and mental emancipation. While Marley sang of unity, Tosh of rebellion, and Banton of survival, Kxng centers the mind as the original battleground. His message is clear: we carry encoded brilliance, spiritual technology, and ancestral memory in our DNA. His lyrics are both ancient scripture and modern manifesto, activating listeners to reclaim the power colonization tried to suppress. Indeed, "Ancient Intelligence" could well be the theme song for this book, perfectly encapsulating the journey of reclaiming inherent wisdom and power.

The synergy between "Ancient Intelligence" and *This Time the Revolution Is Spiritual* lies in their shared call to awaken the sacred self. Though they use different mediums - sound and word - they vibrate with a common frequency of remembrance, like tuning forks resonating across dimensions. Both the song and the book vibrate with a frequency of remembrance - echoing the same ancestral truth. There is a deep spiritual alignment. The song activates the subconscious, stirring ancient codes in the listener's soul, through rhythm and vibration, while the book speaks through narrative and reflection, guiding the conscious mind toward reclaiming spiritual sovereignty. Together, they form a ritual of sound and word. One felt in the body and the other understood in the mind. This is a deep spiritual alignment of mediums each working in its own way to reclaim identity, power, and purpose.

The walls of Babylon will not fall by force, but by the fire of spirit, truth, and remembrance. We have been in Babylon for over 400 years, but now the ancestral drums are calling, and the walls are trembling. Babylon's fall will not come with bombs, but with the rise of awakened souls. When the people remember who they are, Babylon cannot stand. This spiritual revolution is the wind, already swaying the foundations. What chains could not break, remembrance will. The sacred fire is lit, the spirit world is rising, and Babylon's walls are about to come down.

"Babylon will fall not by war, but by the spiritual awakening of a people who remember who they were before the ships came and that this time the revolution is spiritual."
-Winsome Alexander

Fela Kuti
Across the Atlantic in Nigeria, Fela Anikulapo Kuti embodied the spirit of the ancestral warrior.

"Music is the weapon."

Drawing on Yoruba cosmology and revolutionary politics, Fela transformed the stage into a shrine, using Afrobeat to summon ancestral power and call out corrupt systems.

Miriam Makeba, (RIP) often known as "Mama Africa," was arguably *the* most prominent voice for African liberation and against apartheid, both through her music and her activism. Her entire career was deeply intertwined with these themes. *I grew up in Jamaica hearing Miriam Makeba's songs on the radio, though I was too young to fully understand the weight of her cry. Her voice filled our homes with rhythms and melodies that felt joyful, yet beneath them was a call I would only come to recognize later as a cry for freedom, dignity, and the liberation of her people.*

1. "Nkosi Sikelel' iAfrika" (God Bless Africa): This is the definitive African liberation anthem. Makeba performed this song countless times, both on her own and with other artists. It became the national

anthem of post-apartheid South Africa and is used in other African nations. Her singing of this song was a direct, powerful prayer and call for freedom.

2. "Suliram": A lullaby about a mother's love, but given Makeba's context as an exile whose family suffered under apartheid, even a simple song about love and longing could resonate with the pain of separation and the yearning for a free home.

3. "A Luta Continua" (The Struggle Continues): A more explicit liberation song, often associated with the FRELIMO movement in Mozambique. Makeba performed and popularized this phrase and song, making it a rallying cry for anti-colonial struggles across the continent.

Beyond specific songs, Makeba's very presence on the international stage was a political act. She testified against apartheid at the United Nations, her passport was revoked by the South African government, and she lived in exile for over 30 years. Her music consistently highlighted the beauty, resilience, and struggles of Africa and its people, making her an undeniable icon of liberation.

These are not just artists, they are griots. They carry the memory of our people, the heartbeat of our struggles, and the vision of our liberation. Through rhythm, chant, and vibration, they awaken what colonization tried to bury. They remind us: the revolution is not only political. It is profoundly spiritual.

These voices and movements collectively affirm that the current revolution transcends politics and culture, it's a profound spiritual reawakening, guided by ancestral wisdom and a deep yearning for holistic transformation.

This time, the revolution is spiritual... A truth rising from the roots of ancestral memory.

"Life will give you whatever experience is most helpful for the evolution of your consciousness," -Eckhart Tolle (not Black).

At this moment, it seems life itself is summoning us to awaken. The ancestors are speaking and this time, we're listening. From the plantation fires to the prayer altars, the signal is clear: the spirit world is mobilizing. What we are witnessing is more than resistance; it is remembrance. The American Dream, sold as a promise of freedom and prosperity, was a lie built on stolen land and stolen people, and now America is in trouble. Karma has come to collect. The blood, the silence, the erasure, all of it is rising to the surface. When systems fail, the sacred reawakens, calling us back to a deeper knowing, a higher alignment, and a revolutionary truth rooted in spirit.

AUTHOR'S PERSONAL REFLECTION: THE FUTURE IS NOW

As I'm writing this book and claiming that the revolution is spiritual, it's not just a theory. Receive it as a testimony. I'm not speaking as an outsider analyzing trends; I'm speaking as one who has felt the call, who has wept at the altar of remembrance, who has been guided by dreams, omens, intuition, and ancestral whispers. For me, this may not be an academic claim. For me, it is a soul claim. It is a reclaiming of the sacred technologies, truths, and teachings that were stolen, buried, or burned, but never destroyed.

I'm sensing the ancestors calling for visionaries - Ancestral Stewards: who are keepers and guardians of the sacred flame. They're calling for Spirit Warriors and Advocates, Truth-bearers, and Soul Revolutionaries for our spiritual return, recognition, and remembrance.

This book is an ancestral call to those who will listen and harken. I have been chosen not merely as a writer, but as a spiritual vessel, a harbinger of ancestral truth, a messenger of the sacred revolution. I am your spiritual midwife for this birthing and you are being birthed and anointed.

The revolution is spiritual because we are spiritual beings, and the deepest wounds inflicted upon us were not just physical, they were spiritual: the erasure of our names, our gods, our tongues, our rituals. To heal, we must return. To rise, we must remember. This book is part offering, part invocation. And it is my way of saying: the spirit world is not silent and neither am I.

This time the revolution is spiritual... and it's a future they can't foreclose.

DID YOU KNOW

DECODING BABYLON: SYMBOLISM IN RASTAFARI AND REGGAE

In the context of Rastafarianism, reggae music, and the lyrics of artists like Buju Banton, *"Babylon"* is not a literal city, but a multifaceted symbolic term representing:

The Oppressive System: Primarily, Babylon refers to the corrupt, unjust, and oppressive socio-political system of the Western world (and by extension, any system that perpetuates injustice). This includes governments, law enforcement (the police are often directly called "Babylon"), capitalist structures, materialism, and societal norms that are seen as inherently oppressive, particularly towards people of African descent.

Spiritual and Mental Slavery: Beyond physical oppression, Babylon also signifies the mental and spiritual enslavement that prevents people from realizing their true identity, heritage, and connection to the divine (Jah). The "walls of Babylon" represent these mental constructs and systemic barriers that keep people disempowered and unaware of their potential. The "400 years" refers to the transatlantic slave trade and the subsequent period of systemic oppression.

Materialism and Corruption: Babylon is associated with greed, materialism, moral decay, and a departure from natural and spiritual living. It represents a system that values wealth and power over human dignity and spiritual truth.

Biblical Allusion: The term is rooted in the biblical city of Babylon, which famously exiled the Israelites and became a symbol of paganism, wickedness, and oppression in Abrahamic traditions. Rastafarians identify with the Israelites' exile, seeing the African diaspora as a modern-day "Babylonian captivity" in the West.

Therefore, when Buju Banton sings *"till Babylon walls burn down"* or the text states "Babylon's fall will not come with bombs, but with the rise of awakened souls," it is not a call for physical violence against cities. Instead, it is a powerful metaphorical call for:

- The dismantling of oppressive systems.
- A spiritual and mental liberation.
- A collective awakening to truth and self-awareness.
- The rejection of materialistic values and a return to natural, righteous living (often associated with *"Zion,"* the promised land of spiritual freedom and Africa).

The *"fire of spirit, truth, and remembrance"* and *"awakened souls"* are the tools for this revolution, emphasizing a transformative shift in consciousness rather than armed conflict.

THE PROPHETIC VISION OF BOB MARLEY: A REVOLUTION OF SPIRIT

Bob Marley's songs "Chant Down Babylon," "Rastaman Chant (Babylon yuh throne gone down)," and "Babylon System" are unmistakably prophetic, especially when viewed through the lens of the current ancestral spiritual frequency and awakening. His insights, deeply rooted in Rastafarian philosophy, resonate powerfully with contemporary observations of a global spiritual shift.

Here's how these songs are particularly prophetic:

"Babylon System" - The Revelation of Deception and Exploitation

Exposure of Systemic Dehumanization:

1. Marley's iconic line, *"Babylon System is the vampire, sucking the blood of the sufferers,"* is eerily prescient. Today, we witness unprecedented discussions around systemic oppression, economic inequality, and the psychological toll of hyper-consumerism. People are increasingly recognizing how established systems, financial, political, corporate, often drain the life force, creativity, and well-being from individuals for the benefit of a few. This "vampire" imagery feels more apt than ever as people feel exploited and exhausted by the relentless demands of modern life.

2. **Critique of Mental and Spiritual Enslavement:**
The song highlights how Babylon's power isn't just physical but also mental. The line, *"We've been trodding on the winepress much too long,"* speaks to a collective exhaustion from endless cycles of struggle without true liberation. This resonates with the awakening to "mental slavery"- the realization that many societal norms, values, and educational systems have subtly conditioned people away from their true selves, ancestral wisdom, and spiritual power.

3. **The Rise of Disillusionment:**
Marley's raw critique foreshadows the widespread disillusionment with traditional institutions, governments, media, and even some religious bodies, that many are experiencing globally. As information becomes more accessible, people are questioning narratives and systems they once trusted, leading to a deep sense of betrayal that "Babylon System" articulated decades ago.

Here's how these songs are particularly prophetic:

"Chant Down Babylon" - The Blueprint for Spiritual Revolution

4. **The Power of Sound and Vibration:** The very title of Bob's song, *"Chant Down Babylon,"* is profoundly prophetic. It emphasizes the power of vibration, voice, and collective spiritual energy over physical force. In the current awakening, there's a strong focus on frequency, resonance, and the idea that conscious intention, sound healing, and collective spiritual practices can indeed shift realities. This aligns perfectly with the belief that the *"walls of Babylon"* will fall not by bombs, but through a shift in spiritual frequency.

5. **Spiritual, Not Physical, Warfare:** The words, *"Babylon's fall will not come with bombs, but with the rise of awakened souls,"* perfectly encapsulate the core message of *"Chant Down Babylon."* This is the essence of the spiritual revolution. As people awaken to their ancestral power, inherent divinity, and collective consciousness, the old systems built on fear, division, and control simply lose their foundation. We see this reflected in the growing movements for social justice, environmental consciousness, and indigenous rights, which are fundamentally spiritual at their core.

6. **Remembrance as a Weapon:** The idea that "When the people remember who they are, Babylon cannot stand" is crucial. The current ancestral spiritual awakening is deeply about remembrance; remembrance of lineage, forgotten histories, suppressed wisdom, and inherent spiritual gifts. This collective act of re-membering (putting back together what colonization dismembered) generates an unshakable spiritual power that undermines Babylon's psychological and energetic strongholds.

7. **"Rastaman Chant"- The Proclamation of Divine Overthrow:** This song is a prophecy of inevitable collapse. The resolute declaration, **"Babylon yuh throne gone down,"** is not a wish but a prophetic statement of divine certainty. It speaks to the current awakening that oppressive systems, despite their apparent might, are already spiritually undermined and destined to fall, their foundations crumbling from within.

Spiritual Authority Over Material Power: This song asserts that ultimate authority does not lie in physical or political might, but in divine will and spiritual truth. It prophesies an era where Babylon's power is exposed as null and void by an awakened higher consciousness. This resonates with today's understanding that energy and vibration supersede physical control.

Power of Collective Affirmation and Embodiment: The repetitive chant itself becomes a powerful act of spiritual manifestation. It foretells a time when collective faith, vocalized through sacred sounds and unified intention, becomes the unstoppable force that actualizes prophecy and brings about systemic transformation.

8. **Collective Awakening as the Wind:** The phrase, *"This spiritual revolution is the wind, already swaying the foundations,"* captures the subtle yet pervasive nature of this awakening. It is not always a dramatic, visible event, but a deep energetic shift occurring within individuals and communities. This growing collective consciousness, driven by ancestral frequencies and spiritual insight, is indeed creating tremors in the established order.

In essence, Bob Marley's **Babylon** songs serve as both a stark warning and a profound prophecy. They expose the insidious nature of oppressive systems and materialism, while offering a blueprint for liberation through spiritual revolution. His music becomes a call for collective awakening, remembrance of true identity, and a demonstration of the power of unified spiritual vibration.

This aligns perfectly with the rising ancestral spiritual frequencies and the understanding that true societal transformation begins with an inner, spiritual shift. Once again, *reggae is an integral part of the soundtrack of African liberation.*

*With this kind of musical rebellion and spiritual call to revolution, it's no wonder why Bob Marley, articulating the **"Babylon System"** and urging to **"Chant Down Babylon"** was seen as a profound threat, leading to the infamous attempts on his life. His music was never just entertainment; it was a potent force for decolonizing the mind and a direct challenge to established power structures.*

THE ATTEMPTED ASSASSINATION OF BOB MARLEY: MORE THAN A POLITICAL HIT

On December 3, 1976, the world witnessed an event that was far more than a political hit; it was a spiritual attack on a man whose music had become a weapon of truth. The attempt on Bob Marley's life, just two days before his historic Smile Jamaica Concert, was not merely about silencing a reggae artist. *It was about silencing a frequency.* Marley's songs had become anthems of liberation, awakening hearts not only in Jamaica but across the African diaspora. To his oppressors, he wasn't just a musician; he was a movement.

When bullets were fired at Bob Marley, it wasn't just an assault on his body; it was an assault on the message. It was an attempt to mute the frequency of a spiritual revolution that could not be controlled. But Babylon miscalculated. They targeted the man, but the message was already alive in the people. Marley survived, and in a move that defied fear, he stood on stage with his wounds still fresh and delivered a performance that echoed through history.

Bob himself once said, *"The people who are trying to make this world worse are not taking a day off. How can I?"* His survival, his choice to sing even in pain, became a living parable of spiritual resilience. It was proof that while bullets can wound flesh, they cannot kill a vibration once it has taken root in collective consciousness.

The attempt on Marley's life wasn't just about politics, it was a spiritual war. It was Babylon's last desperate gasp to stop a man whose weapon was not a gun, but a song.

PART IV

A NEW WAY FORWARD

CHAPTER 11

LIBERATION BEYOND THE PHYSICAL FREEDOM IN THE FLESH AND FLAME

Revolution is Spiritual. Liberation is Embodied.

THERE IS A truth that has been buried for generations, and it is this: revolution begins not only in the mind, but in the flesh. It is not enough to read about freedom, to chant it with our lips, or to dream of it in the safe confines of our prayers. **True liberation is embodied.** It calls us to bring our full selves; our sacred, breathing bodies into the fight.

The systems of oppression that have sought to break us have always waged war against our physicality. Our bodies have been enslaved, exploited, violated, and controlled. But the same bodies once seen as sites of subjugation are now the vessels of our resistance. We are not just fighting for physical freedom; we are reclaiming the fullness of our divine humanity, our spirits, our cultures, and our sacred flesh.

In this chapter, we will explore the power of the **flesh and the flame**; the physical and spiritual forces that together ignite a new kind of freedom. We will discuss how to awaken our bodies as sites of power, resistance, and transformation, and how to harness the sacred fire of spirit to burn away every chain that has sought to bind us.

RECLAIMING THE SACRED FLESH:
OUR BODIES AS TEMPLES OF POWER

The body, long used as a battlefield, is now the site of our greatest strength. Colonialism, patriarchy, and systemic oppression have worked tirelessly to sever us from our flesh - to make us ashamed of our bodies, to convince us that we are merely vessels for labor, consumption, and submission.

But our bodies are sacred.

In African and Indigenous spiritual traditions, the body is not separate from the soul. It is a living, breathing manifestation of divine power. To honor the body is to honor the divine. Our flesh is not an afterthought of creation; it is a sacred vessel, a temple through which spirit moves.

Within our bodies, the strength of our ancestors lives on. Every breath we take is a continuation of their breath. Every heartbeat carries the rhythm of their songs. Our bodies are repositories of their wisdom, strength, and sacred memory. Through them, we receive not only our physical form but also the spiritual gifts encoded in our lineage.

To reclaim the body is to reclaim our power. It is an act of resistance, a declaration that our flesh is no longer a site of shame or control, but a temple of sovereignty, creativity, and ancestral fire.

EMBODIED RESISTANCE:
THE POWER OF MOVEMENT AND ACTION

To reclaim the body is to move it. Dance, stretch, run, fight, breathe. Through movement, we reclaim our vitality, our joy, our agency. *Movement is one of the most powerful forms of spiritual resistance.* Just as the Maroons of Jamaica resisted enslavement - running through forests, dancing under moonlit skies, using their bodies to disrupt the power structures of their time, we too must move with purpose. Every gesture, every breath becomes an act of defiance.

The Dance of Freedom: Traditional African dances, such as Ghana's *Adowa* or the *Afro-Cuban Orisha dances,* were never just expressions of joy. Trust and believe: they were movements of resistance. Through dance, people carried their history, their pain, and their rebellion in every step. These dances, done in sacred community, called forth the spirits of the ancestors. And the same is true today. Dance becomes an *embodied prayer for freedom* - a rhythmic invocation of remembrance and power.

The Body in Protest: From the Stonewall Riots to the Black Lives Matter uprisings, our bodies have always been instruments of resistance. To stand, to walk, to take up space in the face of oppressive systems is an act of liberation. The body itself becomes the protest sign; unapologetic, visible, alive. *To move freely in a world that seeks to bind you is a radical act of spiritual sovereignty.*

The body is the ultimate weapon in the fight for freedom. When we begin to see it as sacred, we reclaim it from the forces that have sought to control it for centuries. Every breath becomes a refusal. Every step becomes a declaration.

N.B. To begin to make spiritual and reverent connection with the Black body, follow the work of Antoinette Cooper. See her interviews with me on the Big Up YuSelf Show on Youtube titled: "The Black Body as a Sanctuary" and "Medical Racism - Reclaiming Our Bodies - America, the Preexisting Condition" Antoinette is the author of the ground breaking book - UNRULY. Her website is www.antoinettecooper.com

FLAME AS TRANSFORMATION: SPIRITUAL FIRE FOR REVOLUTIONARY CHANGE

Just as our bodies are sacred, so too is the spirit. Across many cultures, fire is the element of transformation, purification, and renewal. It is the living symbol of ancestral power, igniting rituals passed down through generations. The flame consumes the old, the false, the oppressive, making way for the new, the powerful, and the divine.

In Haitian Vodou, fire is used to invoke the spirits (Lwa), its flames carrying messages to the divine realms. In Yoruba traditions, fire serves as a purifier, cleansing the soul and clearing the path for personal and communal transformation. Across these sacred practices, fire is not merely destructive: it is alchemical. It burns to build.

The flame is the heart of revolution. It reminds us that we are not here to passively accept the world as it is. We are here to set ablaze the structures that oppress us and illuminate the path to liberation. Fire is sacred, but it is also revolutionary; a force that consumes, transforms, and renews.

FREEING THE MIND, THE SPIRIT, THE SOUL FROM INTERNALIZED OPPRESSION

The fire of revolution is the fire of the ancestors. When we light candles or offer incense in our homes, when we build altars in their honor, we are inviting their flames to ignite within us. That same spirit of resistance that burned in those who fought before us now seeks to burn within us. The ancestors live in the flames. They dwell in our daily rituals, in our prayers, and in our sacred actions.

Fire Ritual for Liberation: One of the most potent ways to invoke the transformative power of fire is through ritual. This can be a communal fire ceremony, or an intimate moment alone. Write down the things that bind you: fear, doubt, oppression. Offer them to the flames. Watch as the fire transforms them into ash, a symbol of your release. In this act, pain becomes purpose, and suffering becomes fuel for your liberation.

Flame as Protection: In many African spiritual traditions, fire is a shield. When under attack: physically, spiritually, emotionally, you can visualize a ring of fire surrounding you, burning away any forces that seek to harm you. This spiritual defense is more than visualization; it is the embodiment of divine fire, a sacred force that guards and empowers.

The Flame of Creation: Fire is not only destructive; it is profoundly creative. As we burn away the old, we clear space for what must be born. The fire of revolution is not for the sake of destruction, but for transformation. We are not here to burn without purpose. We burn to build. Our revolution is one of creation, birthing new realities even as we dismantle oppressive structures.

THE FLAME OF THE ANCESTORS: CALLING ON THE SACRED FIRE

True liberation will never be achieved in the mind alone. It must be felt, lived, and embodied. We are called not just to imagine freedom but to experience it through our bodies. *We must learn to move, to dance, to fight with our flesh.* We must tap into the sacred flame that burns in our spirits, using it to purify, protect, and transform the world around us.

Our fight is not merely for political or material freedom. It is for spiritual liberation: the freedom to be fully who we are, to live our ancestral truth, and to honor our sacred flesh. The body and the spirit are inseparable in this battle. One cannot rise without the other.

Awaken the Flesh: Begin to see your body as sacred, as a weapon in the revolution. Move it, honor it, care for it. Through physical rituals, dance, exercise, and sacred touch, you will awaken its full power. Your body is the temple of your spirit; treat it as such.

Ignite the Flame: Light a fire in your soul. Reconnect with the rituals of your ancestors, with the sacred flames that have guided them through hardship and triumph. Call on the fire to protect you, to purify you, to transform you. Let it fuel your fight for freedom.

The revolution will not be won in boardrooms or ballot boxes alone. It will be won in the streets, in the homes, in the hearts of those who rise to reclaim their full power. We are not simply fighting for a future where we are free. **We are fighting for a world where we can once again be fully human.**

"My tears began to flow as I wrote this last sentence...a testament to the immense truth and yearning it holds."

A REVOLUTIONARY CALL TO ACTION

As we continue this journey toward liberation, let us remember this: the fight for freedom is spiritual, and it is embodied in the flesh and the flame. Stand in your sacred power. Move with intention. Set the world ablaze with your righteous anger, and let the fires of transformation burn brightly in your soul.

Your body is the battlefield; your spirit is the fire.

The revolution begins within you. It is time to ignite the flame of liberation, to move your body in defiance, and to stand fully in your truth.

This chapter combines the spiritual and physical aspects of resistance and liberation, calling you to embody freedom both in body and in spirit. It brings together ancestral practices and the power of physicality, urging you to actively reclaim your power in the fight against systemic oppression.

RECLAIMING THE COIN

The liberation of the flesh and flame means nothing if we remain enslaved by economic systems that exploit our labor, suppress our value, and rob us of our dignity. But we are awakening. We are reclaiming our economic power: not just as consumers, but as creators, builders, and legacy-makers. We are pulling our dollars from institutions that disregard our lives and investing in each other.

We are teaching financial literacy across generations, practicing cooperative economics, owning land, launching businesses, and refusing to measure our worth by systems never designed to serve us. Every time we hire ourselves, support Black-owned brands, or create wealth rooted in purpose, we are waging war against economic bondage.

This too is sacred resistance.

THE EXODUS IS ECONOMIC,
AND IT IS SPIRITUAL

More and more of us are leaving the very countries that built their empires on our backs. We are finding home elsewhere: where the air is cleaner, the food untainted, the healthcare superior, and the people recognize our humanity. This isn't just migration; it's a spiritual exodus. We are moving to places where we can live with dignity, raise our children in peace, and be well in body and mind.

Don't think we are running. We are returning - returning to ourselves, to sovereignty, and to a rhythm of life that honors our existence. *This, too, is revolution: refusing to die in a land that profits from our pain.* We are choosing life. Choosing freedom. Choosing us.

This time, the revolution is spiritual... and it's a fire they can't extinguish.

This time the revolution is spiritual and...it's a fire they can't extinguish.

Spirit Warriors of Liberation

Before we can reclaim what was taken, we must first understand what was lost and how it was systematically erased. Long before hashtags and healing circles, there were warriors of the mind and spirit who recognized that colonization was not just about land; it was an assault on the soul.

Thinkers like *Frantz Fanon, Amílcar Cabral,* and *Steve Biko* warned that the deepest violence of colonialism was its attack on African identity, culture, and spirit.

Fanon, a Martinican psychiatrist and revolutionary, revealed how colonized people were conditioned to hate their Blackness, their languages, their rhythms; even their gods. Cabral, a freedom fighter from Guinea-Bissau, taught us that true liberation was more than political independence; it demanded a return to the source: our ancestral memory, our cultural wealth, and our spiritual lifelines.

Steve Biko laid the intellectual and spiritual foundation for the global return to African identity, pride, and sacred knowledge, championing "Black Consciousness" as a pathway to psychological liberation and self-reliance.

These men understood that the reclamation of African sacred knowledge is not optional; it is revolutionary.

Frantz Fanon (1925–1961)

Born in Martinique, Frantz Fanon was a psychiatrist, philosopher, and revolutionary. He joined the Algerian struggle for independence from France, working with the FLN (National Liberation Front). His seminal books, *Black Skin, White Masks* (published in 1952) and *The Wretched of the Earth* (1961), exposed the deep psychological trauma caused by colonization, especially the loss of spiritual and cultural identity.

"Imperialism leaves behind germs of rot which we must clinically detect and remove from our land but from our minds as well."

Fanon died in 1961 at the age of 36, but his work continues to guide liberation movements today.

Amílcar Cabral (1924–1973)

Born in Guinea-Bissau to Cape Verdean parents, Cabral was an agronomist, poet, and revolutionary leader of the PAIGC (African Party for the Independence of Guinea and Cape Verde). More than a military strategist, he believed in cultural resistance. For Cabral, reclaiming African spirituality, oral traditions, and ancestral knowledge was essential to true independence.

"Culture is simultaneously the fruit of a people's history and a determinant of history."

He was assassinated in 1973, shortly before Guinea-Bissau and Cape Verde gained independence.

Steve Biko (1946–1977)

Born in South Africa, Steve Biko founded the *Black Consciousness Movement*, which encouraged Black South Africans to embrace their identity, culture, and innate worth. Biko taught that mental liberation must precede political freedom, and that Black people must see themselves through their own sacred lens, not through the eyes of their oppressors.

"The most potent weapon in the hands of the oppressor is the mind of the oppressed."

He was murdered by apartheid police in 1977 at the age of 30. His legacy lives on in every act of Black self-love and resistance.

These three torchbearers understood what many are still learning today: that liberation is not just about territory; it's about memory, culture, and spirit. They helped lay the groundwork for a global return to African sacred knowledge and ancestral power.

Though *Nelson Mandela's long walk to freedom* is widely celebrated and he became the global face of South African liberation, Steve Biko's powerful articulation of Black consciousness offered a distinct, internal pathway to liberation that fundamentally reshaped the struggle.

Steve Biko respected Mandela's courage but felt that the *African National Congress (ANC)'s* earlier approach was too dependent on white liberal allies and failed to address the deep psychological wounds of colonization. Biko believed that Black people had to first reclaim their minds, their pride, and their power: a kind of spiritual self-liberation, before any political alliance could truly succeed.

HOW THEY ULTIMATELY ALIGN

Though their methods differed, Biko laid the psychological and cultural groundwork for the mass mobilizations that would later support Mandela's release and rise to leadership. Many of the youth inspired by Biko went on to join or energize the ANC during the 1980s.

In short:

Mandela fought to change the system. Biko fought to change the soul.
Both were necessary. Both were threats to the regime. And both are ancestors of liberation.

CHAPTER 12

BUILDING SACRED COMMUNITIES: REBIRTHING THE VILLAGE

THIS CHAPTER UNDERSCORES the profound truth that *spiritual resistance and liberation are inherently communal endeavors.* While individual faith sustains us, it is within the embrace of collective community that true transformation takes root and flourishes. We will explore how to recreate and cultivate *'spiritual villages'*- spaces, both physical and digital, meticulously designed for collective care, deep healing, and the harnessing of immense spiritual power.

Through an ancestral lens, we will reimagine the village not merely as a quaint historical concept, but as a dynamic, living blueprint for revolution, protection, and shared purpose in our contemporary world. This is not nostalgia; it is a reclamation and activation of the wisdom embedded in our heritage, forging resilient communities today. We will delve into how these ancestral blueprints guide us in rebuilding the foundational pillars of our spiritual villages: education, health, family, and governance, thereby reclaiming wholeness and paving the path to true liberation.

THE VILLAGE AS THE FOUNDATION OF LIBERATION

In every tradition, across time and cultures, one unbreakable truth remains: our strength is rooted in community. The revolution is not an individual pursuit. It has to be collective. We rise together, or not at all.

Again: *We rise together, or not at all.*

The village is more than a physical place: it is a living, breathing organism that nurtures the spirit, sustains the body, and holds space for the ancestors to walk among us. It is where wisdom is shared, protection is given, and love flows freely. A village is sacred because it honors the interconnectedness of all beings: human, animal, plant, and spirit.

To build sacred communities is to rebirth this village in the modern world, where geography no longer confines us, but shared purpose, mutual care, and collective liberation unite us.

This chapter is a call to return to that village, rooted in the sacred, where every member is held in reverence and every action serves the greater good. Whether rebuilding physical communities or creating virtual ones, we must embody the sacredness, mutual respect, and collective responsibility our ancestors upheld.

This is the collective power of us - the power they so fear.

THE SACRED VILLAGE: A SPACE FOR HEALING, POWER, AND PROTECTION

The village is more than just a gathering of people; it is a sanctuary. It is the space where we can be our full selves, where we are seen, heard, and valued for who we are and who we are becoming. It is where healing happens, where our spiritual practices are nurtured, and where we can step into our power with the support of those who walk beside us.

1.   The Role of Ancestors in Sacred Community

In the traditional African village, the elders were the keepers of wisdom, the guardians of culture, and the intermediaries between the living and the ancestors. Today, as we work to build sacred communities, we must invite the presence of our ancestors into our collective lives once again. Their wisdom, their strength, and their sacrifices must be honored in the way we organize our communities and approach our shared challenges.

Creating Ancestral Altars in the Village: Whether in physical or virtual spaces, the altar serves as a reminder of the sacred presence of our ancestors. Create communal altars where everyone can offer prayers, light candles, or place ancestral symbols. This can be done in a home, in a community center, or even digitally in virtual spaces.

Ancestral Storytelling Circles: Gather together to share the stories of those who have come before us. These stories are not only of triumph, but of adversity, survival, and resistance. In telling and retelling these stories, we reaffirm the bond with our ancestors and draw strength from the collective memory of our people.

2.   The Importance of Mutual Aid and Collective Responsibility

In traditional villages, every member contributed to the well-being of the whole. There was no concept of *"I"* without *"we."* The health of the village depended on the care and protection of every individual. This communal approach is essential in our modern-day spiritual revolution. To build sacred communities, we must foster relationships rooted in mutual aid, respect, and a shared sense of purpose.

Mutual Aid Networks: Build systems of care within your community. This could mean pooling resources to support those in need, offering spiritual guidance or counseling, providing food, shelter, or emotional support. Mutual aid goes beyond charity; it creates systems where we rely on one another, where the well-being of each person is inextricably tied to the well-being of the whole.

Shared Rituals and Practices: One of the most powerful ways to bond a community is through shared ritual. Whether it's a weekly gathering to light candles for the ancestors, a collective prayer, or a monthly ritual of gratitude and intention-setting, these practices generate a collective energy that binds everyone together and reinforces the sacred nature of the community.

3.   Spiritual Parenting and Intergenerational Healing

In the sacred village, the care and upbringing of children is a communal responsibility. *Spiritual parenting* is not just about raising the next generation; it is about passing down cultural knowledge, spiritual practices, and ancestral wisdom. This is how we nurture future leaders to carry the mantle of resistance, honor their heritage, and lead the ongoing fight for liberation.

Mentorship and Ancestral Guidance: Elders in the community must guide the younger generation, not only through words, but by example. Through mentorship, we teach the youth the sacredness of their identity, the power of their ancestry, and the vital role they must play in the revolution. This is more than education; it is the creation of a living tradition of resistance, renewal, and transformation.

Healing the Generations: The wounds of our ancestors live within us as generational trauma. It is our sacred duty to heal these wounds. In the sacred village, healing is a collective act. We hold space for one another's pain, validate each other's struggles, and commit to breaking cycles of trauma together. This healing can take many forms: therapy, prayer, community healing circles, rituals of forgiveness, and ceremonies of reconciliation.

Spiritual Protection and Sacred Boundaries: In the village, spiritual protection is not an individual task but a communal shield. We protect each other through prayer, ritual, and vigilance. Creating safe spaces: physical and spiritual, ensures that the community remains a sanctuary where all members can thrive, free from harm and spiritual attack. Sacred boundaries are established and honored, not as walls of exclusion, but as circles of protection and reverence.

SPIRITUAL PROTECTION AND STRENGTH IN SACRED COMMUNITY

The fight for freedom is not a battle fought alone. We need the protection and strength of the community around us. Just as our ancestors formed intricate networks of resistance, we must build systems of spiritual protection and empowerment that safeguard and sustain our collective journey toward liberation.

Protective Rituals for the Collective: In African traditions, warriors did not enter battle without spiritual fortification - protective charms, incantations, and rituals of empowerment were essential. Likewise, we must establish communal practices that shield us from forces seeking to destabilize and harm us. This could include regular collective prayers, ritual smudging of communal spaces with sacred herbs like sage or African sweetgrass, or creating protective salt circles to cleanse and ward off negative energies. These acts are not symbolic; they are spiritual armor that fortify the community's collective energy.

Sacred Justice Circles: In the traditional village, justice was not imposed by external authorities, but upheld through communal processes rooted in restoration and harmony. Today, we must revive these principles by forming *spiritual justice circles*: spaces where conflicts, harms, and injustices are addressed with the goal of restoring balance. These circles are about accountability, healing, and reconciliation, ensuring that justice is enacted not through punishment, but through communal care, truth-telling, and the sacred responsibility of making things right.

THE ROOTS OF WAYWARDNESS AND DESPAIR AMONG BLACK MEN

While on the point of sacred community, I want to call attention to a group that I have long felt deep compassion for - our Black men. I feel like our men could use some spiritual support While on the point of sacred community, I want to call attention to a group that I have long felt deep compassion for: our Black men. I feel like our men are in urgent need of spiritual support in these times. My heart breaks every day when I scroll past the @Houston13 Instagram page and catch glimpses of Black men involved in petty crimes. It's as though their pain and misdirection are being broadcast for entertainment, consumed like spectacle. What's even more heartbreaking is that sometimes it seems like they, too, have found a twisted sense of pride or defiance in showcasing these incidents, because when dignity is stripped away, bravado becomes the last shield.

We don't have the luxury of turning a blind eye to the plight of the Black man. No, this is a shared burden. Their wounds are our wounds. Their fall is our fall. I am calling for a **spiritual intervention and restoration**, because the waywardness and despair we observe in some of our Black men are not inherent flaws. They are deeply rooted in a complex, brutal interplay of systemic oppression, historical trauma, economic disenfranchisement, and cultural alienation.

If we truly desire to rebuild sacred communities, we must first understand these underlying causes to effectively address them; not with shame, judgment, or abandonment but with love, truth, and spiritual power. Our intervention must be holistic, touching mind, body, and spirit.

It's crucial to understand these underlying causes to truly address them and call for effective spiritual and community intervention:

HISTORICAL TRAUMA AND DISPOSSESSION:

Slavery and Post-Slavery Oppression:

Generations of brutal dehumanization: through slavery, the forced separation of families, denial of education and property, and relentless systemic violence (lynching, Jim Crow, mass incarceration) have deeply fractured traditional family structures and eroded Black men's roles as protectors, providers, and spiritual anchors. This trauma is intergenerational, silently passed down through families and communities, manifesting as cycles of pain, anger, and disconnection.

Economic Disenfranchisement: Redlining, discriminatory lending practices, the strategic disinvestment in Black communities, and limited access to quality education and employment have systematically denied Black men pathways to economic stability and generational wealth. The result is a crushing sense of hopelessness, a feeling of always being "behind," regardless of effort or talent.

Targeted Incarceration and the Justice System: The disproportionate targeting, arrest, and incarceration of Black men dismantle families and communities. Upon release, many face limited opportunities, legal discrimination, and societal stigma, perpetuating cycles of poverty and disenfranchisement. Prisons often become schools for deeper waywardness, not rehabilitation.

Erosion of Identity and Self-Worth:

Miseducation and Negative Stereotypes: Decades of media portrayals depicting Black men as criminals, brutes, or absentee fathers; paired with a deliberate erasure of African history and global contributions, have corroded self-image and fed internalized oppression.

Loss of Traditional Roles and Spiritual Connection: Colonialism and white supremacy sought to sever Black men from their ancestral roles as spiritual leaders, warriors, and cultural custodians. This spiritual dispossession leaves a void, often filled by destructive behaviors or desperate quests for validation through violence, hypermasculinity, or materialism.

Mental Health Neglect: The stigma surrounding mental health in some Black communities, combined with the lack of culturally competent mental healthcare, has left many Black men navigating trauma, depression, and anxiety in silence. Unprocessed pain often surfaces as aggression, emotional withdrawal, or self-sabotage.

Environmental and Social Factors: Gangsta Paradise:

Poverty and Lack of Resources: Communities deliberately starved of resources, plagued by failing schools, inadequate healthcare, and systemic neglect become breeding grounds for desperation, crime, and survivalist mindsets.

Cycle of Violence: Growing up in environments where violence becomes normalized as a survival tactic or a means of respect and control perpetuates the very cycles of destruction designed by oppressive systems. This, tragically, becomes the "gangsta paradise" a warped ecosystem born of external oppression but internalized as cultural reality.

This waywardness is not an inherent flaw but a direct consequence of enduring oppressive systems that seek to disconnect, disempower, and ultimately destroy.

A CALL TO SPIRITUAL INTERCESSION AND RESTORATION

My call to the community to reach out spiritually for Black men, much like the collective intercession we've witnessed for leaders such as Ibrahim Traoré, is a necessary and urgent response to a deepening social crisis. This is the essence of a spiritual revolution: addressing the roots of our suffering not merely through policy reforms but through activated faith, ancestral alignment, and intentional spiritual practice.

The failure to answer the cry of the Black man leads directly to the fracturing of our family structures. This is not incidental; it is a calculated assault, an insidious weapon wielded to weaken our collective resolve, disrupt our legacy, and derail our liberation.

But we have the power to counteract this.

As a community, we can spiritually *cover* our brothers and help restore them to their rightful position as *protectors, providers, spiritual warriors, innovators, inventors, and creative forces* through deliberate collective action:

Collective Prayer and Intention: Organize regular, focused prayer and meditation circles specifically dedicated to the healing, protection, and restoration of Black men. When we gather in unified intention, we create a powerful energetic shield and send a collective petition into the spiritual realm.

Ancestral Veneration and Guidance: Call upon strong, honorable male ancestors to intervene. Invite them to watch over, protect, and gently guide our "lost" brothers back to their sacred path. This act not only strengthens the energetic link across generations but also reactivates the ancestral wisdom encoded in our DNA.

Affirmation and Visualization: Consistently affirm and visualize Black men thriving; standing as loving fathers, diligent providers, insightful innovators, and powerful spiritual leaders. Words create reality. Images birth worlds. Through intentional affirmation and visualization, we call forth the best of our men.

Communal Healing Spaces: Establish culturally safe spaces, both online and in-person, where Black men can share their struggles, receive support, and engage in practices that nurture healing and self-worth. This can include talking circles, rites of passage, mentorship programs, and spiritual brotherhood gatherings. *Healing must happen in community.*

Reactivating Traditional Knowledge: Encourage the study and practice of African spiritual principles that center balance, community, honor, and a man's sacred role within family and society. We must teach our brothers the sacred responsibilities that colonialism sought to erase.

Collective Prayer and Intention: Organize regular, focused prayer or meditation circles specifically dedicated to the healing, protection, and restoration of Black men. This creates a powerful energetic shield and sends collective intention into the spiritual realm.

Ancestral Veneration and Guidance: Call upon the strong, honorable male ancestors for guidance and intervention. Ask them to watch over, protect, and guide the "lost" brothers back to their path. This strengthens the energetic link across generations.

Affirmation and Visualization: Regularly affirm and visualize Black men thriving in their rightful roles - as loving fathers, diligent providers, insightful innovators, and powerful spiritual leaders. Words and images hold creative power.

Communal Healing Spaces: Create culturally safe spaces (online and in-person) for Black men to share their struggles, receive support, and engage in practices that foster healing and self-worth. This can include talking circles, rites of passage, and mentorship programs.

Reactivating Traditional Knowledge: Encourage the study and practice of African spiritual principles that emphasize balance, community, honor, and a man's sacred role within the family and wider society.

*See **Appendix A** for ancestral rituals of intercession that I personally practice on behalf of our men. I hope these will serve as a guiding light as you join this collective spiritual petition for their healing and restoration.*

*Also, see an **invocation of ancestor Tupac Shakur**, calling upon his fiery spirit to intercede on behalf of Black men, reminding them of their warrior lineage and divine purpose.*

REBIRTHING THE VILLAGE IN THE MODERN WORLD

The village must not remain a static, nostalgic ideal; it is a living, evolving concept that must adapt to the modern world. The key to rebirthing the village lies in understanding that we no longer need to inhabit a single physical location to experience its power. Sacred communities can be built wherever we are. Through virtual spaces, social media, and digital platforms, we can create networks of care, healing, and resistance that are just as potent as any physical gathering.

Digital Villages: We must intentionally build online communities that mirror the values of the sacred village. These digital spaces can foster mutual aid, ritual, storytelling, and collective healing. Technology should not be a tool of alienation but a means of bringing us together in solidarity and love. This is precisely my aim with the **Big Up YuSelf Show** on YouTube and my **visualization clinics.**

There are others walking this path as well:

- Marissa Price Heals
- Lifting As We Climb
- Teatime. Beauty
- Stephanie Perry

Each of these channels nurtures a virtual village, creating spaces where we care for, uplift, and heal each other.

Next Chapter Collective (NCC), founded by Tori Prophet (known online as Prophetmother), is a sacred digital village for those ready to heal, evolve, and write their next chapter with intention. NCC is a space where spiritual seekers, healers, and visionaries gather to share ancestral wisdom, engage in deep self-work, and support each other's journeys toward personal and collective liberation.

Global Village of Resistance: We must also recognize that we are part of a global community bound by an ancestral lineage of resistance. Building international connections with like-minded individuals and communities strengthens our collective power. This can include:

- Supporting Indigenous land defenders
- Engaging in global solidarity movements
- Participating in international prayer networks

The village is no longer limited by geography. It is wherever we come together, in spirit and in purpose, to heal, protect, and rise.

THE SACRED CALL TO BUILD COMMUNITY

To build sacred communities is to take the fight for liberation to the next level. It is to understand that the revolution is not only about dismantling external systems of oppression, but also about creating the internal infrastructure to sustain and nurture us as we rise. The village is our foundation.

We do not fight alone. We do not heal alone. We rise together. Through our collective strength, love, and resistance, we reclaim the sacred power that is our birthright.

As you move forward in building your own sacred community, remember this: the village is reborn in every act of care, every prayer, every offering, and every moment of unity. It lives in the breath of the collective, in the power of shared ritual, and in the hands that lift each other up.

The time is now. The revolution is collective.

Rebirth the village.

BUILDING COMMUNITIES ROOTED IN SPIRIT, NOT IN SURVIVAL MODE.

Too often, our communities have been forced to organize around survival, dodging harm, responding to crisis, bracing for the next blow. This survival-based existence is not our natural state; it is a trauma response, shaped by generations of oppression, dislocation, and systemic violence. While survival has kept us alive, it cannot carry us into liberation.

We are not here just to survive. We are here to live. To thrive. To remember. To create.

To build communities rooted in spirit means shifting from crisis-driven connection to sacred intention. It is a conscious departure from scarcity, hustle, and hypervigilance, and a return to rhythm, ritual, and rootedness. Spirit-based communities are built not on fear, but on faith; not on competition, but on communion. They are not simply reactive; they are generative. These communities are seeded with ancestral wisdom, watered with love, and sustained by collective purpose.

When we root our communities in spirit, we no longer measure worth by productivity or pain. We honor rest as resistance. We value joy as justice. We prioritize inner alignment just as much as outward action. In this space, spiritual practice is no longer an afterthought, it becomes our infrastructure. Ritual becomes rhythm. Ceremony becomes center. Prayer becomes policy. And our liberation is lived.

This is what it means to build beyond survival:

- We center spirit, not just solutions.
- We gather for beauty, not just breakdowns.
- We create because we are divine, not just because we are desperate.
- We remember that the sacred is our strategy.

To live in spirit is to live in abundance—not necessarily of wealth, but of connection, meaning, reverence, and power. This kind of community goes beyond merely meeting needs; it awakens souls. It protects not only the body but also the dignity and divinity of its people.

We must ask ourselves:

- What would our communities look like if they were organized around spiritual well-being instead of survival?

- What rituals would we revive?
- What wisdom would we restore?
- What futures would we reimagine?

This is the sacred charge of our time:
To rebirth the village, not only as a refuge from pain, but as a sanctuary of power.
To build not just shelters, but temples.
To gather not just in grief, but in gratitude, prophecy, and purpose.

The new village is here.
It lives in us, through us, and beyond us.
Let us build it, not because we are desperate, but because we are divine.

This time the revolution is spiritual... and it's a current they can't hold back.

JOINING "THE VILLAGE REVOLUTION"

Journeying through the profound truths of ancestral wisdom and the sacred path of reclamation, the spirit of this book ignites a call within us; to remember, to heal, and to rise. Decolonizing our inner landscapes sparks a revolution that ripples far beyond ourselves. The Village Revolution is about creating sacred spaces that embody this power in actionable, transformative ways. It invites you to step into this work, together.

This is the perfect moment to introduce you to the **We Are Creators Visualization Clinic**: a focused, 5-hour virtual mini-retreat designed to empower you as a deliberate co-creator of your reality. In this sacred, healing circle, you will slow down and focus on you - your goals, your dreams - and practice embodying the vessel who attracts desires with effortless ease.

We don't chase. We visualize. We align. We embody. We create. -W.A.

This clinic is a deeply transformative space where visualization transcends material desires. It is sacred inner work - a soul-awakening journey that incorporates ancestral rituals and spiritual practices. When you close your eyes and look within, you meet the part of you that remembers your purpose. That's where true vision lives. It's where real dreaming and real manifestation begin.

"Who looks outside dreams; who looks inside awakens." -C.G. Jung

This is **circle work**, where we hold one another's dreams. The collective energy amplifies the individual experience. Breakthroughs happen in real time, activating faster, more meaningful manifestations.

Join the We Are Creators Visualization Clinic (Clinic 1) where going inward becomes a sacred act of remembering who you are.

Also available:

- Clinic 2: Deep Focus on YOU (2 hours)
  A soulcrafting session combining visualization with deeper inner work, aligning your vision with your soul's purpose and unique gifts.

- Clinic 3: The Science of Visualization (2 hours)
  Explore the dynamics of manifestation: Visionary Imagination, Quantum Visualization, Sacred Visioning, Creative Consciousness, and Dimensional Mapping.

To sign up for the clinic, visit *https://big-up-yuself.ck.page/7306eb022d*. For more information or to subscribe to the newsletter mailing list, email me at *bigup@bigupyuself.com* and to learn more about my work, visit my website at *bigupyuself.com*.

AN INVITATION TO DEEP RECLAMATION: THE SACRED ANCESTRAL ROOTS & LIBERATION CIRCLE

Having journeyed through these pages, witnessed what still sings in the ashes, and begun to understand the profound legacy of our collective wounds, perhaps your spirit now yearns for more than insight.

You are seeking "the village." Let's create it.

Perhaps you long for a space where healing can truly take root; where intellectual understanding transforms into embodied liberation. The path to reclaiming our whole selves, our true joy, and our inherent power is rarely walked alone.

This is why I extend a heartfelt invitation to join a sacred gathering: **The Sacred Roots & Liberation Circle.**

This is not a clinic.
This is a deeply intimate, resonant space crafted for profound spiritual healing, transformative ancestral ritual work, and genuine, soul-nourishing fellowship.

Here, we move beyond knowing about decolonization to embodying its freedom through ancient practices and heartfelt connection. This is where we build "the village."

Imagine a circle where every voice is heard.
Every inherited burden is honored and released.
Every act of remembering is celebrated.

In this sacred space, we will engage in ancestral rituals designed to mend fractured identities, unravel generational trauma, and amplify the spiritual power flowing through your bloodlines. It's a rare and urgent opportunity to feel the presence of those who walked before us, to draw from the collective strength of shared purpose, and to nourish your spirit in a way that heals not only you but generations forward and back.

This is more than a gathering.
It is a living revolution, unfolding within each of us, together.

Come, let us hold space for one another's liberation.
Come, remember who you truly are.
Come, reclaim the sacred freedom that is your birthright.
This is sacred rebellion.

*For more information or to subscribe to the newsletter mailing list, email me at **bigup@bigupyuself.com**.*
*To learn more about my work, visit **www.bigupyuself.com**.*

YouTube Channel: Big Up YuSelf - Celebrating the Original You. This is a circle that encapsulates the overarching message of self reclamation from trauma and self celebration along the healing journey. Big Up Yuhself (Original spelling) is a Jamaican greeting or expression which means, "I see you" and "Celebrate yourself - you're a big deal." On the channel, we hold conversations both solo and with guests, all designed for us to vibrate as our original selves were meant to. Subscribe to the YouTube Channel by visiting, *https://www.youtube.com/@bigupyuself.*

Big Up YuSelf TV Show, presented by Fenix TV.app. Here you'll find episodes which appear on YouTube and others recorded just for the TV channel.

CHAPTER 13

THE REVOLUTION HAS ALREADY BEGUN

The revolution isn't coming. It's here.

Not with blaring trumpets or breaking news, but in whispers, in rituals, in reclaimed names, and in the soft murmur of ancestors calling their children home.
It is quiet but unstoppable. It is intimate and immense.
It is already underway, and we are living in it.

The Proof Is All Around Us

You don't need to look far to witness this sacred uprising. The signs are everywhere—for those who have eyes to see and ears to hear. We are in the midst of a cultural, spiritual, and ancestral resurgence.

Names once stripped from us are being reclaimed. Children now bear names that echo the sounds of their original tongues. Adults are shedding names imposed through colonization and baptism, reclaiming ancestral identifiers that carry meaning, memory, and vibration.

Examples include:

- Sarah → *Sade (Shar-day):* Yoruba name meaning "Honor confers a crown."

- **Swahili Names:**
  Zuberi (Strong), *Amani* (Peace), *Imani* (Faith), *Nia* (Purpose), *Sanaa* (Work of art).
  James → *Jelani:* Swahili for "Mighty" or "Powerful."
- Christopher → *Kwame:* Akan name for boys born on Saturday.

In the **Ifá and Yoruba tradition**:
Names like *Oluwaseun* ("Thank you, God"), *Ayodele* ("Joy has come home"), and *Ifeoluwa* ("God's love") are rising in use.

In **Kemetic (Ancient Egyptian) traditions**:
Names like *Ra'mes* ("Born of Ra"), *Neferet* ("Beautiful one"), and *Anpu* (original name of *Anubis,* god of the afterlife) reconnect descendants to Nile Valley spiritual heritage.

In **Zulu/Xhosa traditions**:
Names like *Thandiwe* ("Beloved") are cherished for their profound meanings.

Among **Akan/Ghanaian day names**, which are widely reclaimed in the diaspora:
Kwame (Saturday-born boy), *Kofi* (Friday-born boy), *Akua* (Wednesday-born girl), and *Afia* (Friday-born girl).

Iconic Name Reclamations:

- Cassius Clay → *Muhammad Ali:* Rejected his "slave name" and embraced a name meaning "Beloved of God" in Arabic, reflecting his Islamic faith and Black pride.
- Malcolm Little → *Malcolm X* → *El-Hajj Malik El-Shabazz:* "X" symbolized his lost African ancestral name. His pilgrimage to Mecca marked a spiritual evolution, adopting El-Hajj Malik El-Shabazz to honor his Islamic faith and global Pan-African consciousness.

- LeRoi Jones → *Amiri Baraka:* Adopted an African name meaning "Blessed Prince," aligning with Black nationalism and cultural revolution.
- Stokely Carmichael → *Kwame Ture:* Chose this name to honor African leaders Kwame Nkrumah and Sekou Touré, symbolizing his deep commitment to Pan-Africanism.
- Ronald Everett → *Maulana Karenga:* Took a Swahili name meaning "Master Teacher," reflecting his leadership in African cultural revitalization and the founding of *Kwanzaa.*
- Yvette Marie Stevens → *Chaka Khan:* Adopted the name of a Central African warrior, channeling ancestral power and cultural pride through her music and persona.
- David Rice → *Mondo we Langa:* Reclaimed his African heritage with a Kikongo name meaning "Power of the Sun," chosen during his political imprisonment.
- Rhonda Eva Harris → *Iyanla Vanzant:* Embraced a Yoruba name meaning "Great Mother" or "Comforter," marking her spiritual initiation and alignment with African ancestral wisdom.

Across the diaspora, people are renaming their children with intention, and in many cases, renaming themselves. These names are chosen not for how they sound to Western ears, but for how they vibrate in the ancestral realm.

This naming is resistance.

It's memory.

It's a declaration that we will not be branded.

We will be remembered.

LANGUAGES ONCE SILENCED ARE BEING SPOKEN AGAIN

Across the diaspora, we see the return of Yoruba, Twi, Igbo, Patois, and Creole tongues. Each word spoken is an act of defiance. Each utterance is a resurrection.

Languages once silenced are being spoken again, marking powerful acts of cultural reclamation and resistance across the African diaspora. Yoruba, spoken widely in Nigeria and by descendants in the Americas, is being revived through religious practices like Ifá and through cultural education. Twi, the language of the Akan people of Ghana, is now taught in schools and celebrated in music and festivals, reconnecting generations to their ancestral roots. Igbo, another major Nigerian language, has seen a resurgence in literature, music, and film, reinforcing ethnic pride and cultural heritage.

In the Caribbean, Jamaican Patois is embraced more than ever as a vibrant symbol of identity and resilience. Jamaicans are rallying for Patois to be recognized as an official language alongside English, asserting its legitimacy as a fully-formed language with its own grammar, lexicon, and rich oral traditions. Similarly, Haitian Creole, once marginalized and dismissed, is now an official language of Haiti and a cornerstone of national identity, flourishing in music, literature, and political discourse.

Each word spoken in these ancestral tongues is an act of defiance against colonial erasure, a resurrection of spirit and culture, and a powerful reminder that language is a vessel of memory, power, and liberation.

ECHOES OF ANCIENT LANDS:
THE VIBRATIONS OF RECLAIMED WORDS

This linguistic resurgence is deeply intertwined with a remembering of sacred geography. When emerging Jamaican songwriter and artiste Skillful Kxng sings about Alkebulan, Kemet, and Kush in his anthem "A.I." (Ancient Intelligence) - a song I consider the very theme song of this book, he's not merely naming places. He's summoning memory, reclaiming divine lineage, and speaking the language of ancestral power. His words, deeply rooted in long-forgotten truths, resonate as prophetic chants, heralding a return to our spiritual origins.

Alkebulan, believed to be the original indigenous name of the African continent, evokes a pre-colonial unity among its diverse peoples and lands, an identity as the "Mother of Mankind" that existed before the imposition of foreign names and narratives. It symbolizes Africa's divine legacy and spiritual depth.

Kemet, the ancient name for Egypt meaning "Black Land," points to one of the world's oldest and most revered wisdom systems, a cradle of knowledge in geometry, astronomy, medicine, and spirituality, including the sacred principles of Ma'at. Many Afrocentric spiritual traditions draw upon Kemet as a foundational source of ancestral teachings and evidence of Africa's global influence.

Kush, the powerful Black African kingdom to the south of Kemet, stands as a symbol of African sovereignty, royalty, and divine rule. Its history is graced by the reign of formidable queens known as Kandakes (Candaces), emblematic of feminine leadership and sacred power.

Skillful Kxng's lyrics are a potent reminder that music is more than sound; it is a vessel of ancestral vibrations. Through his verses, forgotten histories are reawakened, transforming into living, breathing declarations of identity, sovereignty, and sacred power.

SACRED PRACTICES ONCE OUTLAWED
ARE NOW FLOURISHING

Sacred practices once outlawed are now flourishing. People are returning to ancestral spiritual paths such as *Ifá, Vodou, Kemetic wisdom,* and various African mystic traditions. Altars are being raised. Libations are being poured. Orishas are being honored. Ancestors are being remembered: not in secrecy, but in ceremony.

Land is being reclaimed. From urban gardens in the Bronx to community land trusts in Jamaica, from sacred sites safeguarded by Indigenous hands to rewilding movements across the African continent, people are reconnecting with the land as *kin, not commodity.* Across the diaspora, many are purchasing land in Africa, reclaiming both territory and heritage.

Spirit is awakening. The Western religions that once demonized African spirituality are being questioned, examined, and, in many cases, set aside. People are turning inward, remembering that divinity is not confined to books or pulpits but lives within; in our *bones, dreams, drums, and breath.*

This is not a trend. This is not nostalgia. *This is a remembering.*

It is a re-embodiment of who we were before we were broken, boxed, and branded.

FROM PERSONAL REAWAKENING
TO COLLECTIVE POWER

Every story of personal reawakening is a seed planted in the soil of revolution. And the more of us who awaken, the more the sacred canopy grows.

"There was a time I thought I was alone in this remembering. Then I began to see patterns emerging everywhere - a woman renaming herself Oshun; a child learning his great-grandmother's prayers in Ga; a man declaring, "I am no longer a Black man. I am a non-white man." And through my own proud reclaiming of 'Negro' as an identifier - remembering my spiritual and historical identity, I knew the ancestors were stirring. The veil was lifting."

We are no longer looking for permission to exist in wholeness.
We are no longer asking to be seen.
We are reclaiming our place, our purpose, and our power.

We are creating communities of care, building digital villages, and reuniting spirit with strategy. From YouTube channels and WhatsApp groups to healing circles, temples, and tiny homes, we are building the new world within the shell of the old.

This return is also a rebirth.

THE STATUE OF LIBERTY AND THE MUSEUM OF LIES

Let us talk, too, about the symbols they gave us and what they never meant for us to see.

Many don't realize the Statue of Liberty was originally conceived to commemorate the abolition of slavery. The sculptor, Frédéric Auguste Bartholdi, intentionally included broken chains and a shackle at her feet to symbolize this liberation. Her right foot is even lifted, a gesture suggesting she is stepping away from the bondage of the past.

Of course, that's not the story we were told. The true meaning, too "provocative" and too truthful for the American financiers, was conveniently hidden. While the chains are indeed on the statue, not removed and placed elsewhere, they are largely out of sight, obscured by her robes and the high pedestal. This strategic placement has fueled the enduring misconception that they were erased, a sanitized memory for a nation uncomfortable with its history. The narrative we are given instead is a more palatable, universal message of liberty that ignores the chains of the past.

The new Statue of Liberty Museum, opened in 2019, has exhibits that discuss the symbolism of the chains and the statue's connection to abolition. This is where the story gets even more cynical. The very thing they tried to bury is now on display, but in a sanitized, controlled environment; a museum piece, a historical fact, rather than a living truth. It's a testament to the ongoing effort to manage the narrative, to keep the messy parts of history locked away behind glass.

Though the Statue of Liberty may have become a symbol of welcoming immigrants, for many, true liberty was never about copper monuments. We see the broken chains not as relics of the past, but as a living prophecy. True liberty is spiritual, ancestral, and uncontainable. It lives in the breaking of generational curses, in the return to our original selves, and in the powerful act of naming our own divinity. The chains at her feet serve as a powerful, and often unseen, reminder of this ongoing struggle, a truth they tried to bury but we continue to unearth.

THIS REVOLUTION IS SACRED

This revolution is not about taking up physical, tangible arms; it's about taking up space. It's not about overthrowing systems, but about overgrowing them: rooting deeply into our truth, expanding into our power, and embracing our sacred responsibility. This revolution doesn't have to be loud and noisy. It's moving like a quiet storm. *I call it "spiritual stealth."* It's not a big, dramatic event you see coming. It's more like a deep, steady rumble that's gaining strength right under the surface. It's like an ambush: you don't even know it's happening until it breaks free with a force you can't stop.

We are shifting timelines, reclaiming earth-based ways of knowing, and healing both backward and forward. What we are igniting is beyond the reach of any empire. It cannot be legislated, contained, or silenced.

This is not the beginning. It is the **return**.

We are the revolution our ancestors prayed for. And we are already here.

This time the revolution is spiritual... and it's a rhythm they can't disrupt.

CHAPTER 14

MANIFESTING REPARATIONS

Reparations may not come from the White House, but they can rise from our altars, our block parties, our bank accounts, our bedrooms, our art, and our refusal to be broken.

OUR PATH: SPIRIT OVER STRIFE

WE DECLARE, UNEQUIVOCALLY: #LeaveUsAlone. Our desire is for peace, deeply ingrained in the fabric of our being, for fighting is not our intrinsic makeup. We are not driven to fight senselessly, nor do we harbor the inhumane inclinations that fueled the very systems of our oppression. Our minds bloom with creativity, our spirits yearn for community, for building, for advancement, for the boundless realm of invention and innovation from which we came. To engage in the destructive fighting of the oppressor is anathema to the very essence of our creative spirit.

Therefore, this time, the revolution is spiritual. We are done with the same old fight. *Our spiritual warfare is now our weapon of choice.* We dismantle oppressive structures not with brute force or physical conquest, but with the boundless power of awakened souls, ancestral remembrance, and collective intention. We are about community. As we forge our own path of self-reparation (for what is not given, we take), let us begin by gathering in our sacred circles, committing to the profound "circle work" within these pages, and extending profound kindness to one another. For in cultivating peace within and among ourselves, we manifest the world we deserve. Let's look out for each other - the greatest weapon against us is our failure to unite and mobilize as one. Let's be kind to each other.

For in choosing spirit over strife, we reclaim our inherent power and liberate our destiny.

If reparations as we've traditionally imagined them will never come, then we must learn to *manifest* them - spiritually, economically, communally, and psychologically, in ways we *control*. *We may never get what's owed, but we can still take what's ours.*

FIVE WAYS WE CAN CLAIM REPARATIONS WITHOUT INSTITUTIONAL ACKNOWLEDGEMENT OR PAYOUT

1.   Spiritual Reparations: Reclaiming the Sacred

True reparations begin with healing the soul wound. Colonization and slavery didn't just exploit our labor; they severed us from our ancestral practices, languages, and spiritual technologies.

Manifest spiritual reparations by:

- Returning to ancestral rituals. Reconnect with intuitive spirituality, African cosmologies, and the sacred practices passed through our bloodlines.
- Rebuilding connection with nature, the body, dreams, and sacred rest - embracing movements like Tricia Hersey's Rest Is Resistance as revolutionary acts of restoration.
- Honoring Black joy, rage, sensuality, softness, and mysticism; reclaiming the very aspects of our humanity that colonialism sought to demonize and suppress.

They stole more than labor; they tried to steal our soul.

2.   Psychological Reparations: Decolonizing the Mind

The plantation now lives in how we see ourselves.

True reparations demand we free our minds from the inherited shame and white-washed definitions of worth, success, and beauty. Colonization planted lies in our psyche; lies that we must uproot.

Manifest psychological reparations by:

- Teaching our children the fullness of our history - not starting with slavery, but with civilizations, creators, philosophers, healers, and warriors.
- Celebrating Black brilliance in every form - from natural hair to spiritual gifts, from emotional expression to revolutionary thought.
- Undoing the need to prove, perform, or assimilate - rejecting the constant pressure to validate our humanity through the lens of the oppressor.

3.   Communal Reparations: Rebuilding Village

Colonialism destroyed the village. Reparations rebuild it.

True reparations are not limited to financial restitution or individual success; they must include the restoration of our collective strength. Rebuilding the village is a sacred, self-determined act of reparation, a return to the communal ecosystems that once nurtured our wholeness.

Manifest communal reparations by:

- Creating intergenerational spaces of healing, mentorship, and celebration where elders pass wisdom, youth bring fresh vision, and everyone belongs.

- Returning to communal values; reviving shared parenting, ancestral storytelling, grief circles, and food rituals that reconnect us to each other and to the land.
- Making joy and care revolutionary again - understanding that in a world designed to fracture us, community care is an act of resistance and a blueprint for liberation.

4. Energetic Reparations: Living as if We Are Already Whole

Living well is our revolt.

What if reparations begin not with waiting, but with declaring ourselves whole, worthy, and sovereign now? What if we refuse to delay rest, pleasure, safety, and prosperity until someone else deems us deserving? This is energetic reparation; reclaiming the right to live abundantly, even in the face of systems designed to deny it.

Manifest it by:

- Refusing to internalize inferiority or invisibility. You are not a deficit; you are a divine being.
- Claiming luxury, wellness, and softness as a right, not a reward. Rest, joy, and beauty are not frivolous. You must know that they are revolutionary birthrights.
- Building futures where we belong to ourselves, not a system. We build on our terms, rooted in ancestral wisdom, not colonial templates.

One person can't do everything, but if everyone does something, everything will get done.

Contribute your part, however small; even if it's simply supporting someone else's effort. When you watch one of our videos, take a moment to **subscribe, like, and leave a comment.** A simple "♥", "hello," or "thank you" costs nothing but demonstrates invaluable support. Every act of engagement affirms our shared desire for collective success.

Think in terms of the collective.

We are not helpless. Helplessness is not our destiny. Regardless of our differences in faith, expression, or ideology - we are bound by a singular, urgent truth: our ultimate collective liberation. When we fully commit our energy to this purpose, we will shatter the strongholds that perpetuate our oppression, subjugation, and the erasure of our humanity.

Come!
This is spiritual warfare.
And it's time to engage.

5.   Economic Reparations: Redirecting Wealth

If they won't give it, we'll build it.

We may never receive reparations checks from governments, but that does not mean we are powerless. Economic reparations can begin with radical self-investment and the reclamation of wealth through **community-driven economics**. The key is not merely accumulating wealth, but *aligning it with our liberation.*

Manifest it by:

- Supporting Black-owned businesses, land trusts, banks, credit unions, and mutual aid networks. Circulating our dollars within our communities creates sustainable ecosystems of wealth.
- Building financial literacy, inheritance strategies, and group economics. Wealth is not just earned: it's protected, passed down, and collectively grown.

- Shifting from "survival hustle" to "liberated wealth." Wealth that serves *us*, not white validation or assimilation. Wealth that funds our visions, not our distractions.

We do have economic power, albeit misplaced and misaligned. Let's take a look at how we measure up economically.

BLACK SPENDING POWER / BUYING POWER: A SLEEPING GIANT

Black consumers in the United States wield **immense and rapidly growing economic power**. Yet, this power remains underleveraged. Let's look at where we stand:

- Current Spending Power (2024/2025): Projected to reach $1.8 trillion by the end of 2024 and surpass $1.98 trillion in 2025. Some forecasts push this figure up to **$2.1 trillion.**
- Future Growth: Expected to climb toward $2.5 to **$3 trillion by 2030.**
- Global Comparison: If U.S. Black consumer spending were measured as a country's GDP, it would rank among the world's largest economies: comparable to nations like Russia or Canada.
- Economic Footprint vs Population Share: While Black households make up approximately 13.4% of the U.S. population, they contributed nearly 10% of national consumer spending in 2019. This percentage has likely increased with the rise in buying power.
- Cultural Influence: Beyond numbers, Black consumers are global trendsetters. Choices in fashion, beauty, music, entertainment, and digital culture often dictate what becomes mainstream. Brands invest billions trying to capture this influence.

So there's no denying we have some financial power. Here's our problem though...

SPENDING VS. WEALTH: A CRITICAL DISTINCTION

It's essential to understand the difference between **spending power** and **wealth**.

- **Spending Power** is the total amount of money a group has to consume goods and services. It reflects how much we contribute to the economy as buyers.
- **Wealth**, on the other hand, is about assets minus liabilities: homes, businesses, investments, savings, and inheritances. It represents long-term financial security and power.
- While Black consumer spending power is enormous, the wealth gap remains devastatingly wide. According to the Federal Reserve's 2022 Survey of Consumer Finances:
- The median wealth of white households is $285,000.
- For Black households, it is only $44,900.

This stark disparity exposes a hard truth: we are driving the U.S. economy through our consumption, yet far too little of that economic power is reinvested into our own communities.

Why?

- Limited Black-owned businesses and services in many neighborhoods mean our dollars often flow out as quickly as they come in.
- Systemic barriers to wealth building - redlining, discriminatory lending, employment gaps, and educational inequities—continue to choke pathways to generational wealth.

- Consumerism traps: We're often targeted as consumers but excluded as owners.

Thus, while we are a **powerful economic engine**, the wealth generated from our spending primarily enriches systems and corporations that **do not reinvest in our liberation**.

The real challenge lies in transforming our immense spending power into sustainable wealth creation within Black communities. This requires shifting from mere consumption to intentional economic empowerment: owning businesses, investing in our institutions, and building intergenerational wealth.

Movements like **"Buy Black"**, as well as the support of **Black-owned banks, credit unions, and cooperative economics**, are vital strategies to **increase the circulation of Black dollars within our own communities**. These efforts are not just about economics; they are acts of **self-determined reparations**, designed to foster collective prosperity and economic sovereignty.

THE SOLUTION: CIRCULATE BLACK DOLLARS WITH PURPOSE

The **Buy Black movement**, support for **Black-owned banks and credit unions,** and collective investment strategies aren't just trendy hashtags, they are **economic reparations in action**.

- Every dollar spent consciously is a seed planted for collective empowerment.
- Every Black business supported is an institution strengthened.
- Every financial literacy circle is a foundation laid for future generations.

We don't have to wait for external reparations checks to start reclaiming our economic power. The revolution starts with **where we choose to spend, save, and invest our dollars today.**

HOW WE FIX IT

Let's Focus on Intentionality.

We must move beyond mere consumption and, with focused intent, align our spending power with a deliberate strategy for wealth accumulation. Every dollar must contribute to our collective economic liberation. Our collective power is undeniable; now we must strategically deploy it to intentionally close the wealth gap, ensuring that our economic contributions translate into generational assets and true self-determination.

This moment calls upon us, as a people, to align our formidable spending power with our wealth-building goals, consciously directing our resources to create lasting legacies and liberate our economic future.

Here's how Black communities can work towards this, building on the foundation already laid:

STRATEGIC & INTENTIONAL SPENDING: STRENGTHENING THE "BUY BLACK" MOVEMENT

This is the most direct way to keep dollars circulating within our community and it can't be emphasized enough. It requires actively seeking out BOBs for everything - from daily necessities to services, entertainment, and luxury goods.

Stop handing them our wealth! Every time we willingly buy luxury items from our oppressors, we pick the switch for our own beating. This practice transfers our wealth to systems designed to disempower us, directly fueling our poverty and diminishing our collective strength. We cannot afford to be indifferent. Our ancestors bled and sacrificed so we could be strategic with our wealth, ensuring it would never again be weaponized against us. **Wake up.**

How to Prioritize BOBs:

- Use apps and directories like *Official Black Wall Street, Black Owned Everything, WeBuyBlack.com.*
- Follow social media accounts that spotlight BOBs.
- Commit to allocating a percentage of your spending to Black-owned businesses. *Make it a lifestyle, not a trend.*

Conscious Consumerism:

Even when buying from larger corporations, research their Diversity, Equity, and Inclusion (DEI) practices, their investment in Black communities, and who sits at their leadership tables. Spend with companies that align with values of justice and equity.

And when it's time to boycott, **show up!** Don't act indifferent. Don't plead ignorance. There's no excuse not to be aware and supportive of movements for our liberation. Indifference is complicity.

Group Economics: Explore and participate in buying circles, co-ops, and mutual aid collectives where pooled resources and collective purchasing power support BOBs and secure better deals within our communities. Together, we can create our own economies.

LEVERAGING BLACK-OWNED FINANCIAL INSTITUTIONS

Leveraging Black-Owned Financial Institutions

*Until researching this book, I had no idea there were so many Black-owned banks and credit unions. It is my absolute joy to share this knowledge with you. (See **Appendix E** for an extensive list.)*

Bank Black / Credit Union Black:

Shift your banking, saving, and investing from mainstream institutions to Black-owned banks and credit unions.

How:
- Open checking and savings accounts.
- Apply for mortgages and business loans.
- Use their services for retirement and wealth planning.

  These institutions are far more likely to lend within Black communities, fund Black entrepreneurs, and understand the unique financial needs of Black families.

Support Financial Product Development: Champion and utilize institutions that create targeted products aimed at closing the wealth gap, such as:

- First-time homebuyer programs
- Small business micro-loans
- Financial literacy and wealth-building initiatives

BUILDING FINANCIAL LITERACY AND FLUENCY

Education from an Early Age:

We must teach financial principles: saving, budgeting, investing, understanding credit, and managing debt to children and young adults within families and community organizations. Financial literacy is not optional; it is essential for liberation and generational wealth.

How:

- Implement financial education programs in schools, churches, and community centers.
- Normalize financial discussions within households and community gatherings.
- Encourage mentorship, where financially knowledgeable individuals guide and support youth and peers in mastering economic strategies.

Investment Culture: From Consumers to Owners

We must shift from a consumption-heavy mindset to an investment-first mindset. Wealth is not built by how much we spend, but by how much we own and grow.

How:

- Promote participation in **investment clubs**, where community members pool knowledge and resources to build wealth together.
- Educate on **stock market fundamentals**, **real estate investing** (including **REITs**), and **portfolio diversification**.
- Simplify and demystify complex financial instruments like mutual funds, **ETFs,** and bonds through accessible workshops, webinars, and peer-led learning circles.

- Cultivate an investment culture where ownership, asset-building, and long-term planning become standard community practices.

My YouTube sisters: *Sondra Jones Thigpen of From Lack to Legacy* and *Dee Watkins, the financial coach behind Brown Girls Invest Too,* are out here sharing accessible, empowering financial education. Their channels are packed with insights and practical tools.

Sondra is on a mission to help 1,000 Black women open brokerage accounts, and Dee offers eBooks and trainings to help people build financial literacy, achieve independence, and create lasting wealth.

Estate Planning: Emphasize the importance of wills, trusts, and life insurance to ensure intergenerational wealth transfer and protect assets. This is crucial to prevent wealth from dissipating after one generation.

FOSTERING BLACK ENTREPRENEURSHIP AND OWNERSHIP

Support & Mentorship:

Encourage and actively support emerging Black entrepreneurs. The journey to business ownership becomes less daunting when a strong support system is in place.

How:

- Provide mentorship programs where seasoned entrepreneurs guide new business owners through the challenges of startup and growth.

- Create and promote networking opportunities that connect Black entrepreneurs with potential partners, investors, and customers.
- Offer accessible resources for business plan development, marketing strategies, financial literacy, and legal guidance to ensure new ventures are built on solid foundations.

Access to Capital:

One of the most persistent barriers Black entrepreneurs face is the historic and ongoing lack of access to capital.

How:

- Advocate for increased funding for Community Development Financial Institutions **(CDFIs)** that focus on underserved Black communities.
- Utilize **crowdfunding platforms** dedicated to supporting Black-owned businesses, allowing the community to invest directly in its entrepreneurs.
- Encourage angel investors and venture capitalists to **prioritize Black-led ventures** and create funding initiatives specifically designed to close the capital gap.
- Support the growth of **Black-owned financial institutions**: banks, credit unions, and investment firms that are more likely to understand and meet the needs of Black entrepreneurs.

Building Local Black Business Ecosystems:

A thriving Black economy depends on interconnected, self-sustaining ecosystems where Black businesses supply and support one another.

How:

- Identify gaps in local goods and services that Black entrepreneurs can fill, ensuring that community needs are met from within.
- Foster partnerships between Black businesses to create cooperative supply chains, shared services, and collaborative marketing efforts.
- Encourage *"circular spending"* where every dollar spent within the community continues to circulate and multiply before exiting.
- Leverage digital platforms to build directories and marketplaces that make it easier to discover and support local Black-owned businesses.

ADVOCACY FOR SYSTEMIC CHANGE

Policy Reform:

Advocate for policies that dismantle systemic barriers to Black wealth accumulation and economic empowerment.

Examples include:

- Enforcing fair housing policies to combat redlining and discriminatory lending.
- Ensuring equitable access to quality education, from early childhood through higher education.
- Addressing wage disparities and advocating for pay equity.
- Reforming predatory lending practices that disproportionately target Black families.
- Supporting student loan debt relief to alleviate one of the largest financial burdens on Black graduates.
- Pushing for universal access to affordable healthcare, a fundamental component of economic stability.

Community Development: Support and invest in initiatives that build infrastructure, enhance educational opportunities, and expand social services in historically marginalized Black communities. These are not just acts of charity but necessary investments in long-term economic growth and empowerment.

Accountability: Hold mainstream corporations and financial institutions accountable for their commitments to **diversity, equity, and inclusion (DEI).** Demand transparency and tangible action in areas like lending practices, hiring, leadership representation, and investment in Black-owned enterprises and communities.

The Long Game: Strategic Collective Action: Achieving economic equalization is a marathon, not a sprint. It demands a mindset shift; from isolated, individual spending habits to a **collective, coordinated strategy for economic liberation.** Every financial decision we make is an act of power, either reinforcing the status quo or actively reshaping our future.

Your Children's Future: If you are a parent or aspire to be, your engagement in this work is not optional; it's essential. The systems we build (or fail to build) today will directly impact the lives of the next generation. Neglecting this responsibility means your children will likely face even harsher obstacles than you have. Building intentional, sustainable systems of economic empowerment is not just about us, it's about **securing a liberated future for them**.

MANIFESTING REPARATIONS: A SPIRITUAL REBELLION

We may never receive reparations in the form we were promised; not from governments or systems still invested in our silence. But this revolution is not waiting. We are learning to *manifest our own reparations,* right now, in ways that are spiritual, embodied, and generational.

1.   Reclaiming Ancestral Power

We begin by remembering. Our ancestors were not only enslaved; they were dreamers, healers, astronomers, midwives, warriors, and poets. Their brilliance lives in us. When we reconnect to their rituals, stories, and sacred practices, we reawaken a lineage that was never truly lost. Reparations begin with returning to who we were before the disruption.

2.   Creating Sacred Wealth

Reparations are not just financial; they are about access, agency, and self-determination. When we circulate resources among ourselves, build businesses rooted in justice, and teach our children about wealth through a decolonized lens, we're constructing new economies that honor our spirit, not exploit it. This is sacred wealth, not capitalist greed.

We may never receive reparations in the form we were promised - not from governments or systems still invested in our silence. But this revolution is not waiting. *We are learning to manifest our own reparations,* right now, in ways that are spiritual, embodied, and generational.

3.   Refusing to Assimilate

Colonialism taught us that safety lies in sameness. But sameness is a lie. Every time we choose our *natural hair, native tongue, spiritual rituals, and ancestral knowing* over the need to "fit in," we are rejecting assimilation as a survival strategy. Our authenticity is reparations: because it restores dignity where erasure once ruled.

4.   Building Healing Communities

Isolation is a colonial tool. *Connection is resistance.* Healing is not meant to be solitary. Reparations look like safe spaces for grief, joy, prayer, celebration, and radical rest. They look like us gathering around fires, altars, circle spaces, and stages, remembering that our healing has always been communal, not just clinical.

5.   Becoming the Future Our Ancestors Dreamed

Reparations are not only about justice for the past; they are about creating a future that interrupts trauma. Every liberated child, every protected Black woman, every restored relationship with land, body, or spirit; these are receipts. These are the return on an inheritance once stolen. *We are the reparations we've been waiting for.*

AS WE HAVE DECLARED BEFORE: THE MOST RADICAL ACT OF FREEDOM TODAY IS TO STOP APOLOGIZING FOR WHO WE ARE.

For generations, we've been conditioned to validate our existence; stretching ourselves thin, overcompensating, and reshaping our tongues and bodies to fit into molds never meant for us. We've muted our instincts, diluted our truths, and silenced our knowing, all for the fragile promise of acceptance.

But assimilation is not reparations.
It is a lingering phantom of slavery, whispering that survival still depends on our obedience. It seduces us into believing that being "respectable" or "professional" will protect us, even if it costs us our authenticity. This haunting shows up not only in systems, but in how we shrink ourselves in everyday spaces: boardrooms, classrooms, even family gatherings.

But we are no longer bound by those chains.
The revolution we seek is not external validation. It is internal liberation.

This is a spiritual uprising.
Reparations begin when we reclaim what colonialism taught us to hide:
Our joy.
Our roots.
Our language.
Our wildness.
Our intuition.
Our sacred connection.

Every time we choose authenticity over assimilation, we repair what was severed. Every time we prioritize ancestral memory over societal approval, we are restoring what was erased. This is reparations in practice. *It's not a check, but a way of being.*

To stop performing for white comfort is not defiance; it's remembrance.

Living from our spiritual center; not whiteness, not capitalism, not fear - is a form of reparations no institution can grant us. It's a restoration of wholeness, dignity, and self-determination.

We are not here to fit in.
We are here to outgrow systems designed to erase us.
We are here to root ourselves deeply in who we were before the forgetting and to live from that sacred place with unshakable power.

The revolution now is spiritual. And that means reclaiming the parts of us we were taught to hide. *To stop performing for white comfort is to make space for ancestral memory to return.*

To *live from our spiritual center*, not white standards, not capitalism, not fear, is a kind of reparations no one can grant us but ourselves.

The work is not about domination, but about wholeness.

We are not here to fit in.
We are here to *remember who we were before the forgetting began* and live from that place with power.

Cleaning Our Sacred House: A Call to Internal Liberation

HERE'S A PAINFUL truth we must confront: we've unknowingly inherited habits of hatred, deception, and violence from the very systems that tried to destroy us. And tragically, we've turned those same weapons inward; on ourselves, and on each other. But listen closely: *this is not who we are.*

Our true essence is far more sacred, profound, and powerful. It's time to remember that. It's time to truly see ourselves and start showing up in the world, and for one another, from that authentic, unbreakable place.

Think about it: every division among us, every seed of self-hate, every whisper of distrust; these are not accidents. These are the precise tools used to keep us disempowered. Every derogatory word we speak about ourselves, every toxic image we celebrate, every time we tear each other down, we are handing them more ammunition. More proof. More justification to deny us dignity.

To our artists with massive platforms: especially you, Tyler Perry - this is a plea. Stop giving the world front-row seats to our trauma. Stop making a spectacle of our struggles for entertainment. I know you believe these stories reflect parts of our reality, but not every wound needs to be aired for consumption. There are sacred narratives we *must protect.* We don't need to parade our pain to validate our existence. You hold the power to uplift, to inspire, and to present an image of us that heals rather than harms. Please, choose that power.

And to our musicians, content creators, influencers: let's be more responsible with the lyrics we write, the messages we amplify, and the stories we allow to define us. The content we create, consume, and share shapes not only how others see us, but how we see ourselves.

Remember the words of that anthem: *"Ain't No Stoppin' Us Now."*
But first, we have to gather ourselves. We have to polish our act.
We have to *clean house.*

I say this out of deep, unwavering love. My love has deepened since writing this book. I am so proud of us.
But we can and we must do better.

Every time we fight, gossip, condemn, or unfairly criticize each other, we are playing right into their hands. We are doing their work for them. But imagine, just imagine, if we chose instead to radically love one another. If we treated each other with unshakable kindness, gentleness, and respect. If we consciously decided to support each other without exception.

What could stop us then?
Their greatest weapon - our division - would be obliterated.
Their systems would begin to crumble from within.

My people, *wake up.*

They live in constant fear that we will turn on them with the same violence they inflicted upon us. But that's not who we are.

So why are we turning that violence on ourselves?

RESTORING THE INNER SANCTUARY KINGDOM

"Who looks on the outside dreams; who looks on the inside awakes." - C.J.

Brothers and sisters, this radical self-love and love for each other is not some impossible feat. It begins with a deep, personal commitment to reprogramming our minds, a renewing of the heart. Let's simply make a conscious decision to start loving ourselves better, because when we do, we will inevitably love each other better.

If someone disappoints you, let them know lovingly so they can truly understand their actions, and then choose whether to make amends or offer contrition. After that, send them love, peace, and blessings, even if that relationship needs to shift, or if distance becomes the path to your own peace. Don't harbor hate or strife. Please, remove yourself from situations or relationships that aren't nourishing, that drain you, because that toxicity will become a part of you and spill into every other connection.

Forgive yourself for your own missteps, and forgive one another. And please, mind the words you unleash upon each other and to yourself, for that matter. Words have power. They can cast spells.

Get your mind right. Far too many of us need therapy and coaching more than we're willing to admit. And please know this: if someone lovingly encourages you to seek therapy or speak with a professional, it's likely because they see a need that is evident and they care enough to point you toward healing. Let's stop denying our true mental and emotional states.

None of what I'm talking about today will truly connect or make a lasting difference if, mentally, you can't grasp it or respond in your best interest if you can't even begin to exercise or execute this message. I believe that many of the world's deepest problems, past and present, stem from profound mental unwellness.

When you find yourself moving through life with meanness, spite, cruelty, or an absence of compassion, understand this: you are mentally unwell. Hurt people hurt people.

Vote sensibly and objectively. Don't waste your precious vote on a system that openly tells you and shows you they do not care about you or your sovereignty. Always remember the collective. Think beyond what's best for you alone, and consider what elevates our entire community. Of the evils you must choose from, choose the lesser. Don't be swayed by loud, empty promises. Be guided by wisdom, discernment, and at the very least, common decency. "Anti-wokeness" doesn't serve you; it actively works against you. Think critically. We are deeper than superficialities: remember who we are and what our ancestors fought for.

Let us choose to be people who heal ourselves and each other. You, my friend, are a healer if you choose to operate like one. Every day, you have the power to either help heal someone or to contribute to their brokenness. If your choice is to break them, understand that this reflects your own unhealed wounds. Let's practice using our discernment, trust our intuition, and stop doubting our personal power. It's time we start honoring it. *Wisdom is encoded in our DNA. Let's activate it.*

So, first things first: check your mental health. Schedule a mental health evaluation every year you schedule your wellness exam - even if you don't think you have a problem. Health concerns often don't show up until in a routine exam. Prioritize becoming mentally stable, because without it, everything else will suffer. Seek first the Kingdom of God; and remember, that Kingdom resides within you. Seek to be well within yourself, and all other things will align. Tend to that inner world, and the outer world will take care of you.

Love, my friends. Love. Let's take back our power. Remember who you are. You are not criminals and warmongers, hotheads or toxic, low-vibration troublemakers. *Your ancestors are speaking to you,* calling you back to your original self; a people of pride, dignity, creativity, innovation, spiritual depth, communicators with the elements (the land, water, fire, air, and cosmos), keepers of the village, mystics, and sages.

Big up yuself, and big up one another.
Ayibobo. Ashe. Amen.

Let's get ourselves together.
This isn't just about unity and kindness being a "good idea"; it's the ultimate strategic move in our collective liberation. For too long, the most potent weapon used against us hasn't been some external force: it's been our own internal divisions, our failure to truly unite and move as one. Every time we allow discord, mistrust, or petty differences to fester, we hand power to systems designed to keep us fractured.

Even more dangerous is when we begin to mirror the very tactics our oppressors used against us: violence, deception, and internal strife. *We must refuse to become our own oppressors.* We must reject those low frequencies. This is where we must exercise spiritual discernment, trust our intuition, and stop second-guessing our divine intelligence. Let's honor our personal power rather than deny it. Each of us is equipped with inner wisdom; our ancestors encoded it in us. Now is the time to use it.

Let's commit, wholeheartedly, to being kind, empathetic, and respectful to each other. Every single act of solidarity strengthens our foundation. Let's think in terms of community. Our individual well-being is inseparably linked to the health of our collective. True power emerges only when we genuinely look out for each other, moving as a unified force toward our shared destiny.

This, my friends, is where the spiritual revolution truly begins.
It demands awareness, self-governance, and personal responsibility. Every single one of us has a crucial role to play in this revolutionary liberation. We are all

interconnected, and the stark truth is: **none of us are truly free until we are all liberated.** This isn't just a fight. It's a profound transformation of spirit, mind, and collective action. And this would be the behavior of a people who believe they are free.

Ayibobo. Ashe. Amen.

This time the revolution is spiritual... and it's a unity they feared but now it's here.

FINAL THOUGHTS: ON UNITY, COMMUNITY, AND THE COMPLEXITIES OF LIBERATION

The anger among my people is palpable. Some call for separation, even segregation, as the only path to reclaim our power and safety. I understand that anger deeply. And yes, I absolutely recognize the *necessity of exclusive spaces* where we can heal, build, and thrive. These are not mere preferences; they are vital sanctuaries in a world that relentlessly erects barriers against us, because the systems designed to exclude and marginalize us are still overwhelmingly active.

But I do not believe broad segregation is our ultimate path forward. To embrace it as such risks repeating the very cycles of division that have historically shackled us, rather than advancing a true, expansive liberation and unity.

White supremacy and systemic oppression have inflicted immeasurable, undeniable harm. This is a fact, and as systems, they are inherently evil. Yet, I also know that not every single so-called "white" person is an enemy. Many have genuinely extended kindness, allyship, and solidarity. For those relationships in my life, I am grateful. While oppressive forces have and still shape much of the struggle we face today, I reject a worldview confined to a simplistic "us versus them." I hold to a greater vision: a dream where we live as a united human family, transcending race and division, where our sovereignty is honored, and we freely practice our spirituality, traditions, and unique ways without malicious interference or exploitation.

To reach that future, a *spiritual revolution* is essential. This revolution cannot be merely physical or political; it must be an inward and upward transformation, one that restores *balance and justice* from within. When reclaiming truths that were once forbidden, resistance is inevitable. But I am not just telling stories. I am lighting torches, so others can find their way back home.

We cannot afford silence. Silence is complicity. Disengagement is surrender. Our ancestors are calling us to remember who we are, to honor their sacrifices not just with words, but with action. We must raise our voices, reclaim our power, and actively participate in the shaping of our future. Our liberation depends on it.

I understand not everyone will agree with me and I respect the full spectrum of thought within our community. But this vision of unity, sovereignty, and spiritual restoration is what guides my heart and my work. I believe that true freedom must be collective and inclusive. It cannot be just personal but shared.

ON THE IRREVERENT COMMODIFICATION OF SACREDNESS

When it comes to our spirituality and sacred symbols however, I draw a firm line. Sacred is sacred. These are not fashion trends. These are not accessories for profit. It deeply troubles me, frankly, when I see models who do not look like us wearing shirts with our ancient symbols simply because it's "cool." That is not reverence. That is *exploitation.*

And this isn't about isolation; it's about *protecting the sanctity of our spiritual heritage.* Our symbols and practices carry a profound lineage, an inherent power that cannot be separated from those of us who are direct descendants of their origin.

They are not meant for fleeting trends or external profit. It is unsettling, to say the least, when sacred symbols are reduced to casual decor, worn without understanding, or taught by those outside our community for personal gain. For us, these practices are more than aesthetics. They are affirmations of identity, acts of ancestral veneration, remembrance, and declarations of our rightful place in the world. The ankh for example is a living symbol of identity, cultural reclamation and resistance. And sankofa symbolizes reclamation of our heritage.

So let me be unequivocally clear: *Hands off our stuff!*

Our spiritual practices and symbols are sacred conduits. They deserve to be honored, protected, and carried forward by those who hold an authentic, generational connection to them. Their potency, meaning, and purpose must never be diluted by careless commodification.

This is not gatekeeping. This is safeguarding.

SOVEREIGNTY WITHOUT DOMINATION: A VISION FOR COLLECTIVE LIBERATION

1.   Sovereignty is Self-Rule, But Self-Rule Exists in Relation
Your sovereignty, whether personal or communal, does not require domination over others. True sovereignty means being free to live by your own values, truths, and spiritual laws without external interference. This is the essence of the revolution we are calling for.

However, genuine sovereignty for all demands that everyone's sovereignty is equally recognized and respected. Collective sovereignty envisions a world where each person, and each people, has the space to self-govern. It is not about one group's supremacy, but about many sovereigns coexisting in mutual respect.

2.   Collective Sovereignty Means Shared Liberation, Not Shared Identity
     I am not asking us to assimilate, erase our culture, identity, history, or sacred ways for the sake of harmony. On the contrary, I affirm that we all deserve to live sovereign lives, especially those of us whose sovereignty was stolen.

     In my ideal world, there would be a collective recognition of each group's sacred right to exist, thrive, and live freely. This vision is not about assimilation. It is about mutual liberation, where no one's freedom requires another's erasure.

3.   Inclusivity Means No Domination
     When I speak of inclusivity, I am not suggesting we embrace harmful systems or welcome those who seek to oppress us. I am calling for a world where no group's sovereignty is built upon the suppression of another.

     That is how a united human family becomes possible; not through forced sameness or erasure, but through mutual respect of distinct sacred identities. That vision sits right in my spirit; it feels far more liberating than the alternative of segregated, perpetual hate and rage.

I do not believe sovereignty is about isolation. True sovereignty is sacred self-rule. And part of that sacredness is honoring it in others as well.

We have a long journey ahead before reaching this dream, and I believe this spiritual revolution will be the path that gets us there. My dream is not of one group ruling over another, but of a world where many sovereign peoples live freely: spiritually, culturally, and politically, without interference or domination.

That is the collective liberation I speak of.

But that would be a whole other revolution. Maybe someone else in that future will get to write that book.

SACRED TECHNOLOGIES: RITUALS AND SPIRITUAL PRACTICES

"Some may question the accuracy or legitimacy of these practices. I understand - and encourage discernment. But remember: colonialism tried to erase these ways, not because they lacked power, but because they held too much. This book is part of reclaiming that power - not to exploit it, but to honor it."

RITUAL BASICS

Ancestral Light Invocation

Purpose: Call upon benevolent ancestors for protection and clarity.

What You Need: White cloth, glass of water, candle, ancestral photo or item.

How to Perform:

Place all items on a clean surface.

Light the candle, call names of known and unknown ancestors.

Pour a libation and speak your request or gratitude aloud.

Sit in silence and journal what arises.

CHANTS & SPOKEN WORD FOR ANCESTRAL WORK

Kemetian Offering Words *(reconstructed)*
"Hotep di nesu, en Anpu, neb ta Djeser..."
Translation: *A royal offering to Anubis, lord of the sacred land...*
Use during spiritual offerings or when invoking safe passage for the dead.

Yoruba Praise Chant (Oriki Example)
"Oshun, iya mi, omi tutu, aya Orunmila..."
Translation: *Oshun, my mother, cool water, wife of Orunmila...*
Use when honoring feminine power, rivers, healing, or beauty.

Visual Guide: Basic Altar Layout

- Center: Ancestral photo or sacred symbol (e.g., Ankh or Nsoromma)
- Left Side: Candle or fire element
- Right Side: Water (bowl or glass)
- Front Corners: Offerings (e.g., fruit, herbs, shea, coins)
- Back Center: Cloth in white, gold, or kente fabric

VODOU PRACTICES, OFFERINGS, AND LIVING TRADITION

Now that we've placed Vodou in the larger context of global resistance and sacred survival, we'll return to it this time, to explore how it is practiced. How the *lwa* are served, what the rituals look like and how you might listen if they are calling to you.

Entering This sacred space...

ANCESTRAL RITUAL: CALLING ON OGOU FOR STRENGTH AND PROTECTION

For those who are tired, under attack, or on the front lines of change, this ritual is for you. For the ones fighting systems too heavy to carry alone. For the freedom fighters, the survivors, the builders of something better, call **Ogou.**

Use This Ritual When: You're preparing to protest, speak truth, or protect your community. Use it if you're experiencing burnout or despair, if you feel spiritually attacked or destabilized or when you want to reconnect with the fire of your ancestors.

Who is Ogou?

In Haitian Vodou, Ogou (also spelled Ogoun) is a powerful warrior *lwa.* He governs:

- Iron and weaponry
- Political revolution
- Righteous anger
- Strategic wisdom
- Protection of the oppressed

He was present at *Bois Caïman,* invoked by enslaved Africans as they prepared to rebel. When you call Ogou, you're calling the spirit of the rebel who wins.

OGOU RITUAL FOR PROTECTION & RESISTANCE

"Ogou, you who do not back down. Ogou, iron of the people. Ogou, protector of the fire-hearted. Come."

What You'll Need:

- A red candle (Ogou's color)
- A machete, knife, piece of iron, or nail (symbol of his power)
- A small glass of rum, with a splash poured out as offering
- A cigar or incense (optional)
- Red cloth or scarf
- A metal bowl or dish
- Drumming or warrior music (live or recorded)
- Your voice

Before You Begin:

Clean your space with Florida water or herbal smoke (basil, sage, or bay leaf).

Take three deep breaths and stand tall. This is not a ritual of begging. This is a summoning of strength already within you.

Performing The Ritual:

1. Light the red candle. Place the iron object beside it. Say:

    "Ogou, warrior of justice, come stand beside me. I light this flame in honor of your fire, your fight, your fury. Let your sword cut through the lies. Let your strength lift what I cannot carry alone."

2. Pour the rum slowly into the bowl. Clap three times. Say:

    "This is for you, Ogou. Drink and remember. You who fought at Bois Caïman. You who defend the oppressed. Be with me now."

3.   Touch your forehead, heart, and stomach, calling on his energy to enter you:

"In mind, in spirit, in gut, I carry the fire of Ogou."

4.   Speak your truth. Aloud. This is where ritual becomes resistance. Say what you are fighting for. Name what you will no longer tolerate. Speak for those who can't. Call out the systems that harm.

5.   Drum or move your body. If you're alone, stomp your feet, tap a rhythm, or play warrior music. Let the fire build in you.

6.   Close with:

"Ogou, you walk with me. I fear nothing. My spirit is armored. My hands are sacred. My path is protected.
Asé. Ayibobo."

7.   Let the candle burn down safely (or snuff it after it's burned for a while). Dispose of offerings respectfully. Pour rum into the earth, return iron to your altar, or bury it.

If for iron or metal you use a household item (like your kitchen knife):

1.   Cleanse it afterward.

Wipe it down physically, then spiritually - using one or more of the following:
Pass it through incense or sage smoke. Sprinkle with saltwater or Florida Water. Speak a simple releasing phrase like:
"Thank you, Ogou. This tool now returns to daily use. The ritual is closed."

2.   Be clear in your spirit.

Know that while it served as a sacred object for the ritual, it now returns to its secular function. That intentional shift matters. Just honor it first. Cleanse it. Thank it. And release the energy. Rituals are made sacred not just by the objects but by the way we treat them.

3.   Alternative option for ongoing work:

If you plan to call on Ogou regularly, consider dedicating a separate knife or iron object that's *just* for ritual use. This builds spiritual consistency and makes your altar more powerful over time.

ANCESTRAL RITUAL: CALLING ON EZILI DANTOR FOR PROTECTION, COURAGE & SACRED RAGE

Ezili Dantor: The fierce Black mother and maternal protector of Black womanhood and children. She's another revolutionary force, especially for readers reclaiming sacred anger, feminine strength and righteous vengeance. Covers love of children, community, freedom and the wounded heart that still chooses to fight.

For every woman, femme, mother, survivor, or daughter who has been silenced, erased, or violated. For the protectors. For those who burn and bleed but keep rising. For those who love fiercely and fight harder. This is for you.

She is often represented by the Black Madonna of Częstochowa, scarred and sacred. She is also connected to the Petro family of spirits, those spirits born of fire and rebellion.

She was present at the Haitian Revolution, said to have ridden a woman into trance at the Bois Caïman ceremony, crying out for liberation. She is the mother who fights for her children's future with teeth, with blood, with spirit.

Use This Ritual When:

You're facing personal or systemic violence. Use it when you're carrying grief, ancestral pain, or deep spiritual anger. Draw for it when you need to reclaim your power as a mother, daughter, femme, or survivor. And when calling protection for your children or community.

Ezili Dantor Ritual: To Protect, To Reclaim, To Rise

> *"Mama Dantor, scarred but unbroken, come into this space. Wrap your arms around the wounded. Sharpen the knives of the warriors. Bring fire to our blood and justice to our hearts."*

What You'll Need:

- A blue and red candle (her colors)
- A picture of the Black Madonna or a fierce mother figure
- A glass of cremas (or milk, or rum with condensed milk) as offering
- A knife, blade, or mirror (symbol of protection and reflection)
- A sacred object representing your womb, pain, or voice (a stone, a feather, a photo, a poem)
- A drumbeat or song of mourning and resistance (or silence if needed)

Before You Begin:

Sit in front of your altar or a quiet space.
Place the candles and offerings before you.
Hold whatever pain or injustice you carry. Let it rise.

Performing The Ritual:

1.   Light the candles. Say:

"Ezili Dantor, Black mother, I call to you. You who were wounded and kept loving. You who were exiled and kept fighting. Enter this space. Enter my blood. Enter my voice."

2.   Offer the drink. Pour some on the ground or in a bowl. Say:

"I pour this for the mothers who never saw justice. For the children taken. For the bodies hurt. For the stories buried. May your fire rise in me."

3.   Hold the mirror or blade. Look into it. Say:

"I am not weak. I am not voiceless. I am not alone. The mother stands behind me. The protector walks with me. The wound does not shame me, it serves as my altar."

4.   Speak or scream your truth. Don't hold back. Let your sacred rage rise. Let your grief come. Let your voice return. Dantor wants your honesty, your fire, your brokenness. This is the part that *heals* and *arms* you.

5.   Call on her protection:

"Dantor, wrap your arms around this body. Guard my children. Guard my voice. Guard my spirit. Let no system touch me without reckoning. Let no wound remain without rising. I am protected. I am sacred. I am fire. Ayibobo."

6.   Sit in stillness or dance if you feel moved. Close when you feel complete.

Ezili Dantor reminds us that sacred rage is a spiritual weapon. That the womb is a source of divine fire. That survival is not submission, it is warriorhood. And that you do not fight alone.

Other Haitian Lwa:

- Erzulie Fréda (Èzili Freda): This Lwa is the spirit of love, beauty, luxury, and prosperity. She is known to bestow material riches, finery, and a lavish lifestyle upon her devotees. While her focus is often on material wealth and sensuality, a comfortable and beautiful life can certainly contribute to overall well-being.

- Kouzen Zaka (Azaka Mede): He is the Lwa of agriculture, harvests, and the rural working class. Kouzen Zaka is invoked for abundance, success in labor, and a bountiful harvest, which directly translates to financial stability and sustenance. He represents the wealth that comes from hard work and the land.

- Lasiren and Labalenn: These are mermaid Lwa who embody the wealth and abundance of the ocean. Lasiren can grant prosperity and good fortune. Labalenn is a more powerful, often unconscious force of strength and deep wealth.

- Damballa Wedo: The serpent Lwa, associated with creation, wisdom, fertility, and purity. While not directly linked to wealth, Damballa often brings blessings, peace, and spiritual well-being, which are fundamental to a healthy and prosperous life.

Yoruba Orisha:

- Oshun (Osun): This is probably the most prominent Orisha for what you're describing. Oshun is the Orisha of sweet waters, love, beauty, sensuality, fertility, and wealth/prosperity. She is often invoked for financial blessings, abundance, and to overcome obstacles to well-being. She is also associated with healing, particularly related to women's health and fertility. Her colors are yellow and gold, and her offerings often include honey.

- Olokun: This Orisha (who can be seen as male, female, or androgynous depending on the tradition) rules the depths of the ocean and is considered the source of all wealth and abundance. Olokun is also highly revered for their ability to bring health and prosperity. In some traditions, Aje (see below) is considered the daughter of Olokun.
- Aje (pronounced Ah-jeh): Aje is specifically the Orisha of wealth, trade, and economic prosperity. She is often invoked for business success, financial stability, and the accumulation of resources. She is considered a powerful facilitator of wealth creation for those who are willing to work.
- Babalu Aye (Shopona): While primarily associated with disease, healing, and epidemics (especially smallpox in the past), Babalu Aye is often invoked for healing and to ward off sickness. Appeasing him can bring relief from illness and good health.

CHANNELING NANNY: RITUALS FOR MODERN FREEDOM FIGHTERS

SAMPLE RITUAL FOR CHANNELING NANNY OF THE MAROONS: IGNITING THE SPIRIT OF RESISTANCE

This ritual is designed to connect with the fierce, protective, and strategic spirit of Queen Nanny of the Maroons, inviting her energy to fortify modern freedom fighters. It integrates the elements, (ashes/clay/charcoal, natural elements for an altar) with intentions of protection, vision, and sustained resistance.

Preparation:

1. Sacred Space: Choose a quiet, undisturbed space, ideally outdoors in nature, or a place where you feel connected to the earth. Clear it physically and energetically (you might use a simple sweep or light cleansing smoke like sage if you have it).

2.   Gather Materials:

For Markings: A small amount of ashes (from burnt natural material if possible, or even a burnt matchstick), clay (natural, non-toxic), or charcoal (activated charcoal powder mixed with a little water, or a piece of drawing charcoal). A small dish or shell to hold it.

For the Altar:

Leaves: Fresh, vibrant leaves, perhaps from a sturdy tree.

Stones: A few smooth, grounding stones.

Names of Freedom Fighters: Small slips of paper with the names of Nanny, other historical freedom fighters (known or nameless), and contemporary figures or causes you wish to invoke.

Water: A small cup or bowl of fresh water.

Fire: A small, safe candle or a representation of fire (like a red cloth or red flower). I use battery operated candles too.

Personal Offering (Optional): Something simple and meaningful to you, like a piece of fruit, a flower, or a few grains of corn.

Journal and Pen: To record insights.

Performing The Ritual:

1.   Centering and Invocation:

Sit or stand comfortably before your sacred space. Close your eyes. Take three deep, grounding breaths, inhaling strength and exhaling tension.

Connect with the earth beneath you, feeling its stability and ancient wisdom.

Gently open your eyes. Light your candle (if using).

Speak aloud, clearly and with conviction: *"Ancestors, I call upon you. Spirit of Nanny, I invite your presence into this sacred space. Guide me, teach me, empower me."*

2.   Building the Resistance Altar:

Arrange the leaves and stones on your altar space. Feel their connection to enduring nature and resilience.

Take your slips of paper with the names of freedom fighters. Hold each one, silently or softly speaking the name, acknowledging their sacrifice and spirit. Place them carefully on the altar.

Place the water and fire (or its representation) on the altar, honoring the elements of life and transformation.

Place your personal offering (if using), dedicating it to the spirit of resistance.

3. Protective Markings and Affirmation:

Take your ashes, clay, or charcoal. Mix it with a tiny bit of water if needed to create a paste.

Using your finger, apply the mixture to your body as protective markings. Common places include:

Forehead (third eye area): For vision, clarity, and discernment.

Cheekbones: For strength and courage in facing the world.

Over your heart: For protecting your spiritual core and intentions.

Wrists: For empowered action and creation.

As you apply each mark, speak your intention and affirmations:

"With these markings, I am protected from all harm, seen and unseen."
"With these markings, my vision is clear to discern truth from deception."
"With these markings, my voice is strong to speak truth to power."
"With these markings, my spirit is fortified for the journey ahead."

Look at your reflection if possible, or feel the marks on your skin. Embody their protective power.

4. Channeling Nanny's Spirit (Meditation & Petition):

Return to a seated position before your altar. Close your eyes.

Visualize Queen Nanny. See her strength, her strategic mind, her unwavering commitment to freedom. Feel her fierce love for her people.

Imagine her presence surrounding you, empowering you. Feel her wisdom flow into you.

In your mind or softly aloud, make your petition to her. Be specific about what kind of guidance or strength you seek as a modern freedom fighter.

"Nanny, wrap your arms around this body. Guard my children. Guard my voice. Guard my spirit. Let no system touch me without reckoning."

"Let no wound remain without rising. I am protected. I am sacred. I am fire."

"Help me embody your courage, your strategy, and your unwavering resolve in my work for liberation. Guide me to dismantle oppression with vision, not vengeance."

Allow yourself to sit in silence, listening for any messages, feelings, or images that arise.

5.   Closing the Ritual:

When you feel complete, offer thanks. *"Thank you, Queen Nanny. Thank you, Ancestors. Thank you for your presence, your guidance, and your power."*

Extinguish the candle safely.

Journal any insights, feelings, or instructions you received during the ritual. This helps to integrate the experience.

You can leave your altar as a sacred space for a period or respectfully return the natural elements to the earth when ready.

This ritual is a template. Feel free to adapt it with your own prayers, songs, or specific elements that resonate deeply with your connection to Nanny and your purpose. The key is sincere intention and reverence.

Use ashes, clay, or charcoal on your body during ritual as protective markings.

Build a resistance altar with natural elements: leaves, stones, and names of freedom fighters.

Create coded affirmations for modern resistance, phrases only your circle understands, rooted in your spiritual lineage.

RITUAL FOR REMOVING HEXES

In July 2025, my dreams were particularly vivid - alive in a way I couldn't ignore. One night, I was awakened multiple times with the same clear instruction: I was to heal people, both physically and spiritually of hexes. This calling to be a healer isn't new - I've heard it before, many times. But I've resisted. Out of fear. Out of not feeling ready. But there is no room for resistance anymore. I accept. People are suffering. And who am I to withhold medicine I've been given because of fear? It's time. I am here to help.

I'll share more about this in my follow up book but for now, I'll simply share a ritual.

But a word of warning, caution and power:

These practices are not to "play dress up" - they awaken living spirits. Always ask permission and give offerings before working with Loa, spirits, or ancestors. Keep a journal of what you experience - dreams, visions, unexpected visits. The path of healing, especially with roots in African diasporic traditions like Obeah, Vodou, and Hoodoo, is sacred and requires intention, ancestral permission, and ethical use.

And remember: the same spirit that can be used for good can be used for harm. Whatever energy you release will likely return to you. This is the Law of Karma or the Law of Return - spiritual truth based on reciprocity: the idea that spiritual forces, ancestors, and energies are *watching*, and that imbalance or misuse will eventually call for rebalancing. Protect yourself and use your powers only for good.

Do not be afraid to work with ancestral spirits and ancient, sacred technologies - they exist to help you. They were robbed from us and weaponized because they were powerful.

Below is a deep, intense and spiritually potent clearing ritual drawn with reverence from Vodou and Obeah. It is designed for removal of hexes, spiritual clearing, and anointing as a healer. Use them carefully, always asking for guidance from your ancestors and the spirits that walk with you.

HEX NEUTRALIZING RITUAL (VODOU & OBEAH BLEND) FOR THE CLEARING OF HEXES, DARK ATTACHMENTS, AND ENERGETIC CROSSINGS

N.B: In traditional language, these energetic crossings are what our elders often call 'crosses' - (pronounced *crawsiz* in Jamaican patois) those heavy burdens, bad luck, and unseen forces that cling and block our paths until they are cleared.

N.B: *Ayizan: Spirit of initiation and purity.*

Though not mentioned earlier in this book, I have chosen to invoke *Ayizan,* a revered female *loa* from Haitian Vodou, for this ritual. She is known as the guardian of sacred mysteries, the protector of spiritual workers, and a powerful presence during rites of cleansing, purification, and new beginnings.

You may call her name aloud during the ritual or simply attune to her qualities - truth, spiritual order, and deep cleansing.

RITUAL OVERVIEW:

This ritual blends practices rooted in both Vodou and Obeah and is intended to clear the body and spirit of spiritual contamination, fear energy, and hexes without returning harm to the sender. It is ideal for healers, empaths, and spiritual workers who suspect they've been crossed, drained, or spiritually targeted.

Supplies Needed

- 1 lime or bitter orange
- Sea salt
- Florida Water (or white rum + basil)
- Camphor block (or frankincense as substitute)
- Garlic (3 cloves)
- Black pepper
- White candle
- 1 uncooked egg
- Cascarilla (or white chalk)
- Coconut or castor oil infused with basil and rosemary
- Charcoal + fireproof bowl
- Optional: Small mirror, white cloth

Step-by-Step Instructions:

1.   Prepare a Spiritual Bath

Squeeze lime juice into warm water, add sea salt and a splash of Florida Water or rum. Stir clockwise. Bathe from head to toe while reciting:

> *"Spirit of Ayizan, opener of sacred ways,*
> *Obeah fire, ancestral hand - come wash me clean today.*
> *Anything sent that is not of light,*
> *Be pulled from my bones and cast into night."*

Allow yourself to air dry if possible.

2.   Smoke Cleansing with Spirit Fire

Light a charcoal disc. Burn garlic peel, camphor, and black pepper. Fan smoke over your body and space. If using a mirror, place it facing outward as you say:

> *"Smoke of truth, burn what binds.*
> *Not with hate, but love that blinds.*
> *Let what was sent return to none*
> *Let it be undone, let it be gone."*

3.   Egg Sweep

Pass the uncooked egg slowly from crown to soles of your feet, praying:

> *"Spirit that clings, thought that weighs,*
> *Out you go, no more stays.*
> *From crown to root, from soul to skin,*
> *You have no place here, nor way back in."*

Wrap the egg in brown paper and dispose of it at a crossroads or bury it under a tree away from your home.

4.   Sealing the Energy

Use cascarilla or chalk to draw protective symbols on your body - especially your chest, back of neck, and soles of your feet. Anoint your crown, third eye, and palms with your herb-infused oil, saying:

> *"By oil and herb, I seal what's mine.*
> *My spirit is sovereign. My soul divine.*
> *No shadow walks where I have claimed.*
> *I walk in power, healed and named."*

5.   Sit in Stillness and Light

Light your white candle. Wrap your head in white cloth. Sit quietly, breathing, affirming:

> *"All that clung is now released.*
> *All that harmed has now ceased.*
> *I am free. I am clear. I am whole."*

Aftercare:

Burn lemongrass, bay leaf, or sandalwood the next day to bless your space.
Eat grounding foods (yam, callaloo, root vegetables).
Sleep with a blue cloth or white handkerchief near your head.
Give thanks to your ancestors and Ayizan for protection.

Optional Adaptation:

If Ayizan is unfamiliar or not resonant, replace her invocation with a prayer to your own ancestral mothers, to Spirit, or to the Divine Force of Light and Truth in your tradition.

ANCESTRAL SPIRITUAL RITUALS FOR INTERCESSION

Here are some ancestral spiritual rituals you can explore and adapt on behalf of our brothers, always emphasizing respect for lineage and intention:

Libation Ceremony:

Purpose: To honor ancestors, call upon their wisdom and blessings, and request their intercession.

How: Pour water or a culturally appropriate drink (like rum or liquor) onto the earth (or into a plant/bowl if indoors) while speaking aloud the names of honorable male ancestors (known or unknown). Ask them to guide, protect, and intervene for our struggling brothers, calling them back to their divine purpose. Speak their names and the virtues you wish to see manifest. (Call on any names that move you. I invoke Tupac on behalf of young brothers)

Light-Setting/Candle Rituals:

Purpose: To bring light, clarity, purification, and spiritual guidance.

How: Use candles of specific colors (e.g., white for purity/peace, blue for healing/protection, gold for prosperity/divine connection). Carve names or intentions into the candle. Anoint with natural oils. Light the candle while offering prayers or chants for the spiritual cleansing, restoration, and protection of Black men. Allow the candle to burn down completely (safely).

Altar Building for Restoration:

Purpose: To create a dedicated space for spiritual focus, offering, and connection.

How: Set up a small altar with meaningful items: photos of strong Black men (ancestors or living examples), symbols of protection (like ankhs, cowrie shells), natural elements (water, earth, a plant), and offerings (fruit, flowers, incense). Use this space for daily or regular prayers, meditations, and intentions for the restoration of Black men.

Smudging/Cleansing Rituals:

Purpose: To clear negative energy, release blockages, and invite positive spiritual forces.

How: Use sacred smoke from herbs like sage, frankincense, or myrrh. Intentionally smudge spaces where negative energy has been pervasive, or even objects, while speaking affirmations of cleansing, healing, and spiritual renewal for Black men. You can visualize the smoke lifting away despair and confusion.

Drumming and Chanting:

Purpose: To raise spiritual vibrations, connect to ancestral rhythms, and create a powerful energetic call for change.

How: Gather with drums (djembe, conga, or even hand drums) and engage in rhythmic drumming. Integrate chants or songs that speak to healing, strength, unity, and the reclaiming of Black masculinity. The vibration of the drum is deeply transformative and calls to ancient memory.

When performing any ritual, the most important elements are *sincere intention, focused belief, and a heart full of compassion and clarity.* These spiritual actions, combined with sustained community effort, can indeed create a powerful ripple effect, helping to restore our Black brothers to their rightful, sacred positions within our community and the world.

A NOTE ON PRACTICES & AUTHENTICITY

The spiritual practices and rituals included in this appendix are based on a blend of ancestral knowledge, oral traditions, scholarly research, and personal spiritual experience. They are shared in the spirit of cultural remembrance and sacred reclamation. Many of these ancestral practices come from oral traditions - living, breathing wisdom passed down through generations, dreams, rituals, and lived experience. These traditions are not monolithic; they shift across families, regions, and lineages. What I share here reflects what has been shared with me through research, interviews, and spiritual experience, not as fixed doctrine, but as an offering.

I share these practices not as a high priestess or spiritual authority, but as a daughter of the diaspora reclaiming what was stolen, hidden, and demonized. These are not prescriptive formulas but invitations to reconnect with your roots, respect the divine, and explore further with qualified elders and spiritual guides. I offer them with deep reverence and always encourage readers to go deeper with trusted elders, practitioners, and spiritual guides in their own journey.

Refer to the disclaimer in the front of this book prior to practicing any of the rituals presented.

TRIBUTE TO TUPAC

He Left a Cultural Legacy

Tupac was more than a rapper. He was a poet, revolutionary, and truth-teller. His work centered on social justice, racism, poverty, Black liberation, and inner struggle. Many people invoke his words and spirit for strength, awareness, or insight. That's ancestor-level influence.

Tupac spoke from the Soul of the People. He represented a generation's pain, pride, rage, and hope. In doing so, he became part of the collective spiritual memory of Black people around the world. Ancestors aren't just those who birthed us, they're also those who *inspired* us, *defended* us, and *gave voice* to our struggles.

People call his name with reverence. When they say "Tupac was a prophet" or "Tupac still speaks to us," they are keeping his spiritual presence alive. Calling the names of the dead with love and respect is a form of ancestral veneration.

BETWEEN WORLDS: AN INVOCATION THROUGH THE DOORWAY TO ANCESTOR TUPAC

Tupac Amaru Shakur, son of the struggle, voice of the voiceless, we call your name with power and purpose. You who walked with fire in your chest and truth on your tongue, Come sit with us. Rise in us and speak through us.

You who danced with death but lived for life, whose pen was a blade and whose words were balm, come. Warrior poet, child of revolution, we honor the fight you carried in your soul and the love you bled onto every beat.

May your restless spirit find rest in our remembrance. May your courage awaken our own. May your vision of justice and truth stretch beyond the grave and guide us still through the darkness.

On this day, we call you not only in praise but in petition.
Intercede for our brothers who've lost their way.
Those wandering in shadow, forgetting their crown,
Remind them of their worth, their fire, their purpose.
Call them back to the drumbeat of their destiny.
Let your spirit speak freedom into their bones.

You showed us what it means to cry and still rise, to rage and still create, to question, to feel, to stand up even when broken.

Ancestor Tupac, *we pour libation in your name.*
We rise in your memory and we continue in your fire.

Asé. Ayibobo. Amen.

Healing Affirmations for Ancestor Work

To speak during ritual, prayer, meditation, altar work, or daily remembrance.

To Open the Way

- I call on my honorable ancestors, known and unknown - with love, respect, and gratitude.
- Ancestors, I welcome your presence and your wisdom into this sacred space.
- As I remember you, I remember myself. As I honor you, I grow stronger.

For Guidance & Protection

- Walk with me, guide my steps, light my path.
- Your strength lives in me. Your prayers are still working.
- Protect me as you protected your own. Help me make wise decisions.

For Healing Generational Wounds

- I am the one who chooses healing for those who came before and those yet to come.
- With love and intention, I break cycles of pain and restore our sacred power.

- I release inherited burdens and carry forward only what is worthy and whole.

For Connection and Sacred Purpose

- I am a living altar. My life is a continuation of your legacy.
- I move forward with clarity, knowing I am backed by generations of wisdom.
- Your blood runs through mine. Your dreams live in me. I walk in purpose because of you.

To Close Rituals or Affirm Daily

- Thank you, Ancestors, for walking with me today. I honor your presence.
- May my actions be a prayer. May my life be a blessing in your name.
- I rise because you rose. I am because you were. And I remember. Asé.

How We've Fought Historically and How We Fight Today

Honoring the Spirit that Could Not Be Broken: From Colonization to Continuum, The Fire Still Burns

The concept that now we must fight racial and colonial injustices with more than physical retaliation but with spirituality invoking the spiritual practices and understandings of our ancestors is powerful and deeply timely. Historically, resistance to racial and colonial injustices has taken many forms, and understanding these helps set the stage for why a spiritual revolution is both necessary and transformative. So, how have we been fighting and resisting historically?

Here's a broad overview.

TIMELINE OF AFRICAN SACRED KNOWLEDGE SUPPRESSION, RESISTANCE & SURVIVAL

Pre-1500s: Ancient Origins and Sacred Wisdom

- **Before 3000 BCE - Kemet (Ancient Egypt):** African civilizations developed spiritual systems, sacred geometry, and healing practices based on cosmologies like Ma'at and ancestor veneration. Priests and priestesses served as scientists and spiritual leaders.

- **2000 BCE–500 CE - Nubia, Ethiopia, Mali, Yoruba, and Akan Civilizations:** Sacred knowledge, including divination (Ifá), herbal medicine, and spirit communication, was passed down through oral tradition by griots, priests, and elders. These indigenous African religions formed the spiritual foundation for resilience and identity.
- **700 CE - Arab Invasions of North Africa:** Islam was introduced, sometimes merging with but often suppressing indigenous practices and marginalizing traditional spiritual leaders.

1500s-1800s: Suppression and Slave Revolts

- **1492–1800s** - Transatlantic Slave Trade & European Colonization: Millions of Africans were enslaved, their languages, rituals, and spiritual practices violently suppressed. Colonizers and missionaries demonized African cosmologies as "witchcraft."
- **1500s-1800s - Enslavement in the Americas:** Africans brought their traditions, such as Ifá, Vodun, and Palo, to the Americas. These practices survived underground, hidden in music, dance, and coded within Christian forms.
- **1532–1697 - Maroon Communities:** Escaped Africans formed independent communities in the Caribbean and Americas, preserving traditional rites, herbs, and spiritual leadership. Spiritual resistance became a key tool for survival and rebellion.
- **1739: Stono Rebellion (South Carolina, USA):** An organized slave uprising.
- **1791–1804: Haitian Revolution:** The only successful slave revolt that led to a nation, using Vodou as a unifying spiritual force to overthrow French colonial power.
- **1831: Nat Turner's Rebellion (USA):** A significant armed rebellion by enslaved people.

- **1832: Baptist War (Jamaica):** A slave revolt led by Samuel Sharpe.

1800s–1960s: Colonial and Political Resistance

- **1857: Indian Rebellion:** A major uprising against British rule.
- **1896: Battle of Adwa (Ethiopia):** The Ethiopian army, led by Emperor Menelik II, decisively defeated Italian forces, making Ethiopia the only African nation to successfully repel a European colonial power with military force.
- **1905–1957:** African Nationalist Movements: Movements for independence rose across the continent, culminating in Ghana's independence in 1957.
- **1909: Formation of the NAACP (USA):** The National Association for the Advancement of Colored People was founded by an interracial group of activists, including W.E.B. Du Bois and Ida B. Wells, to fight for legal and political equality.
- **1912: African National Congress (ANC) founded (South Africa):** An organization formed to resist racial injustice and advocate for the rights of the Black majority.
- **1952–1960: Mau Mau Uprising (Kenya):** An anti-colonial military rebellion against British rule.
- **1954: Brown v. Board of Education (USA):** A landmark Supreme Court ruling that declared state-sponsored segregation in public schools unconstitutional.
- **1954–1962: Algerian War of Independence:** A military and political struggle against French colonial rule.
- **1955–1956: Montgomery Bus Boycott (USA):** A major nonviolent protest and act of economic resistance led by Martin Luther King Jr.
- **1963: March on Washington:** A key moment in the Civil Rights Movement where Martin Luther King Jr. delivered his "I Have a Dream" speech.

- **1964: U.S. Civil Rights Act passed:** A landmark legal victory that outlawed discrimination based on race, color, religion, sex, or national origin.

1920s-Present: Ideological and Cultural Reclamation

- **1920s: Marcus Garvey's UNIA:** A movement promoting Pan-Africanism and Black-owned businesses.
- **1930s: Rastafari:** The emergence of this spiritual-political movement in Jamaica.
- **1952: Frantz Fanon publishes Black Skin, White Masks:** A foundational text of decolonial thought.
- **1950s-1960s: Rise of Black Power Ideologies:** Malcolm X emerged as a powerful voice for Black empowerment and self-defense, offering an ideological alternative to nonviolent resistance.
- **1960s–70s: Black Consciousness & Afrospiritual Movements:** The Civil Rights and Black Power movements in the U.S. and the Black Consciousness Movement in South Africa reawakened interest in African roots. This era also saw the formation of Black banks and cooperatives.
- **1994: End of Apartheid (South Africa):** The legal system of racial segregation ends, and Nelson Mandela becomes president.
- **1990s-Present: Global Revival:** Ancestral veneration, divination, and plant medicine are resurging among people of African descent worldwide, supported by modern platforms and retreats.
- **2000s-Present: Spiritual Revolution:** African spirituality reclaims its sacred place as not "new age" but original age. A growing focus on ancestral healing and decolonizing the mind and spirit. People are integrating spiritual traditions, like collective meditation, ritual, and Afro-Indigenous cosmologies, into activism as tools for liberation.
- **2020: #BuyBlack movements:** Economic resistance efforts surge following global protests.

Today: Let's use psychological reversal. Let's refuse to internalize inferiority. Let's project strength rooted in identity and sacred knowledge. Use our symbols, stories, and rituals to disrupt the narrative of white supremacy. We prevail.

Closing Reflection:

Despite centuries of erasure, the drum still beats. The ancestors still whisper. And the sacred knowledge lives hidden in plain sight, awaiting those who remember to listen.

SELECTED BIBLIOGRAPHY: SOURCES & INSPIRATIONS

- Hurston, Zora Neale. *Tell My Horse: Voodoo and Life in Haiti and Jamaica.* Harper Perennial, 1990.

- Deren, Maya. *Divine Horsemen: The Living Gods of Haiti.* McPherson & Company, 1983.

- Penniman, Leah. *Farming While Black: Soul Fire Farm's Practical Guide to Liberation on the Land.* Chelsea Green Publishing, 2018.

- Somé, Malidoma Patrice. *Of Water and the Spirit: Ritual, Magic, and Initiation in the Life of an African Shaman.* Penguin Books, 1995.

- Teish, Luisah. *Jambalaya: The Natural Woman's Book of Personal Charms and Practical Rituals.* HarperOne, 1985.

- Wilmot, Swithin. *The Maroons of Jamaica 1655–1796: A History of Resistance, Collaboration & Betrayal.* Ian Randle Publishers, 2020.

- Beckwith, Martha Warren. *Jamaica Anansi Stories.* Dover Publications, 1969.

- Smith, Michael W. *Voodoo in Haiti: Catholicism, Protestantism and a Model of Effective Ministry.* University Press of America, 2007.

- Thompson, Robert Farris. *Flash of the Spirit: African and Afro-American Art and Philosophy.* Vintage, 1984.

- Brown, Vincent. *The Reaper's Garden: Death and Power in the World of Atlantic Slavery.* Harvard University Press, 2008.

- León, Lizabeth Paravisini-Gebert and Margarite Fernández Olmos (eds). *Sacred Possessions: Vodou, Santería, Obeah, and the Caribbean.* Rutgers University Press, 1997.

- Hill, Napoleon. *Outwitting the Devil: The Secret to Freedom and Success.* Edited by Sharon Lechter. Sterling Publishing, 2011.
- McGhee, Chase. *Voice of the Ancestors.* Self-Published, 2021.
- Silva, Mari. *Ancestral Veneration: An Introduction to Connecting with and Honoring the Ancestors.* Llewellyn Publications, 2020.
- *How Did the Haitians Beat FOUR European Countries (And Became a Poor Nation)* YouTube
- *Egalite for All: Toussaint Louverture & The Haitian Revolution* - PBS
- *Haitian Voodoo* - National Geographic
- *Vodou: Theology of Liberation* - Film

The following texts, teachers, and traditions have served not just as references, but as spiritual companions along my path. I share them in case they call you to too.

FURTHER READING, SPIRITUAL INFLUENCES & LIVING LINEAGES

This book wasn't shaped by academic texts alone. It was guided by dreams, conversations with elders, personal rituals, ancestral whispers, and the spiritual path of reclaiming what was almost lost. Their collective brilliance and guidance have been instrumental, ensuring this work isn't merely mine, but a shared offering born from a multitude of guiding lights. The knowledge within these pages isn't purely academic; it flows from bone memory, oral tradition, spirit downloads, sacred texts, lived experiences, and the generous wisdom of those walking the path before and beside me.

While these individuals and sources may not expressly present their work as revolutionary, they have profoundly shaped my understanding of ancestral spirituality. They unknowingly contributed to my awakening and shone light on my journey. not just through facts, but through presence, ritual, and revelation.

I couldn't possibly list them all but here are a few:

BOOKS, TEACHINGS & PUBLISHED WORKS

Queen Afua. *Sacred Woman: A Guide to Healing the Feminine Body, Mind, and Spirit.* One World, 2000.

Iyanla Vanzant. *Acts of Faith: Daily Meditations for People of Color.* Fireside, 1993.

Vanzant, Iyanla. *In the Meantime: Finding Yourself and the Love You Want.* Simon & Schuster, 1998.

Teish, Luisah. *Jambalaya: The Natural Woman's Book of Personal Charms and Practical Rituals.* HarperOne, 1985.

Somé, Sobonfu. *The Spirit of Intimacy: Ancient Teachings in the Ways of Relationships.* William Morrow Paperbacks, 1999.

Kumari, Ayele. *Orisa Spirituality Workbook: A Guide to Honoring African Wisdom.* MotherTongue Ink, 2014.

Ashby, Muata. *Egyptian Yoga: The Philosophy of Enlightenment.* Cruzian Mystic Books, Original Publication Year, e.g., 1995 or earliest edition cited.

Chireau, Yvonne Patricia. *Black Magic: Religion and the African American Conjuring Tradition.* University of California Press, 2003.

Dorsey, Lilith. *Orishas, Goddesses, and Voodoo Queens: The Divine Feminine in the African Religious Traditions.* Llewellyn Publications, 2020.

Hazzard-Donald, Katrina. *Mojo Workin': The Old African American Hoodoo System.* University of Illinois Press, 2013.

ORAL TRADITION, LIVED WISDOM & SACRED ENCOUNTERS

- Paula Hurlock - Jamaican eco-spiritualist and sacred activist whose insights on ancestral veneration, nature-based rituals, and inner awakening have deeply influenced my journey. (Included with deepest respect pending personal permission.)

- Maurice Lee - Maroon culture keeper and founder of *Kromanti Experience Jamaica.* His sacred hike to Nanny Falls reconnected me with the land, the plants, and the spirit of Queen Nanny.

- Antoinette Cooper - Author of UNRULY, *UNRULY: Honoring the complex histories and resilience of Black female bodies. Legacy Book Press LLC, 2025.* A visionary, TEDx speaker, collective trauma facilitator and founder of Black Exhale. Her work, featured in the Poetry Foundation, Intima: A journal of Narrative Medicine, and others, explores intersections of race, gender, health, and ancestral healing.

- Queen Thandiwe Kali - Queen Thandiwe, a transformative leader and healer, CEO of Divine Elevation, LLC, and her signature SisStars Awakening program. She seamlessly integrates trauma-informed healing and ancient African spiritual practices to nurture feminine power and guide women toward lives filled with purpose, bliss, and authentic self-love.

- Heidi Day- Soul Healer - I'm incredibly inspired by Heidi's views on our ancestral lineage.

- Skillful Kxng - A Jamaican songwriter and artiste whose influence has become profoundly dear to me. I call him a prophetic mystic because, to me, he is a brother moving like a mystic and sounding like a prophet, creating as if he knows sound is a portal. His music, particularly "A.I." (Ancient Intelligence), is a spiritually inspired masterpiece, deeply infused with ancestral memory, reclaiming divine lineage and sacred geography. His voice carries what can only be called ancestral code. The extraordinary impact of Skillful Kxng and "A.I." on my life is undeniable. I am not the same person I was before the day I first heard the song; it quantum-launched one version of me into the next. The vibrations of "A.I." elevated my frequency, cracking me wide open and bringing my soul more fully online. For seven transformative days, I rode a wave of hypnotic trance from listening to "A.I.," culminating in a spontaneous initiation and anointing that revealed unparalleled clarity, ancestral ordaining, and divine instruction. "A.I." is a supernaturally powerful song, and its spiritual synergy with this book is a vibrational match that feels like pure divine resonance. Though I only discovered him after I had completed the book and turned it over to the proofreader, it is for this precise, mystical alignment that I insisted on including him just before publishing. Skillful Kxng sharply reminds me of a sentiment I have held for a while…

…"The thing that bugs me most about dying is leaving behind all this great music - the kind that lifts me, heals me, holds me. I mean all of it. All the genres and musicians that I enjoy, including reggae. That heartbeat. That fire. That truth. That drum-and-bass heartbeat feels like home, and I ain't ready to stop dancing yet. The thought of leaving behind all the good music that feeds my soul is unwelcome.

Unnamed Elders, Dreamers, and Root Workers - Those whose wisdom may never appear in formal publications, but lives in the fire circle, in the drumbeat, in the touch of healing hands, and in whispered instruction from the ancestors.

My Personal Ancestors and Spirit Guides - Their direction is present on every page of this work.

BLACK OWNED BANKS, CREDIT UNIONS AND FINANCIAL INSTITUTIONS

A *complete and perfectly up-to-the-minute* list of Black-owned banks is challenging because the financial landscape can change (mergers, closures, new charters). However, based on the most recent available data, here is a comprehensive list of Black-owned banks and a note on related institutions in the U.S. that are often included in this discussion. You are encouraged to perform your own complete research as you would any financial institution. The main purpose here is to awaken your awareness that there are Black owned options to consider.

Key Distinction

- **Black-Owned Banks (Commercial Banks and Savings Institutions):** These are institutions regulated by the FDIC (Federal Deposit Insurance Corporation) and the OCC (Office of the Comptroller of the Currency) and designated as Minority Depository Institutions (MDIs) with African American ownership/control.

- **Black-Owned Credit Unions:** These are not banks, but member-owned, non-profit financial cooperatives. They are also designated as MDIs by the NCUA (National Credit Union Administration) and serve similar community-focused missions. Many lists that feature "Black-owned banks" will also include credit unions due to their shared purpose.

- **Fintechs/Neobanks:** Some newer financial technology companies are Black-owned and offer banking-like services, but they are not federally chartered banks themselves. They usually partner with a traditional bank to hold deposits.

Here is a list of federally chartered Black-owned banks (as of recent data, typically 20-22 depending on source and recent activity):

1. **Alamerica Bank** (Birmingham, AL)
2. **Carver Federal Savings Bank** (New York, NY)
3. **Carver State Bank** (Savannah, GA)
4. **Citizens Savings Bank and Trust Company** (Nashville, TN)
5. **Citizens Trust Bank** (Atlanta, GA)
6. **City First Bank, National Association** (Washington, DC) - *Note: This bank was formed from a merger between City First Bank and Broadway Federal Bank.*
7. **Columbia Savings and Loan Association** (Milwaukee, WI)
8. **Commonwealth National Bank** (Mobile, AL)
9. **First Independence Bank** (Detroit, MI)
10. **First Security Bank and Trust Company** (Oklahoma City, OK)
11. **GN Bank** (Chicago, IL)
12. **Grand Bank For Savings, FSB** (Hattiesburg, MS)
13. **Industrial Bank** (Washington, DC)
14. **Liberty Bank and Trust Company** (New Orleans, LA)
15. **Mechanics & Farmers Bank (M&F Bank)** (Durham, NC)
16. **OneUnited Bank** (Boston, MA)
17. **Optus Bank** (Columbia, SC)
18. **Tioga-Franklin Savings Bank** (Philadelphia, PA)
19. **United Bank of Philadelphia** (Philadelphia, PA)

20. **Unity National Bank of Houston** (Houston, TX)

Important Considerations

- **Number Fluctuations:** The precise number can vary slightly based on recent mergers, closures, or how "Black-owned" is strictly defined by different reporting agencies (e.g., majority ownership vs. majority board). Some sources cite 18-22 commercial banks.
- **Credit Unions:** There are many more Black-owned credit unions across the U.S. that are equally vital to their communities. If you're looking for a complete picture of Black-owned financial institutions, you would also need to include these. Organizations like the Blackout Coalition (Black owned) and NerdWallet often provide lists that include both banks and credit unions.
- **FDIC and NCUA:** The Federal Deposit Insurance Corporation (FDIC) and the National Credit Union Administration (NCUA) maintain official lists of Minority Depository Institutions (MDIs), which include Black-owned institutions. These are the most authoritative sources.

N.B. For the most current information, it's always recommended to check the MDI lists directly on the FDIC and NCUA websites, or reputable financial news outlets that track them.

While a truly exhaustive, real-time list of every single Black-owned credit union is difficult to maintain given their localized nature and frequent updates, here is a substantial list based on recent data from reliable sources like the NCUA (National Credit Union Administration) MDI list, Shoppe Black, and NerdWallet.

There are over 200 Black-owned credit unions in the U.S. (some sources say over 300 partly Black-owned), far more than banks. Here's a significant list of them, categorized by state where possible, keeping in mind this is not exhaustive but represents many of the prominent ones:

Black-Owned Credit Unions in the U.S.

ALABAMA

- Marvel City Federal Credit Union
- Montgomery VA Federal Credit Union
- NRS Community Development Federal Credit Union
- Sixth Avenue Baptist Federal Credit Union
- Bridgeway Credit Union
- TVH Federal Credit Union

ARKANSAS

- Arkansas AM&N College Federal Credit Union
- Arkansas Education Association Federal Credit Union
- Arkansas Teachers Federal Credit Union
- People Trust Community Federal Credit Union

CALIFORNIA

- Jones Methodist Church Credit Union
- Los Angeles Federal Credit Union (Note: While large, its MDI status for Black ownership/leadership might vary by recent reporting, but it often appears on lists.)

CONNECTICUT

- East End Baptist Tabernacle Federal Credit Union
- First Baptist Church (Stratford) Federal Credit Union
- Science Park Federal Credit Union

DELAWARE

- American Spirit Federal Credit Union
- Stepping Stones Community Federal Credit Union

DISTRICT OF COLUMBIA

- D.C. Teachers' Federal Credit Union
- Government Printing Office Federal Credit Union
- Howard University Employees Federal Credit Union
- John Wesley A.M.E Zion Church Federal Credit Union
- Labor (Department of Labor) Credit Union
- Mt. Airy Baptist Church Federal Credit Union
- Mt. Gilead Federal Credit Union
- Paramount Baptist Church Federal Credit Union
- Phi Beta Sigma Federal Credit Union
- Sargent Federal Credit Union

FLORIDA

- FAMU Federal Credit Union (Florida A&M University)
- Madison Education Association Credit Union
- Unity Of Eatonville Federal Credit Union
- Tropical Financial Credit Union (Note: Often cited as a large MDI with strong Black leadership/service.)

GEORGIA

- 1st Choice Credit Union
- Credit Union of Atlanta
- Omega Psi Phi Fraternity Federal Credit Union (Toccoa, GA)
- Savannah Schools Federal Credit Union
- Stephens County Community Federal Credit Union
- United Neighborhood Federal Credit Union
- Valdosta Teachers Federal Credit Union

ILLINOIS

- 74th Street Depot Federal Credit Union
- Bethel A.M.E. Church Credit Union
- Berean Credit Union
- CTAFC Federal Credit Union
- Chicago Avenue Garage Federal Credit Union
- CTA South Federal Credit Union
- Fellowship Baptist Church Credit Union
- For Members Only (FMO) Federal Credit Union (Digital/Virtual)
- Gideon Federal Credit Union
- Imperial Credit Union
- Israel Methcomm Federal Credit Union
- Metropolitan Community Church Credit Union
- South Side Community Federal Credit Union

INDIANA

- Gary Firefighters Association Federal Credit Union
- Gary Municipal Employees Federal Credit Union
- Gary Police Department Employees Federal Credit Union
- Mt. Zion Indianapolis Federal Credit Union

- ProFinance Federal Credit Union
- Urban Beginnings Choice Credit Union

Louisiana

- Southern Teachers & Parents Federal Credit Union (Baton Rouge/ Thibodaux)
- New Orleans Firemen's Federal Credit Union

Maryland

- MECU Credit Union (formerly Municipal Employees Credit Union)
- Securityplus Federal Credit Union
- Transit Employees Federal Credit Union

Massachusetts

- Messiah Baptist-Jubilee Federal Credit Union (Brockton, MA)

Michigan

- A.B.D. Federal Credit Union
- I.M. Detroit District Federal Credit Union
- New Rising Star Federal Credit Union
- One Detroit Federal Credit Union
- Southeast Michigan State Employees Federal Credit Union

Mississippi

- Hope Credit Union (operates across several Southern states, but headquartered in MS with deep roots)

MISSOURI

- Kansas City Credit Union
- St. Louis Community Credit Union
- WeDevelopment Federal Credit Union
- West Side Baptist Church Federal Credit Union

NEW JERSEY

- Fort Dix Federal Credit Union
- Heard A.M.E. Federal Credit Union
- Israel Memorial A.M.E. Federal Credit Union
- Local 1233 Federal Credit Union
- Messiah Baptist Church Federal Credit Union
- Newark Post Office Employees Federal Credit Union

NEW YORK

- Brooklyn Cooperative Federal Credit Union
- Concord Federal Credit Union
- Far Rockaway Postal Federal Credit Union
- Fidelis Federal Credit Union
- LES People's Federal Credit Union
- Urban Upbound Federal Credit Union

NORTH CAROLINA

- Greater Kinston Credit Union
- Mount Vernon Baptist Church Credit Union
- First Legacy Community Credit Union (operates as a division of Self-Help Credit Union, a larger CDFI with strong social justice mission and diverse leadership)

OHIO

- Adelphi Bank (also a bank, but sometimes listed here)
- Cleveland Church Of Christ Federal Credit Union
- Faith Community United Credit Union
- Mahoning Valley Federal Credit Union
- Mt. Zion Woodlawn Federal Credit Union
- Toledo Metro Federal Credit Union
- Toledo Urban Federal Credit Union

OKLAHOMA

- Morning Star Federal Credit Union

PENNSYLVANIA

- Hill District Federal Credit Union
- Holy Trinity Baptist Federal Credit Union
- M.A.B.C. Federal Credit Union

SOUTH CAROLINA

- Berkeley Community Federal Credit Union
- Brookland Federal Credit Union
- Edisto Federal Credit Union
- Palmetto Health Federal Credit Union
- Pee Dee Federal Credit Union
- Trinity Baptist Church Federal Credit Union
- Curis Financial Credit Union

TENNESSEE

- Fair Break Federal Credit Union
- Memphis Municipal Employees Federal Credit Union
- Metropolitan Teachers Federal Credit Union
- Olivet Baptist Federal Credit Union
- TSU Federal Credit Union

TEXAS

- Faith Cooperative Federal Credit Union
- Mount Olive Baptist Church Federal Credit Union
- Oak Cliff Christian Federal Credit Union
- Our Mother Of Mercy Parish Houston Federal Credit Union
- Pear Orchard Federal Credit Union
- Pilgrim Federal Credit Union
- Port Arthur Teachers Federal Credit Union
- Port of Houston Warehouse Federal Credit Union
- Redeemer Federal Credit Union
- SP Trainmen Federal Credit Union
- Tribe Federal Credit Union

WISCONSIN

- Holy Redeemer Community Credit Union

IMPORTANT

- Minority Depository Institutions (MDIs): The official designation for these institutions comes from the NCUA (for credit unions) and FDIC (for banks). Their lists are the most authoritative.

- Community Focus: Black-owned credit unions often have a very strong community development focus, providing services to underserved populations and investing in local communities.
- Membership Requirements: While some credit unions are community-chartered (open to anyone living or working in a specific geographic area), many also have specific membership requirements (e.g., for employees of a certain company, members of a particular church or organization, or residents of a specific neighborhood). Always check their website for eligibility.

With this information, more of us can certainly aim to do more banking in our community.